What Readers Are Saying About

# The Whispered Teachings of Grandmother Trout

"Fast-paced, filled with enough Southern coastal Texas lure, nature, fly fishing, humor, sex, drama, and clever surprises all the way to the last page to make it thoroughly entertaining. This is what GREAT movies are made of."

~ WANDA TAYLOR,
"The South's 1st Lady of Fly Fishing"

"I had a hard time putting this book down. Kathy's words drew me in with her expressive writing style and alluring storyline. She takes you on this in-depth journey through the lives of these wonderful characters and paints a beautiful inviting picture of South Texas and the Laguna Madre."

~ ALEX RAMIREZ,
CEO of Outdoor Specialty Products, a manufacturing rep in the fly-fishing industry including Far Bank Enterprises (parent of Sage, Redington, and RIO)

"I have a stack of books next to my bed that I've been very gradually working my way through. They're all non-fiction, "personal growth" books, to help me gain a better grasp of that, ever-elusive, inner peace or to learn something new to share with my clients, readers, and radio show listeners. But, as the warmer weather arrived, I was thinking more and more about playfulness and giving in to guilty pleasures. I began to crave a good piece of fiction, one where I could relate to the main character and get lost in the story.

"Kathy Sparrow's book has fulfilled this craving. I became so wrapped up in the story that I stayed up late at night, unable to put the book down, emotionally wrapped up in the character and all of her personal ups and downs. In the end, I didn't feel so guilty about this pleasure because I could feel a subtle shift inside. Perhaps, I had achieved a bit of that 'personal growth' while enjoying the read, learning some of the lessons with Sparrow's protagonist, Ali, from the whisperings of Grandmother Trout."

~ Dr. Mara Karpel,
psychologist, radio show host, and author of,
*The Passionate Life: Creating Vitality & Joy at Any Age*

"Kathy Sparrow's The *Whispered Teachings of Grandmother Trout* offered me a challenge. As I became engrossed in the lives of Ali and Jack, their thoughts felt like they became my own. My mind filled with their options and fought with the same emotions. The turning point for me was when the trout said, 'I'm over here.' I spend a fair amount of time outdoors as a sanctuary from daily life and a place to gather my thoughts. I wonder if I am really listening. Ali did not get it right away and had to let go of her fears to understand the whispers.

"Having made a significant career transition, I would say I have not let go of my fears. Perhaps if I listen more closely, I can learn from 'whispered teachings' and challenge the edge of comfort and fear."

~ Mike McCleish,
former Army Special Forces, veteran, and Media/
Photographer Coordinator for Project Healing
Waters Fly Fishing - Colorado Springs

"I so enjoyed *The Whispered Teaching of Grandmother Trout* for many reasons. First, I love it when I forget where I am sitting and what I am doing as I was transported to the Laguna Madre and became deeply engrossed in the happenings of Ali, Kate, Gus, Joe, Jack, and Skipper, The well-developed characters were not just names, but people I got to know. I was drawn into the captivating connection to nature and the solace it gave to so many. There was great depth to the storyline with instruction on fly fishing, development of characters, and an alluring writing style that read easily!"

~MERRIL BORUCHIN SPIELMAN,
Dean of Refugee Film School,
Holistic Life Coach, and Global Traveler

"Only a woman who deeply knows the true anatomy and soul of fly fishing could so wisely reel us into this parallel world of the anatomy and very soul of human challenge, passion, and the call to surrender. Sparrow brings feminine divinity home to roost in the waters of Southern Texas. Brilliant."

~ MOLLY LORD,
TUNED-IN Productions

# The Whispered Teachings of Grandmother Trout

# The Whispered Teachings of

# Grandmother

# Trout

Kathy Sparrow

A Writable Life
San Diego, CA

A Writable Life™ Publishing
3796 Curlew Street
San Diego, CA 92013
www.awritablelife.com

Publisher's Note: This is a work of fiction. Names, characters, places, and incidents are a product of the author's imagination. Locales and public names are sometimes used for atmospheric purposes. Any resemblance to actual people, living or dead, or to businesses, companies, events, institutions, or locales is completely coincidental.

**The Whispered Teachings of Grandmother Trout/Kathy Sparrow**
-- 1st ed.

ISBN 978-0-9982492-1-6
Cover Design by Karen Floyd
Cover Photo by G. Scott Sparrow
Interior Design Book Layout Marko Markovic *(5mediadesign)*

# Dedication

*To my grandchildren — Jude Aaron, Maximus Rockwell,*
*Abigail Grace, and Naomi Azalea —*
*May you always follow*
*the whispers of your heart.*

# Chapter One

Ali Stephenson bolted upright in her bed and looked around the darkroom, barely making out the edges of her dresser and the chair in the corner by the sliding glass door. No sounds of birds greeted her from the patio, where she had filled the feeder the night before. No sliver of sunlight emerged from the morning sky. Taking a deep breath, she swung her lean legs off the bed and pulled back the drapes. A gentle pink glow was just beginning to wash across the horizon. She searched for the images from the dream that woke her with a start, and none emerged. Sighing, she turned away from the window.

Thirty minutes later, she emerged from her bedroom, dressed for the day in white linen pants and a navy blouse. The coffee had automatically brewed, and as she poured the cup of the steaming ebony liquid, she remembered she needed to buy a baby shower gift for a friend and added that to the list on her phone. She sighed, again.

*Just put it behind you, once and for all, Ali Mae.* Her grandmother's words echoed in her mind. It was her grandmother's way of dealing with anything troublesome. Shove it aside. Ali had learned that one well. Shaking her head, she filled her travel mug, grabbed a green juice from the refrigerator, and headed toward the front door. Ali once again skipped a leisurely moment on the patio with her coffee, to enjoy the birds that visited her feeder. With a glance back toward the patio door, she couldn't remember the last time she actually sat out there enjoying the view of the dunes and the Atlantic Ocean beyond.

Pausing to put her juice in her bag and take the keys from the drawer of the pine gate-leg table, one of her grandmother's prized possessions, she spotted her fly rod in the tall woven Taghkanic trapping basket, made by a family friend out of maple reeds, many years before. She'd gone out casting the night before on the bay behind the condos and hadn't put it back in her car. She checked her watch and decided she was early enough to go to the pond in the corporate complex and cast for a while. That, at least, would make up for skipping coffee with the birds. It was much like a meditation for her, sometimes better than yoga or running. Casting took her to another place, a safe place.

Ali inhaled the moist ocean air as she took her first cast, oblivious that she was being watched. She was immersed in her practice, having become one with her rod. Joe Driscoll parted the blinds, allowing the early morning sun to stream through the window. Placing his hand against the glass, he estimated temperatures to be in the mid-seventies, warmer than when he arrived at dawn. For a moment, he allowed himself to imagine the warm breeze dancing on his face. The view was pleasant. From here, he could watch the surf roll to the shore. It moved him, much like the sight of a beautiful woman.

He lowered his gaze, and such a woman was below him. Ali was a little earlier than usual. He never grew tired of watching her practice casting at the beginning of the day. Her graceful form, her lithe body, and her powerful stroke told a lot about her. She repeated the action over and over again, sailing a chartreuse speck at the end of a fluorescent orange fly line through the air. She appeared to be using the fountain as a target, taking care to miss the ducks and geese swimming in the manmade pond.

Removing his dark wire-rimmed glasses, Joe rubbed his brow. His feelings about her were complex—more than a daughter, less than a lover. It was that way from that very first day she came into his office. That day began her career at the magazine, his magazine. That day seemed like a lifetime ago. They'd been through a lot together.

The alarm on his watch sounded, shaking him from his thoughts. Glancing at the gold face, he tapped it lightly and nervously cleared his throat. He took a set of keys from the pocket of his gray trousers. Bending his tall frame, he opened the drawer of his mahogany desk. Inside, several prescriptions stood perfectly upright in a black metal basket. He methodically opened each, removing one or two pills in different shapes and colors as he went down the line. He had a matching set at home.

Reaching for the crystal decanter with his tanned hand, speckled with liver spots, he poured a glass of water and then washed down each of the pills without hesitation. After wiping his mouth with a handkerchief, which he had removed from his back pocket, he refolded it with care and studied the gold monogram JED in one corner. There was no junior. The Driscoll family would soon draw to a close. But hopefully not too soon, not before his affairs had been put in order. He hated the sound of that phrase, but it was one that had remained in the forefront of his mind for some time now.

After closing the drawer, careful to once again secure its contents, he returned to the window. Ali was still there. Her chestnut hair, which fell below her shoulders, glistened in the sun. This time she had company. Joe tensed as he watched her movements lose their grace until they ceased. The man next to her paced back and forth, his arms flailing about. She appeared to be silent—unable, or perhaps unwilling, to respond. He loathed the resignation in her posture.

She retreated from the water's edge, carrying her rod, with her head hanging. The man followed her, with his mouth moving with exaggeration. Joe watched until they disappeared from his view.

Turning back to his desk, he picked up the assignment file for the following few issues. He reviewed his typed notes until he came to "Fly Fishing South Texas Style." He took his red pen, crossed out a name, and replaced it with Ali's, topping it off with an exclamation point. She needed a break, not only from what he'd just witnessed but before...He wouldn't allow himself to finish his own sentence. He still had time, perhaps more than he deserved, but he was determined to take every second of it and live to the fullest, only now in a more mindful manner.

He hoped that his example would inspire others to do likewise, particularly Ali. While he admired her dedication and spirit for the magazine, he worried about her drive. It seemed, at times, a matter of will rather than passion. He wondered if he had expected too much of her. Shaking his head, he hoped that that wasn't the case. He needed her now more than ever.

And she needed a reprieve from Sam. He never approved of their courtship, and he'd like to do anything he could to sabotage it once and for all. Yet, if Joe could draw anything from the scene below his window, the end was likely near. His temples vibrated. He wanted better for her, always had. If only she could desire that for herself.

Reaching across his desk, Joe picked up the phone and dialed a four-digit extension. "Ali, when you have a moment, would you come by my office? Thanks, my dear." His drawl testified to his heritage and his manners to his upbringing.

He ran his fingers through his silver hair, a little sparse on top, but thicker on the sides, at least for now. He sighed as he rolled down the cuffs of his starched white shirt, covering the forearm that was once darkened from hours spent surfing but now bruised from repeated tests and transfusions. He leaned back in his black leather chair and stared at the ceiling, opting to spend the time until her arrival contemplating his words. They were important. They always were, only there were times in his life when he couldn't perceive just how impactful his words, or his actions, really were. The error of his ways had caught up with him, and he had only himself to blame.

A knock on the door ended his reverie.

"Come in."

Ali showed no signs of the exchange he observed, except for the drawn expression and pale complexion that had become her trademark of late. Rising from his chair, he greeted her, "You have a lovely cast. Timing is impeccable." He motioned toward the chair.

A hint of color tinted Ali's cheeks. "Perhaps your timing was a bit off."

"My timing was perfect for witnessing yet another scuffle with your beau."

Ali groaned.

He stared at her over the top of his glasses. "It's difficult to see you make another poor choice in a suitor."

"Seems to be my destiny." Exasperated, she tucked a lock of hair behind her right ear, exposing a single pearl stud. "Is this all you called me in for?" The impatience in her voice was evident. Her steely expression was a shot across the bow, warning him not to dive deeper into that conversation.

"Not at all." He stretched out in his chair, leaning back just slightly. Clasping his hands behind his head, he deliberately set the tone for a more relaxed exchange. "Been to the farm?"

She crossed her right leg over her left and began tapping her foot wildly, loosening the heel of her navy pump from her foot. "Not in a while."

"It's been years, according to my estimation."

"Maybe so." She bit the side of her lip.

"Done anything for fun lately?" His grayish-green eyes twinkled.

"Joe, what is this all about?" Her brow was now deeply furrowed.

"When's the last time you spent any significant amount of time outdoors? And I'm not talking about your fifteen-minute forays on the corporate pond."

"I actually went casting last night." She looked defiantly into his eyes.

"What happened to the young woman who finagled her way into a four-day workweek just so she could spend most of her weekends at her family farm, walking in the woods, inhaling the aroma from the carpet of decaying leaves and blooming dogwood along a bustling stream?"

Ali sighed. "I guess she grew up."

"Dried up is more like it." He leaned forward with a mischievous grin. "But I'm going to change all that." He handed her a file. "I have an assignment for you—one that will put some sunshine in your smile, some color in your cheeks, and while it isn't the mountains, you'll get to wield your fly rod at fish, rather than the ducks in the pond, and perhaps rekindle your desire to honor your roots again."

She looked at the red handwriting on the tab of the manila folder. "You're kidding."

"There's a list of contacts, deadlines, word count, and the advertisers are already in place."

"Why me?" She asked suspiciously before turning her attention to the file.

"You need a solo adventure." He resumed his relaxed posture, studying her face as she read over the file.

Her face softened as she flipped through the pages, and then a smile formed on her thick lips. She closed the folder. "I have only freshwater equipment."

"Buy what you need." He rose, his lean frame towering above her. "Take ten days. Enjoy yourself."

Ali glanced out the window. "Are you hitting me with more staff cuts?"

"Not in the foreseeable future."

She eyed him warily. "Then I'd better take a look at my schedule and reshuffle my priorities."

"Any idea when you might like to go?"

She rose to leave. "My birthday's coming up."

"A momentous one if I remember correctly." He moved to the front of the desk and stood before her. He peered into her bright blue eyes and, for a moment, regretted that he wasn't younger. Things could have been different between them.

"Forty is a great time to contemplate changes in your life."

Ali frowned. "I prefer not thinking about it right now."

"Any regrets?"

"A few, but none that I can do anything about." She edged toward the door, put her hand on the doorknob, and then paused to look back at him. "Thanks, Joe." She waved the file folder.

"Just have fun. You write better when you're relaxed, just like your casting."

"Aye, aye, captain." She saluted and left the room.

\* \* \*

The afternoon sun filtered through the white vertical blinds, leaving shards of light on Ali's office floor. Hers was the corner office, with views of the ocean on one side and glimpses of the bay on another. A vacant look rested upon her face, as she stared momentarily out the window as if searching for something. The dream had stayed with Ali throughout the morning, with vague images flitting through her mind as she went about her tasks. She tried to force them into greater clarity, but it did little good. This was one of those moments as she searched the skyline with her arms crossed. The dream wasn't disturbing. She'd had her share of those and was never tempted to revisit them in the daylight hours. This one was inviting.

Scanning the office, she knew why she wanted to retreat into the dream. Stacks of files framed two corners of her desk, and a pile of messages lay upon the desk blotter. The voice mail light was flickering, and an unfinished story stared back at her from the computer screen. She'd lost her ability to concentrate over a week ago. Her thoughts continually drifted to her upcoming trip. The idea of being away—from the office, from Sam, and even from Joe—brought with it relief. He had been right. She was drying up. She pushed her bangs away from her forehead and straightened in her chair, determined to get back to work. A knock on her door ended her contemplation.

"Come in." She stood behind her desk, poised for her visitor's entrance. With her shoulders squared and her head erect, she felt ready for whatever came her way. A young man, no more than twenty-five, carrying a rod tube, about two feet long, and a green paper bag with a rope handle entered the room.

"Ms. Stephenson."

She nodded. "Yes?"

"Delivery from River Run Outfitters."

Her face brightened, and her shoulders relaxed as she moved to the front of the desk.

"Mr. Haskins said it's all set. Line has been put on your reel and all."

Reaching for the package and the rod tube, Ali felt another image from the dream fill her with warmth, but once again, the vision was unclear.

"He wants a fishing report as soon as you get back." The young man chuckled nervously.

She studied the young man standing before her for a moment, staring at his tall, muscular body. His tanned face was framed with curly blond hair, and he had a dimple on his right cheek when he smiled. She envied his youth and wanted him to stay so she could bask in his freshness in his carefree exuberance. His presence was a nice distraction, from her lack of motivation.

Steeling herself against her temptation, she reached behind her desk and into her purse. "Tell Mr. Haskins that I'll even provide photo support with my fish tales," she said as she pressed twenty dollars into the palm of his hand. "Have a great afternoon."

The door closed behind him, and she leaned against her desk. She glanced around the room. It was much like Joe's office. Same size and layout, with cherry furnishings instead of mahogany. Even her power wall was a close match to his, complete with regional and national awards. Her gaze fell to one side, where a cluster of prizes for stories she'd written hung neatly. Compared to the others, they meant the most. But managing the magazine and editing had filled her time for the past several years. Only occasionally did she write a story. Most of those were fillers, needed in a pinch to fill space.

Ali closed her eyes and crossed her arms, hugging herself tightly. Something was taking hold of her. A force that had the power to turn her life into a complete mess or transform it into something far better than she could ever imagine. She couldn't tell which.

"I'm ready," she whispered aloud, wondering what she was ready for. The dream came back, clearly this time. She was standing in water up to her knees, holding a fly rod. Beside her was a man whose face she could not see. But he felt older, wiser. Ahead of her stood another man, about her age, perhaps a few years older—also wielding a rod. Looking into the water, she saw fish swimming toward her, large fish, either in singles or in pairs. Their dark bodies glimmered through the surface. The man next to her whispered. "Speckled Sea Trout." His voice was reverent. The younger man went on ahead and cast but failed time and time again to hook up. "He can't do it alone," the older man whispered. "No one can." He looked at her; his hazel eyes pierced through her soul. "Not even you."

\* \* \*

The door opened behind her with a burst and closed with a loud thud. Sam Hagen took off his glasses and frowned. "You stood me up. We were supposed to meet a half-hour ago."

Ali jumped. "I've got a lot to do in the next few days." She slipped the fly rod from its case, running her fingers lovingly along the glossy black surface.

"You're really going?" Sam came up beside her and wrapped his arms around her waist.

She gripped the rod until her knuckles turned white.

"I thought I could convince you to spend your birthday with me, somewhere in the mountains, perhaps the farm." He nibbled her ear, sinking his teeth into her skin. "You've never taken me there."

"Not here." Ali pried his hands from her waist, feeling trapped.

His fingers clung to her black sweater. "What gives?"

"I like to keep my private life private." She stepped away.

"It's a little late for that, isn't it?"

He was right. Ali had done little to hide their romance. This one or any other. Not even with Nigel. Her stomach churned at the thought of him, and she quickly directed her attention back to Sam. Ali regarded him for a moment and was startled by her revelation. His physical features did little for her. He had a thick face and was far too polished. His shoes were never smudged, and his clothes were always immaculately pressed, even his jeans.

She fought the urge to laugh aloud at the absurdity of what she'd settled for this time. She studied the rod again, pausing for a moment before propping it against the wall.

"I don't understand this obsession," Sam quipped.

A dreamy look fell upon her countenance. "Grandpa would get so excited when a fish hit his fly. He would squeal like a little boy. Brought back his youth." She paused, and her voice softened. "And his rhythm as he cast the line. He was so graceful. There was just something very magical about the way he moved."

"Magic is what happens when you and I go to the mountains."

"Not lately, Sam." Ali wasn't the type to be cruel, but she was beginning to have a hard time playing games to keep others happy.

He winced. "You've changed."

"I know."

"It's all that yoga and meditating," he said snidely.

They were the only activities that could bring peace to her troubled mind lately, and she found herself turning to them more and more. That and her long walks on the beach. "Maybe you should try it sometime." Her words vibrated with the sting of a scorpion.

Sam abhorred the outdoors or anything that resembled self-development. His idea of a trek to the mountains was sleeping late and then sitting by the fireplace for hours on end reading Thoreau, sipping wine, and then sucking her into endless literary debates by evening's arrival. For a time, she found them thrilling, matching wits with a man she thought was her intellectual equal. Of late, she preferred Pam Houston, Brené Brown, or Joy Harjo much to his disdain. He said he couldn't relate to a feminine voice, particularly of strong women. Ali knew he didn't even try.

"Send someone else on the assignment." His husky voice bordered on threatening.

"Joe wouldn't hear of it."

"Oh, yes, our illustrious leader. We can't override *his* decisions."

"Why should we?" Her piercing expression could send a chill up the spine of the most hardened criminal, but Sam seemed oblivious to it.

"I'll plan a special celebration for you upon your return." He clasped her arm.

"That won't be necessary." She lowered her eyes, aware that the pressure beneath his fingers had increased. Her heart raced, knowing she needed to make an exit. "I've got to go to production."

She pried herself from his grasp. The sensation of his fingers on her skin remained, reminding her of the other times when he tried to sway her into his way of thinking, always in private. When they were alone, she did whatever was necessary to appease him. But in the office, she felt safe and subsequently courageous. She peered at her reflection in the mirror, pausing to tuck a few strands of her chestnut hair into the bun which rested on the nape of her neck. Clutching the doorknob, she paused. "I can't see you anymore. It's just not been right for me for a long time."

Out of the corner of her eyes, she saw a wave of shock wash over his face. Then the anger took hold, and Ali knew a hasty retreat was in order, or she'd suffer another cold slap on the face, perhaps worse. She hadn't seen the initial blow coming, and she chastised herself for being so stupid—and staying with a man who had harmed her. She wrote it off as a familial flaw that she learned to live with early in her life. With the others, it had been just words, and as an editor, she could erase them from her mind, at least most of the time. But with Sam, the stakes were elevated, and she knew she was no match for him in the end. She placated him for a time, sucking in her pride and suckling his.

With her hand still gripping the doorknob, panic seeped under her skin. But then the essence of the dream shrouded her with its cloak. It was time to move on. To what, she just didn't know. She whisked out of the door, with a subtle sense of freedom following in her wake.

# Chapter Two

The heat of deep South Texas greeted Ali like a warm embrace. Standing on the walkway outside the airport, she relished the sweetness of the afternoon air. Great-tailed grackles, with their black feathers glistening in the sunlight, serenaded her arrival with their boisterous cackles from atop of the palms as she headed toward her rental car.

For a girl raised in the mountains with oaks and maples, South Texas should have seemed foreign. But as Ali settled in behind the wheel of the car and aimed for the hamlet of Arroyo City, she had the odd sensation of going home. As she left the airport, the scenery around her shifted. Development gave way to mesquite and cactus. Spanish daggers stood like sentinels along the highway, ushering her to a new adventure.

Entering the little town of Rio Hondo, she stopped at a traffic light. She surveyed the sleepy village, deserted in the afternoon heat, except for a few people moving slowly about their business. On one corner stood a bakery, boasting fresh tortillas. Two women, with their silver hair wound in buns, carrying colorful market baskets, silently made their way through the threshold.

On the opposite side of the street, a tall, teenaged boy with dark cropped hair, dressed in jeans and a red t-shirt, gathered abandoned shopping carts from the parking lot of a small grocery store. Immediately to Ali's left, a two-story brick schoolhouse stood empty except for a bedraggled dog seeking shelter from the blazing sun and sleeping on the front entryway. And to her right was a cafe and gas station.

A little girl with long, curly, dark hair and big brown eyes, gripping a dripping ice cream cone, grinned broadly at Ali as she and her mom, no more than a teenager, stepped onto the curb and prepared to cross the street. After meeting the little girl's gaze, sadness crept into Ali's heart. Six years is a long time to carry the pain of a past mistake, but this was one Ali knew would follow her to her grave. She reached for her bottle of water and took a long sip. There was a time when she did the same with a fine bottle of wine, night after night until enough time had passed, and the demons had been tamed. Screwing the top back on the bottle, she switched on the radio to drown out any lingering thoughts. Lively Tejano music, with swift guitar rifts and dancing trumpets, floated through the speakers. Ali's mood brightened as she waited for the light to turn green.

A light toot of a horn sounded behind her. In the rearview mirror, she spotted a white pickup truck. The driver gave her a friendly wave. She returned the gesture and stepped on the gas, forgetting the vehicle behind her. She continued her leisurely pace and made note of other significant landmarks as she crept through town. There were two more cafes, a dollar store, a beauty salon, and then the post office and a hardware store on the next block. Life's basic necessities could be satisfied in just a few blocks.

The town limits passed quickly, and the driver of the truck moved by her on the open highway. She glanced at the pickup as it passed. It was towing a classy shallow water skiff that immediately reminded her of a 5-series BMW, white and spotless, as was the truck. The man again waved as he pulled back into the lane in front of her and then sped away, leaving Ali to her steady, slower pace.

She began looking for the next intersection, noted as FM 106 to FM 2925. At first, perplexed about the FM, she soon discovered it meant farm to market. Mama Kate's directions were precise, down to "the white house on the corner of the intersection," where she was to take a left. After doing so, Ali drove along the highway for several miles. Horses grazed along the road, dogs slept lazily under porches, and scissor-tailed flycatchers darted overhead, seizing their prey in midair. Crops of milo, cotton, and sugar cane stretched for as far as she could see, broken only by occasional mesquite or ebony reaching skyward above the fields of green.

And, the sky—vaster than Ali had ever seen before—hung like an azure umbrella over it all. Something stirred deep within her that was both exciting and frightening as she watched huge white puffy clouds float along on the backdrop of blue. She felt connected to everything within her field of vision and beyond.

The sign for the Arroyo Baptist Church alerted Ali that she was nearing her destination. The beat of her heart increased, and she inched the gas pedal a little closer to the floor. She wasn't one to know exactly what was right or wrong at any given moment without lengthy periods of contemplation. This time was different. She knew in every square inch of her body and soul that this trip was in alignment with anything and everything that could be aligned—stars, moons, planets, or tea leaves. She glanced at the directions and began watching for the next set of landmarks. On the corner of one intersection, she passed Chili Willies, a rustic building with half a dozen pickup trucks parked in front. She was told the place had the best burgers around. She knew she was close and eagerly awaited her first glimpse of Mama Kate's.

Exactly one mile beyond the steel gray water tower, she pulled into the driveway of a quaint seaside farmhouse with a large black Labrador sprawled on the front porch. Adjacent was a two-story guesthouse with the same red doors and terra cotta trim.

She took it all in, memorizing the details that she would later write about and also becoming very aware of her racing heart. Emerging from the car, Ali was again greeted by the humid afternoon air. She inhaled deeply and savored the salty, sweet, earthy smell of the plants and grasses—and saltwater.

The door to the main house opened, and a woman, a bit stocky and small of stature, in her late sixties approached her. "You must be Ali. I was expecting you 'bout now." She extended her delicate hand, brown from the sun and a bit gnarled from arthritis. "I'm Kate McGregor, known around these parts as Mama Kate."

"Ali Stephenson." As she clasped the woman's hand, she was transported to her grandparents' farm, comforted by the memory. "It's a pleasure to meet you." Ali surveyed the yard. Lush vegetation with flowers in hues of yellow, melon, and scarlet lined the fence. A wild patch of yucca, palms, and cactus graced the open space near the road. And in front of the porch, bloomed several roses in pinks, yellows, and reds. "So many roses!" Ali exclaimed.

"Mary's favorite flower." Kate glanced toward the towering mesquite tree in the side yard. Ali followed her gaze where a statue of the Holy Mother held forth among a bevy of bird feeders and more plants, including a pink shrub rose.

"Catholic?" Ali inquired.

Mama Kate shook her head. "Just know a wise woman when I see one." She looked deeply into Ali's eyes, letting her words linger between them. "C'mon in." The woman turned toward the house, with Ali following. The Labrador lazily sauntered behind the two women. Without turning, Kate said, "Max, you leave her be."

"He's fine. I love dogs."

"Let me warn you now. He'll most likely follow you to your room in hopes of getting in your bed." Mama Kate chuckled. "I doubt if he'll be the only one. Not many pretty ladies like you descend these parts, especially to go fishin'."

Ali chuckled. "I've had my fill of men for a while." The flatness of her voice was startling. "My work is much safer."

Mama Kate put her hands in the pockets of her flowered cotton tunic. She studied Ali. "Right...Your room is up the stairs and to the right. Gus is usually here to help my guests with their bags, but I sent him to town for groceries."

"Your husband?"

"Not married. Did that once. The love of my life. Hard to replace a man like that."

A reverent silence fell between them. Ali followed Mama Kate's gaze. This time she noticed not a statue, but an expanse of water about a hundred yards wide, meandering past the dock—the Arroyo Colorado, with the thick, native brush of sage, mesquite, and Spanish daggers lining the far bank.

Mama Kate spoke first. "The Lord called him, and ...well, I stayed and made the best of what we had going...which is this." She pointed to a boat on the slip. "Cy used to do all the guiding. Now I hire them. Keep that thing around just in case I get a wild hair to go for a boat ride." She grinned and then made a move to end the conversation.

"I'm going to take me a siesta before supper. I suggest you do the same. The sun and wind will likely beat you to death out there on the bay. Come week's end, you'll be thankful to go back home..." She peered intently at Ali once again. "Most folks are." Mama Kate nodded her head, appearing to have listened to a voice inaudible to Ali. "But then again, some stay longer than they expect. One look at the Mother Lagoon, and I knew I'd found home."

The smell of fresh-baked bread and roasted chicken roused Ali from a deep sleep. She sat up and observed the room, more closely than when she first arrived. The off-white lace curtains hung loosely from metal rods framing a single window. An overstuffed chair sporting blue hydrangeas with a matching ottoman was placed nearby, affording a view of both the yard and the television. After a big stretch, Ali swung her legs off the bed and sunk her toes into the celery green Berber carpet. Leaving her shoes behind, Ali exited the room and descended the stairs. The noises from her stomach reminded her that she hadn't eaten since morning. She entered the kitchen to see a multicourse meal in full production.

"Mama Kate, I thought you napped."

The older woman had smudges of flour on her face. "I did, twenty minutes. Any more than that, then you waste the day away." She raised her eyes to meet Ali's.

"I guess the trip took a bit out of me."

Mama Kate shrugged. "Concrete and glass zap the life right out of most people. All that old air, foul energy, bad moods, and such gets trapped inside them buildings. I see it on my guests' faces all the time." Kate flashed a knowing look at Ali. "Everybody thinks they come here to catch fish." She chuckled.

"May I help with anything?" Ali asked, averting Kate's observation.

"Set the table if you'd like. There will be four of us. Jack Cooper will be stopping by. She rolled the pie crust onto the rolling pin and then gently placed it on the pie plate. "I wanted him to meet you before the two of you set off in the morning. Thought it might make it easier to get to know each other over dinner than on the water with that dang motor running."

"She's matchmaking again." An older gentleman wearing brown and green plaid shorts and a freshly ironed khaki fishing shirt strolled through the kitchen door. "Hates seeing other people live lonely lives. Jack's a loner, living on the edge of the bay. Kinda like Kate and me." His eyes danced as he patted Kate on the shoulder.

Mama Kate scowled. "Gus, this is Ali, the magazine writer."

Gus extended his hand and smiled. "Nice to meet you, Ali. Gus Lammons, the gopher around these parts." He winked and then glanced around the house. "Jack not here yet, huh? Heard he got into some big trout earlier this week. Came up empty again, as usual."

With weathered skin and deep creases around his eyes, Gus appeared several years older than Mama Kate. He looked pointedly at Ali. "That man is obsessed with big trout. When he's not guiding clients, he's out there pounding those waters looking for her." He set a bag down on the counter. "Kate, can I help you with anything?"

"Keep talking. I'll let you know if something's needin' to be done."

Gus sat down at the table as Ali set the plates with a bright blue, yellow, and orange mandala pattern on each of the sage green placemats. "He just don't get it yet."

"Get what?" Ali asked while placing the yellow linen napkins next to the plates.

He leaned one elbow on the table and waved a finger at Ali. "The secret to catching big trout."

"Which is?" Ali slid into a chair, listening intently to Gus.

"It's not that easy to say." Gus paused, struggling for the right words. "Not trying too hard comes close."

"It's really about letting the trout teach you how to come into relationship with her." Mama Kate put a plate of carrots, celery sticks, and cucumbers on the table.

Ali picked up a cucumber and nibbled on it. "Now, I *really* don't get it."

Mama Kate put a hand on Ali's shoulder. "I have a feeling you'll get it before Jack does."

Gus took a bite of a celery stick. "Let me tell you a little bit about sea trout." His eyes twinkled, and his features softened. "They're special creatures. And the big ones are all females."

"Wise women of the bay," Mama Kate added.

Ali's face brightened. "My grandpa loved trout too—the freshwater kind. He said they spoke to him in whispers as he fished the streams. There were times when I'd find him sitting on a rock just staring in the water. When I'd ask him what he was doing, he'd say that he was listening to the trout."

Gus peered intently into Ali's eyes. "Ain't nothin' like it."

"And you say Jack Cooper is obsessed with them." She raised her right brow.

"Yep, and he don't know why either, not the real reason," Mama Kate said as she poured sliced apples into the crust. "All the men think they're out to catch a big fish, add another notch to their belts. Well, most of them." A smile crossed her lips. "What they're really after is communion."

"If they learn what that fish can teach them, they'll know what real love is all about," Gus explained.

"Have you caught the big one, Gus?"

He looked out toward the water. "I have indeed. All eighteen pounds of her. The record. It was a gift that will never come again."

Ali sensed sadness coming from Gus. "What about love?"

"Just not in the cards, I guess, not in the usual sense. But I can't complain. Life's been good to me. Come to know lots of good folks." He chuckled. "A couple of shysters, too." He abruptly rose and headed for the door. "Kate, I'm going out to check something on the dock."

Gus lumbered down the slope with a slight limp in his gate. It was the only thing that hinted at his age. He sported strong arms, muscular calves, and a sturdy back. He took the pebbled stone steps with ease, occasionally stopping to remove a dead leaf from a bougainvillea. The lush foliage, with the purple and crimson blossoms, lined a fence and ended about a third of the way to the dock, where it was met by an open expanse of thick, wide-bladed, carpet grass.

As Ali soaked in her surroundings, a ruby-throated hummingbird hovered at the orange bell-shaped blossoms of the cape honeysuckle. That single bird reminded her of the day on the farm where she counted a dozen of its cousins buzzing like bees around her grandmother's honeysuckle near the kitchen window. It had been a long time since she took note of such things. Too long.

"Jack's here."

"I didn't hear your doorbell." Ali turned from the window to find Mama Kate staring at her once again.

"I don't need that."

Kate had an air of wisdom about her. Her confidence beamed through her eyes, and the fact that she ran a tight ship was evident to Ali upon her arrival. Ali pondered the complexity of the woman who would be her host for the next few days. Kate seemed at ease and guarded at the same time. She realized Mama Kate was much like herself and wondered if it was the single event of her husband's passing or the culmination of many of life's disappointments that built the invisible, but palpable, wall around her. A light tap at the front door pulled her from her thoughts.

Max jumped up from his spot by the sofa, tail wagging, as he approached the door. Jack Cooper rounded the corner and entered the dining room, followed by a dog that resembled Max, much smaller and with a large white, star-like patch on her chest. He paused for a moment before her, startled by her presence. She extended her hand. "Ali Stephenson."

He shook her hand. "Jack Cooper," and then nodded toward the dog sitting obediently at his feet. "This is Lily."

Ali scratched the dog's ears, feeling Jack's eyes upon her. She met his gaze, taking note of his pronounced cheekbones and soft brown eyes. He looked uneasy, almost like he'd seen a ghost.    "Thanks for helping me with my assignment."

"Mama Kate set it up. Made me an offer I couldn't refuse." He moved by Ali and into the kitchen.

"I plum told him he had to take this one or never work for me again."

"Smells good, Mama Kate." He put his hands on Kate's shoulders.

"Don't go sweet talkin' me now. I'm busy." She glanced at Lily and Max. "Let your poor dog out for a romp with Max. Do him some good to stretch his old bones." She winked at Ali. "Then you take Ali out on the porch, get acquainted. Wine is on the counter yonder. Beer's in the fridge. Help yourselves." She glared at Jack. "Might loosen you up a bit."

Reluctantly, Jack did as he was told. He poured two glasses of wine and beckoned Ali to follow him to the porch. Jack took a sip of his wine, leaning his elbow on the green mosaic table between them. "Ever fly fished?"

She studied his profile while contemplating her answer. His skin was bronzed from the sun, and his hair was medium brown, with a hit of gray in his sideburns. "As my grandpa would say, I cut my eye teeth on cold water streams in Virginia."

Jack squirmed in his seat. "This is different."

"I know what I'm in for." Ali was annoyed that she felt like she had to prove herself and her abilities to this man she just met and knew nothing about her. And whom she was paying for his services.

Jack raised a brow and took another sip from his green-hued glass. "We'll see."

Mama Kate slipped out onto the porch, hearing just the last part of their conversation. She took a seat opposite Jack, which allowed her a perfect view of the pair.

For the first time since setting foot in South Texas, a sinking feeling settled into Ali's stomach. Gus was casting his rod, as gentle and graceful as her grandfather had. As she watched the rhythmic action, she began to regain her confidence.

"Can you double haul?" Jack interrupted her thoughts.

"Yes." She met his eye with a challenge.

"How far is your best cast?"

"Seventy-five feet—and *accurate*," She snipped.

Jack pursed his lips. Their conversation was suspended. Only the bright yellow-bellied kiskadees, with their black mask-like markings, dared to break the silence with their raucous calls. One sat on the piling high above the boat; another remained out of sight but sang from the far banks of the Arroyo. Evening was descending upon them, and nature was unleashing a burst of glory in the western sky.

"Jack, go get Gus. He's got a feather out of place about something." Mama Kate observed the older man, with concern. "It's time to eat, anyway."

Ali watched Jack saunter down the hill, her eyes settling on the shape of his shoulders beneath his sage fishing shirt. Max and Lily stayed close at his heels. "Seems like Captain Cooper has a feather or two out of place as well."

Mama Kate squinted in his direction. "He'll most likely warm up after he's had some time with you out on the water."

"I hope so. Or else it's going to be a very long week."

# Chapter Three

The stars twinkled brightly against the midnight blue backdrop. No hint of the day was yet to be seen, and the moon, just slightly past full, hung low on the horizon, an orange orb beckoning to be witnessed. Kate stood on the dock with her arms outstretched, soaking up the night's energy. She loved this time of day, especially these few days of each month when the moon was full. The feminine force more evident at this time to her.

Standing alone under the canopy of stars with the full moon shining upon her face, it was easy for her to sense that she was part of a seamless web of the Divine. It restored her faith and allowed her to believe that her presence was indeed significant on this planet. She had more work to do. If she didn't, she would have perished with Cy. There were many times when she wished she had.

Kate placed her hands over her heart. In a voice, loud and strong, she beckoned the Holy Mother, her Guardian Angels, and anyone else who would listen, to come forth and fill her heart and mind with the knowledge of what she needed to do that day and in the coming week. Ali was special. Kate could feel it. And she saw a spark of recognition in Jack Cooper's eyes when he first laid eyes on the woman. She knew he would.

The sound of a motor droning in the distance caught Kate's attention. She cocked her head and then nodded. It was Jack, and she was waiting for him. "Lord, let me be kind to that fool when he arrives." She bowed her head and then took a seat on the bench to await his appearance from beneath the cloak of the night's last breath.

Jack eased up to the dock, unaware of Kate's presence. It gave her time to look at him, really look at him. The mantle of sadness and anger that was evident when they first met still shrouded him. It kept him from living completely. They had something in common. But she had learned to move on, mostly, and although it had taken years, she now could say that she enjoyed life again.

"Morning, Jack." She rose as he tied the boat to the dock.

His mouth dropped open, obviously not expecting to find the dock occupied. "Morning, Kate. Why aren't you in the kitchen?"

"Already been there. Everythin's in the oven."

Jack hopped onto the dock. "Looks like it'll be a nice day for fishin'."

"It'll be nicer if you get that thorn out of your side," she chastised him.

He put his hands in his pocket and looked up at the sky. "I was a bit of a creep last night."

"I'll say." She tugged at the sleeve of his shirt. "Ali seems nice enough. Knows her stuff about fishin' too. Give it a chance."

"So, is this why you're here? To give me my morning preachin'?"

They strolled toward the house. "People come into our lives for a reason, Jack."

Jack put his arm around Kate's shoulder. "I'm still trying to figure out why you are in my life."

She paused, turning to face him and placing both hands on his shoulders. "You gotta listen to me on this one." The urgency in her tone startled both of them.

Ali's eyes sprung open several minutes before her alarm, and she momentarily forgot where she was. Remembering her exchange with Jack, brought it all back, she silently prayed for the strength to get on with her day. Flinging back the covers, she noticed the pit in her stomach. It was not from hunger but from the thought of spending five days with a man whose behavior the night before was not very attractive. Kate's attempt to keep the cordial conversation going had been thwarted by Jack's silence. *Great assignment, Joe.* Sinking her toes into the carpet, she fought back a sudden urge to flee.

Contemplating the day ahead and mentally reviewing her list of questions about the fishery, Ali slipped into her clothes. She opted for a pair of beige pants and a long-sleeved sky-blue shirt, with a matching blue buff to cover her neck. Slowly making her way down the stairs, Ali was greeted with the sounds of several voices, including Jack's. She had no time to wake up over a leisurely cup of coffee before facing him.

"Morning, Miss Ali," Kate called from behind her kitchen helm.

"Good morning, everyone." Ali picked up a cup and poured her coffee. "This kitchen always smells delightful."

"Frittata and cornbread." Kate carried two serving plates piled high with the morning fare to the table. "Keep you fueled up for the day's fishin'."

"Are you ready?" Gus asked as he leaned against the counter, his arms folded.

"As I'm ever going to be, I guess."

"You look dressed for the part." Jack nodded his approval.

"And as soon as I have some of this coffee, I'll probably remember how to cast my rod as well." A hint of sarcasm lingered on her words as she raised her mug in the air.

Ali strode to the table and took her place across from Jack. Looking into his eyes, she noticed that the edge from the prior evening had worn off, and they hinted of boyish mischievousness. She immediately felt guilty for her flippant remark.

Gus crossed the room, carrying his cup of coffee, and sat down at the table. "Where you heading first?"

Jack reached for the plate of cornbread, handing it to Ali before taking some for himself. "Trout Bar. Thought we'd work the channel for a bit before the sun comes up."

"Outgoing tide?"

Jack nodded.

"I saw a six or seven pounder hanging close to the channel marker there last week." Gus buttered his cornbread. "Then she snaked out onto the flat and started tailing right in front of my eyes."

"Catch her?" Jack asked, as he took a helping of the frittata.

"Didn't even cast to her."

"Out of range?"

Gus chuckled. "No, I just watched her."

"Why didn't you go after her?" Jack shook his head in disbelief.

"I figured I'd learn more by watching her for a while than I would by casting to her." He took a swig of coffee. "I'll be ready for her next time."

Gus took a bite of his eggs and turned toward Ali. "It's not as hard as you think. You gotta get in the zone. And try not to overthink it."

"You're talking nonsense." Jack put a heap of jelly on his cornbread. "It's technique, presentation. If you don't get that fly right on her nose, she'll ignore you."

Ali hid her amusement behind her coffee cup as the two continued their debate.

"And how many have you caught?" Gus taunted.

"A little early for this level of testosterone, isn't boys?" Kate joined them, untying her apron and laying it across the back of her chair. "Settle down. Besides, we need to say grace." She bowed her head. "Almighty Father, Blessed Mother, we thank you for this beautiful morning and the company of all at this table. Thank you for the bounty you've set before us. Bring blessings to all who made it possible. Be with us this day as we go about our business. Keep care of these two young folks as they head out on the water. Guide them and bring your wisdom and goodness into their lives. Amen."

An echo of "amens" followed.

"Now eat up," Kate commanded. "The sun is rising, and fish await." Then she caught Ali's eye and winked.

Following the path to the dock with Max by her side, Ali focused on a mantra to calm herself with each step. Her stomach churned, and her heart raced as she drew closer to the boat. She paused at the edge, where the lawn and the dock met, and took one deep breath. Jack extended his hand to take her gear.

"What kind of line you got on there?"

"Tropic line, weight forward."

"Seven weight." Jack tested the rod's action with a quick, short wave back and forth. "Nice. You have good taste."

"What? no sarcasm?" She stepped into the boat without his help. "You must be ill. Let me check your temperature." Spontaneously, she touched his cheek. "Cool as a cucumber." The sensation of the curves of his cheek lingered on the tips of her fingers. An awkward silence hung between them as the sky grew lighter in the east. "Our lunches." She handed him a canvas bag she carried in one hand. "Kate says you have the drinks."

His hand brushed hers in the exchange. "I'm sorry about last night. I'm a little nervous about this charter. I've never had a writer aboard my boat." He chanced a look in her eyes before putting the bag in the cooler. "Makes my job a lot harder than it usually is."

Ali was taken aback by his confession. "Well, I'm a little nervous about this assignment. I've never fished saltwater before. It's a new challenge for me." She extended her hand. "Truce."

As his hand met hers, the right corner of his mouth curved upward, creating a perfect dimple in his cheek. "Deal." He untied the rope from the cleat on the dock. "Let's go fishin'."

Ali settled into the seat beside Jack. With the wind and the motor making it difficult for easy conversation, she simply observed the scenery. The sky blossomed into shades of pink and lavender as they boated east on the Arroyo Colorado. They passed a couple of dozen fishing cottages. Some were grand in design, others were simple huts, and one or two could be described as "dilapidated" at best.

The Arroyo was undergoing a transformation. Evidence of a humble past hung on as newer buildings sprung forth on vacant lots. It all spoke of a simpler life—a slower pace. The appeal surprised her. The cottages came to an abrupt halt at the boundary of the Adolph Thomae Park. Onward, nothing but South Texas landscape, dotted with ebony, *huisache*, and agave, caught the eye, except for a couple of stone buildings and an equal number of piers at the park's launch.

As Ali tucked the information into her memory, she studied his features, more for herself than the article. Her fingers tingled as she recalled the sensation of his cheek against her hand. She returned her attention to the landscape, determined to keep her mind on her work.

"This is all part of Laguna Atascosa Wildlife Refuge," Jack shouted over the din of the motor. "This land will never be developed, at least it shouldn't be."

Ali watched flocks of gulls approach on their way inland to the dumps and parking lots of the nearby towns. At times they hung close to the water, swooping upward just before reaching the boat. Great blue herons and great egrets maintained their positions along the shore as the boat zoomed by. Dolphins rose before them, chasing bait and occasionally playfully flipping out of the water.

"It's beautiful," Ali shouted above the motor. The terrain was a woven canvas of open spaces with clumps of sea oxeye daisies and purslane, as well as areas of thick virgin brush, with sage, mesquite, and prickly pear cactus. She inhaled deeply, allowing the salty-sweet aroma of the flats to fill her lungs.

"Nothing like it." Jack glanced at her. "But wait until you see the Laguna Madre." He pointed ahead of them. "The largest shallow-water estuary in North America. A real treasure."

The mouth of the Arroyo opened into an expanse of water and sky for as far as the eye could see. An occasional spoil island dotted the landscape. Birds of all species and colors flew about or nestled on the sandy banks of the spoils.

"That's Bird Island." He pointed to a large mass of land straight ahead of them. "Those are Roseates." As they turned north, he pointed to a group of pink birds with spoon-like bills at the northern tip of the island.

"What are they?" Ali shouted.

"Roseate Spoonbills. Most folks think they're flamingos. But only one flamingo has been seen around here, and the rangers at the refuge think it blew here in a storm."

He slowed the boat and drew closer as he handed her a pair of binoculars. "They have spoon-like bills."

The birds lowered their heads to the water, moving their bills like a pendulum, first to the left and then to the right, sifting through the water for food. Many of the birds were barely a blush of pink; others were nearly crimson. "How come some are pinker than others?"

"Some say it's maturity; others say it's the amount of shrimp they eat." He shrugged. "Probably a little of both."

Jack and Ali continued onward for about a mile along the Intracoastal Waterway. As they passed a long, narrow spoil about thirty feet wide and a hundred feet long, Jack slowed the engine and allowed the boat to float slowly off the channel to the right. They came to rest twenty feet from the spoil island, sending gulls and terns into a frenzy. Some circled above the boat, voicing their displeasure with raucous squawks at the encroachment.

Reddish Egrets kept watch on an area of water about a hundred yards to the east. With their reddish-brown heads and blue-gray bodies, they danced in the water with their wings elegantly extended. Occasionally, their pointed beaks darted into the water and emerged with a silvery minnow.

"The Trout Bar. When the tide is really low, a sandy bar is exposed. We never boat across it — sacred ground." Jack explained as he staked the boat.

Another skiff veered out onto the flat to the south of the spoil, about fifty yards from them. "That's Skipper." He pointed to a large blue flats boat in a similar shape as Jack's.

"I'm actually meeting with him later in the week to speak about the guides' association."

"He's a good source, knows everybody." Jack handed her the rod and then a plastic bag with several flies in it. "Might want to put these in your fly box." He took another from his pocket. "And you might want to start with this one," he said. He reached for her rod and bit off the fly that she had earlier tied on.

"No nippers."

"Never know where they are." His eyes twinkled in the morning light as he tied on the popper.

Ali carefully studied the fly's construction: a thin block of black foam situated behind the eye of the hook, with a section of green deer hair and rubbery pink stretchy material resembling wobbly legs dangling beneath. "Does this have a name?"

"I call it the VIP," he mentioned while focusing on his own rod.

Sitting on the boat's edge, Ali eased into the water.

"Shuffle your feet," he warned. "Stingrays."

She cringed, hesitating to put her other foot in the water.

"As long as you don't step directly on them, they won't sting," Jack added with a touch of authority.

"Are they aggressive?"

"No. They just don't take too kindly to being stepped on." He pulled his rod out of its holder from behind the seat. "Good news is, they're usually accompanied by a redfish or trout."

Ali took a few cautious steps with Jack by her side. She pulled out line and readied herself for an opportunity. "What am I looking for?"

"Tails, surface disturbance, nervous water." He used his rod to point to an area twenty feet from the spoil. See that choppy water. Most likely baitfish."

Ali strained to identify the movement. "I don't see what you're looking at."

"The wind is making a pattern in the water heading away from us. The nervous water looks like it's coming toward us." He leaned closer. "There, to the right."

Ali fought hard to concentrate on the water and not the closeness of his presence. She could smell the mixture of soap and sunscreen on his skin. *Get a grip, Ali. You're here to fish.* "Got it."

"This is like hunting. We're looking for our prey. Although occasionally, we'll blind cast, like off the edge of the flats into the channel."

She took a step and sloshed the water.

"Move slowly. If you can hear yourself moving through the water, the fish can, too."

They waded slowly along the inside of the spoil, letting the sounds of the morning filter between them. Ali tightly held her line between her fingers, waiting nervously for Jack's command to cast.

"There, she's moving left to right about forty feet out," Jack said.

"What?"

"A tailing trout," Jack pointed his rod in the direction of the fish.

"I don't see it."

"Look for a little black triangle and the body snaking through the water."

Staring intently on the surface of the water, Ali attempted to imprint a mental image of his description in her mind. "Found her." She took a deep breath and brought her rod up for her back cast. Suddenly, Gus's voice echoed in her ear. *I just watched her.*

Holding her rod in place, Ali did just that. As she stared at the creature moving through the water, she fell into a meditative trance, letting the fish's movement imprint upon her mind.

"Cast!"

Jack's voice startled her, and she lowered her rod, blinking to regain her composure. "I thought it would be better to take Gus's advice."

"Damn, girl!" He whipped his hat off in frustration and slapped it on the water. That's not what I'm out here for. You missed the chance of a lifetime."

"There will be others." Ali stripped the line in and reached for the leader. She looked down at the fly and pretended to check the knot, seething over his reaction and being called "girl." Releasing the line and taking a step away from him, she called over her shoulder. "Besides, I'm paying you, so relax."

He let her comment sink in before switching his attention to the edge of the channel. "I don't make a practice of fishing with clients, but Kate wants fish for dinner."

"What about catch and release?" She waded toward him.

"I make exceptions now and again."

Jack positioned Ali along the channel and walked fifty feet upwind of her. They cast rhythmically into the deeper water, stripping their flies back toward the edge of the flat.

She hooked up, "I'm on." Her reel sang as the fish ran deep into the channel. She carefully played the fish, gingerly bringing it within reach. She lifted it out of the water with a grin on her face. It was a nice trout about twenty inches long. "I believe I caught my share of supper." She reached into her pack for the stringer. Reverently, she closed her eyes and said a prayer of thanksgiving for her catch.

"Need help?"

"No, I can do it." With the surety of movement, she slipped the metal spike of the stringer through the fish's lip and then tied the rope end to her belt.

After an hour of dancing with trout on the ends of their rods, they headed back to the boat with enough fish for the table. "Time to go after some redfish," Jack said as he stepped alongside her.

Ali felt his eyes rest upon her for a time, as if studying her for some closely guarded secret. She giggled nervously. "Even if I don't catch another fish today, it's been great. Thank you."

"The day is far from over," he said, untying the stringer from her wading bag.

Kate rested on the porch, with her feet propped up on a chair. She wasn't one to read much, preferring to nurture her connection with God, which she did by praying the rosary and witnessing the magic of nature in her yard. The turkeys were back for a late afternoon snack. The sunlight illuminated their feathers, transforming them into a rainbow of coppers and greens. Two hens gathered with several chicks, nearly full-grown now, under the mesquite. The toms rested near the garden, unable to enter and feast upon the ripe tomatoes because of the waist-high fence Gus had erected to keep them out, topped off with a fine mesh netting.

With the sound of a motor approaching, Kate focused on the Arroyo. Jack had lengthened his guiding day by more than an hour. She took it as a good sign. If things were miserable out there, no doubt they'd be back at the dock in a more punctual manner.

"You're late," Mama Kate called from the porch as Ali and Jack pulled up to the dock.

"I told him a couple of hours ago we needed to call it a day," Ali responded, "He's relentless."

"Stubborn's more like it," Kate chuckled.

"Hey, you two, stop ganging up on me," Jack smiled as he tied up to the dock.

Ali reached for her rod and her gear. "That was one heck of a workout."

"You'll sleep good tonight." Kate wandered down to the dock. "Catch supper?"

"Ali caught her share—and more." Jack held up the trout.

Gus sauntered up behind them. "That girl can fish!"

"No redfish, though," Ali stepped up to the cleaning station and hosed off her rod, acutely aware that hearing Gus refer to her as a "girl" had less of a string than when Jack did.

"Jack put me on several, but I just couldn't seem to connect." The ease at which she tended to her tasks made it seem as if she'd been doing them for years.

Gus took the fish from Jack and prepared to clean them.

"Stay for supper, Jack?" Kate eyed him from beneath her straw hat that looked like it had seen a hurricane or two.

Jack pondered Kate's offer. "I'd like that."

"You can clean up after Ali's had her shower." Kate looked pleased. "Gus will fetch you a clean shirt from his place."

Kate took Ali by the hand. "C'mon, girl. Gotta get you cleaned up, so you can relax with a nice glass of cabernet on the porch."

Ali chuckled. "You are spoiling me, Kate."

"That's my job." The older woman smiled as she led Ali into the house.

✳ ✳ ✳

Stepping out of the shower, Ali stared at her reflection. Her freckles had sprouted, despite repeated doses of sunscreen. But it was her eyes that intrigued her most. They sparkled. She hadn't seen that look on her face in a long time. After combing her fingers through her hair, she applied a little mascara and some light plum lipstick before donning a pair of khaki shorts and a short-sleeved pink t-shirt. She nodded her approval. Jack Cooper was working on her, despite some hesitation and his occasional thoughtless remark.

Sauntering down the stairs, she listened closely for the sound of voices. All that she heard, however, was the sound of Kate humming and the sizzling of oil in a frying pan.

"All cleaned up?" Kate asked, even before Ali rounded the corner into the living room.

"How do you do that?" Ali picked up a carrot stick.

"Do what?"

"Know people are here before you see them?"

"Well, in this case, I heard you coming down the stairs." She dipped a fish fillet into the mixture of cornmeal and flour. "Other times, it's just good old woman's intuition."

After pouring a glass of water, Ali turned to Kate. "Need help?"

"No, this is my job. Yours is to relax and enjoy the place. Jack will be back in a bit. Gus took him to his house for clothes and a shower. I set the wine glasses out on the screened porch to the side here. Out of the sun. Figure you had enough of that for one day."

Ali nodded. "I must admit I'm a little tired. I might not be able to keep my eyes open very long tonight."

"No need. We'll have supper shortly, and you and Jack can go your separate ways and get ready for tomorrow." Kate put the fillet in the oil. "Not that I'd mind if the two of you made other plans, and I had an extra guest for the night." Kate chuckled.

"That's not my style."

"I've heard that before."

"Not from me."

"I see you struggling. Your head's telling you one thing, and your heart's whispering another." Kate wiped her hands on her apron and then turned her attention to the pot of green beans steaming on the stove. "Would you take my advice on something that's probably none of my business?"

"Do I have a choice?" Ali chuckled.

Kate shrugged. "Put yourself in God's hands. See what's in the cards." She plucked a bean from the pot and then took a little bite. "Just about done." She turned off the burner and then surveyed Ali. "Jack has taken a liking to you. I can see it in his eyes."

"Gus mentioned he lives alone," Ali paused thoughtfully. "He's not in a relationship?"

Kate picked up the lid of another pot and stuck a fork in the potatoes. "I hear he sees a waitress from a café that the guides all go to, but I don't get the sense that it's anything serious. More like a matter of convenience, if you know what I mean."

The door opened, and Gus came in, followed by Jack and Max. Jack was clean, but the scruffy growth of his beard remained.

Kate eyed Jack. "You sure look all gussied up."

"I guess that's what happens when you wear Gus's clothes," Jack quipped.

"Ooh," Ali groaned. "That's so bad."

"Wine's on the screened porch. Crackers and cheese as well." Kate turned a fillet. "Gus, pour us a glass and come back to help me out."

"Anything you say, boss." He followed Ali and Jack onto the porch. "If you ask me, she just wants you two to be alone."

Ali blushed, hoping that Jack wouldn't notice. Picking up the bottle of wine, she poured four glasses and turned to Gus. "Please feel free to join us."

"You don't know Kate like I do." He winked at Jack and then retreated to the kitchen.

Jack grinned. "Let's sit. I don't know about you, but the day is catching up with me."

Resting on two wicker lounge chairs, they let silence enfold them for a while.

"So, what are we in for tomorrow?"

"Perhaps your first redfish on a fly." He peered out at the Australian Pines in the corner of Kate's property. "Wind is supposed to die down. We should find tailers in the morning."

"I look forward to it."

"So do I." Jack peered into Ali's eyes and was about to say something when Kate's voice boomed from inside, calling them to dinner.

# Chapter Four

Ali reached over the side of the boat and gave Jack her rod and gear bag. "Missed you at breakfast." She handed him a brown paper bag. "Kate made you an egg muffin sandwich."

"Running a little slower than usual this morning." He stowed the food in the ice chest. "Sleep well?"

"Like a baby." She handed him a thermos. "And you?"

"I've had better nights." He averted her scrutiny.

"Kate must have known. She's filled this thermos with coffee."

Jack winced. "She knows a lot more than she lets on."

"I've noticed."

He chanced a look in her direction and started to say something, but a passing boat diverted his attention. "We'd better get going."

\* \* \*

Ali perched in front of the console, with her camera poised for action. As they journeyed eastward toward the mouth of the Arroyo, she shot photos of the vast cactus and mesquite populated banks. Then, she turned in her seat and took a shot of Jack at the helm. He posed perfectly for several and then playfully made a face, which she captured as well. It gave her a reason to pause. He was a complex man, but he was beginning to reveal a lighter side that she sensed most didn't see.

Turning her attention back to her photography, she noted several brown pelicans perched upon the tug tie-ups near the mouth of the Arroyo. "Would you slow down and move closer to the birds?" She pointed to the large white cylinders riding high above the water. Two or three pelicans rested on each, some preening their feathers with their long beaks. Jack eased the boat closer, and Ali was able to snap a few shots, without disturbing the birds.

The morning sky was awash with pinks, lavenders, and blues as they approached Bird Island. Jack veered the boat to the right and eased south for a few hundred yards before angling to the east. The water had the appearance of a mirror. The distinction between the sky and the water was indiscernible. They were alone on the flats, with the exception of a handful of great blue herons, with their stately gray feathers and white plumage upon their heads. Most stood their ground as the boat approached; others took to flight, squawking their indignation at the intrusion. Great egrets, of nearly the same stature as their cousins, the blue herons, were milling about as well. Their bright white feathers contrasted sharply with the shimmery slate blue backdrop of the water.

Ali snapped away, catching some birds in flight, others standing perfectly still with their heads leaning to one side, eyes peering intently into the water. She lowered her camera to her lap and stored the image into her memory, not only to write about but to revisit whenever she needed a connection with nature. A wave of sadness crept into her psyche. Joe had been right. She needed this trip more than she realized.

"We'll wait to see if the tails come up." Jack roused her from her thoughts as he staked the boat. "I saw several wakes as we were coming in, so they should be here," he added as he surveyed the horizon.

Ali took several photos of the horizon and a couple more of Jack as he continued his watch for tails. "There's one." He pointed to an area about a hundred yards from them. The redfish's tail waved like a flag above the water. He noted several others closer in. "They have an anterior mouth, and so they're naturally bottom feeders. When they're rooting the bottom, their tails stick out of the water. When they tail, it's a sign that they're very comfortable." In the distance, a boat advanced toward them. "When that boat gets closer, they'll stop tailing." Ali quickly switched to a zoom lens and caught several tailing reds in action.

The boat passed, and the tails disappeared as if on cue. Taking advantage of the break in the action, Jack urged her to get her rod.

"Joining me?" she asked.

He shook his head. "Not today." He climbed off the side and put his hand out to help her into the water.

"Then be my cameraman?" She handed him the camera.

As she stepped into the water, Jack reminded her to move very slowly, noting the particularly challenging wading conditions created by the calm morning. The mirror-like surface rippled at even the slightest intrusion. She slowed her pace and suddenly felt more connected to her body than she had in years. Something had shifted, and she saw her surroundings in a way she hadn't before, with much more clarity. "I see four tails."

"It's a pod." Jack nodded in their direction. "Wade out a few feet and wait until they get within your range. Then place your fly right in the center of the pod."

She took one sure-footed step toward the fish. Her heartbeat quickened, and her hands shook as she checked that her fly was correctly tied to the tippet. Fifty feet of the line lay in her stripping basket; another twenty loosely draped off the end of the rod. She took another step and then prepared to cast. Dropped the fly, she made two false casts before laying the fly precisely in the middle of the tailing pod. A large bronze head emerged from beneath the surface of the water. Its fleshy lips grazed the fly, and then it turned away. Ali gasped at the scene as the pod dispersed in all directions.

"What happened?" Jack came up behind her.

"I don't know. I did exactly as you said." She stripped in her line as she recounted the scene. "I waited until they were within range, and then I dropped the fly right in the middle of the pod. One fish came out of the water, looked at it, and then turned away."

"Did you strip the fly?"

Ali was astounded. "You didn't tell me that!"

"My bad!" He bellowed, tilting his head back. Then he glanced around to see if there were any opportunities nearby for a repeat performance.

"I should have asked," she quickly responded. "It's my job to ask the important questions."

"I shouldn't have assumed that you'd know what to do." He turned toward her. "How about we go back to the boat, have some coffee, and one of Kate's muffins. I'll lay out several scenarios on what you'll need to do to catch your first redfish. Maybe the tailing action will resume here shortly."

Jack began his treatise on presenting to tailing redfish as they waded side by side to the boat. Ali noted the details of his explanations, watching his expressions and the movement of his hands.

Then, he stopped abruptly, grabbing her wrist to keep her from advancing. "There's a large trout about ten feet from us, a little to the right." His voice was barely above a whisper.

Turning her head slowly, Ali pinpointed a large trout, over two feet long, suspended in the water, peering back at them.

"Let's just watch her," he whispered.

"Just like Gus said."

"You're too close to cast."

They stood motionless as the fish observed them. Her pectoral fins barely moved as she held herself in place. Then she slowly passed in front of them no more than an arms reach away. Ali's heart beat wildly as the fish came closer. Time seemed suspended as she observed the creature, noting the spots on her skin and the snake-like motion of the fish's body. Ali followed her departure until she could no longer be seen.

Jack was the first to let out an audible breath. "That was incredible." He looked at Ali. "I do believe you're going to have a relationship with big trout."

"What makes you say that?" She was puzzled.

"They don't just do that to anyone."

"Are you saying she wanted us to see her?"

"She wanted *you* to see her."

They climbed aboard the boat, each lost in their own thoughts. Jack stowed the gear as Ali placed the muffins on two green cloth napkins. Jack poured the coffee, and the two sat facing each other on the boat's broad flush deck. Ali took a bite of the muffin as she made a few notes on her pad. "The information you've given me this morning will be very beneficial."

"Now that I've remembered to tell you everything." He smiled apologetically.

"This whole experience is so similar to how my grandpa taught me to see rising trout on the Rapidan."

The color washed from Jack's face, and silence fell between them for several moments until Ali felt compelled to inquire about his obvious reaction.

"You seem to have a connection to that area." She sipped her coffee. "I saw your face change the other night when I mentioned it as well."

Jack stared off into the eastern horizon. "I fished there for many years."

"I thought I detected a northern accent."

"I made my home in Virginia for over twenty-five years." He folded the napkin over the muffin and took a swig of his coffee, looking like he was about to end the conversation.

"Would it be so bad to share a little about who you are, Jack Cooper?" Ali touched his hand. "Off the record."

"Are you always so inquisitive about your subjects?" He regarded her thoughtfully.

"On occasion." Her mind flitted briefly over her past to the one—and *only time*—she let an interview cross the line. It was the beginning of the best and the worst four years of her life.

"So, where did you grow up?" Jack turned the tables on her.

"At the base of Old Ragg Mountain, on Overlook Road, near a two-horse town called Shayville. My grandpa and grandma sold organic vegetables, fruits, and even some honey. We had a little farm stand out by the road, and that was my job during the summer and into the fall after school."

Jack lowered his gaze, peering into his coffee. "The Stephenson Farm."

"You know my place?"

"Best honey I ever tasted."

"I don't remember ever seeing you before."

"Nor I, you." He glanced at her. "My wife's parents own a house around the bend."

"The Wilsons?" Ali's voiced trailed off as she remembered their daughter, who was her weekend buddy.

"Jenna was like my big sister." She pushed the hair away from her ear. "See that scar." Ali pointed to a raised bump just above her pearl earring. "Jenna pierced my second hole. Grandma got so mad. Said it was the workings of the devil to have more than one earring. She made me take it out. So each night I would put it back in until finally I got tired of the routine and let it heal over."

Jack's silence, coupled with Kate's belief that he was unmarried, piqued Ali's curiosity. "I haven't seen her since she left for college. How is she?"

"She passed away three years ago." His voice was barely above a whisper.

Ali's heart stopped momentarily as she reeled with the news. "I'm sorry. I'd always hoped that one day our paths would cross again."

The occasional splash of a leaping mullet and the lapping of the waves provided a backdrop for their thoughts. Ali focused on her present surroundings to stave off the blanket of loneliness that always crept up on her whenever she was transported to the past. "How did you come to be here?"

"I couldn't bear being anyplace that reminded me of her."

"And then I show up on your boat." Her voice trailed off as she pondered the strange turn of events. "I don't understand why things happen like this."

Abruptly, he rose, reaching out to help her up. "We better go find you another group of redfish."

Ali stepped off the boat behind him, wondering how she ended up with a guide so closely tied to her past—one that she too tried to avoid. Shaking her head, she stripped line back into the water and made a few false casts. She readied herself for more fishing, refusing to allow her thoughts to think of anything other than catching fish.

Jack had a wealth of knowledge about the bay, and Ali used every chance she could to ask questions, returning to the task at hand and leaving the personal revelations tucked in the back of her mind. In addition to taking photos, she also made copious notes each time they stopped. Their earlier conversation was neatly encased in that one shared moment. Their uncanny connection was unsettling, and she felt more than a little guilty about her attraction to her friend's husband. Jenna was the only person who encouraged her to leave Old Ragg and go onto college—to be more than a secretary, the way most people expected. *After all, common folk don't have high falutin' ideas about life. They live simply and stay close to family.* Her grandmother's voice echoed in her mind. Jenna provided Ali with the belief that life could be different.

After exhausting their possibilities in the area, Jack and Ali once again boarded the boat. This time Ali sat in front of the console and closed her eyes, taking a brief respite from the sensory and emotional overload. Focusing on the salty-sweet aroma filtering through her nose with each breath, any anxiety that had been building melted away.

Jack stopped the boat just a mile off Padre Island in an area known as the White Sand. In the distance, the high-rise motels in the city of South Padre Island marked the far southern tip of the island. The causeway jutted upward, forming an arc that joined the island to the mainland. Ali spotted cars moving to and fro between the two points. The development on the island extended for about four miles. It then abruptly stopped, leaving the remaining sand flats and dunes to the wildlife and native plants.

"We'll wade here," Jack said after he killed the motor. "This is our version of the Bahamas."

Walking along the firm sandy bottom, Jack helped Ali spot the fish in the rippled water. "They'll appear as clearly defined, dark shapes against the light background. Redfish will be darker and larger than trout. Trout have a greenish tint to them."

"What are those fish?" Ali asked, pointing to the darting shapes passing her.

"Mullet, they act like puppy dogs, kind of frenetic."

"There's a redfish." She pointed at it with her rod.

"Nice! Now watch him, and when he's in range, make your cast. Don't be timid."

Ali tracked the large body, warily moving from left to right about a hundred feet from them. Jack crouched beside her to minimize his profile. Slowly, she raised the tip of her rod, and then as the fish eased in closer, she increased the power of her back cast and presented the fly with determination. Before the line hit the water, the fish darted by them. She looked at Jack, "What happened?"

"He saw you or the line." He rose out of his crouching position. "There will be others." He began walking, cueing Ali to do the same.

With her senses on full alert, Ali spied a small creature floating along on a clump of grass. "A seahorse!" She cupped the hippocampus in the palm of her hand but kept it fully submerged.

Jack bent down for a closer look, and in doing so, the brims of their hats touched. "That's a special find," he whispered as Ali allowed the seahorse to resume its journey.

"I've always loved seahorses. My grandpa once bought me a bracelet with seahorses on it...." Her unfinished thoughts drifted away much like the seahorse.

"He was a special man," Jack said softly.

"That he was, and I didn't appreciate him as much as he deserved to be," Ali turned away, choking back the rise of tears.

For the rest of the day, their conversation was sparse. When the sun settled lower in the sky, they returned to the boat and headed back to Mama Kate's. A comfortable silence bookended the space around them. It had been some time since Ali felt this at ease with anyone besides Joe and her grandpa. She spent much of the evening pondering the characteristics of all the men she'd been with in her life—the ones where she was free to be herself and those whose expectations she forced herself to live up to, only to die a little each moment they were together. As she drifted off to sleep, she reflected on her grandpa and life on the farm, comforted by the memory.

Daybreak was an hour away as Ali sauntered down the stairs, carrying her fishing pack. She wore a sage green fishing shirt and a pink and green tie-dyed buff around her neck. Her beige pants swished as she walked through the room, announcing her arrival. Max beat his tail against the light peach tile as she approached his space. She bent down and scratched his ears, "Morning, Max." He rolled over on his belly, and she rubbed it a few times as well.

"Morning, Kate."

"You're up early," Kate raised her brow in surprise.

"I guess my two-hour nap yesterday restored my reserves," Ali responded softly.

"Ready to head back home yet?"

"Not at all," Ali said. The pitch of her voice startled her. *What's that about?*

Kate watched Ali's expression. "I doubt he's ready for anything serious."

Ali poured a cup of coffee and returned to the dining table. "I'm not talking about Jack, Kate. I'm talking about this land, the wildlife, the plants, the smells—all of it, especially you and Gus. It feels so much like home here."

"Uh, huh." Kate spooned a pot of oatmeal into a Talavera bowl, its blues, oranges, and yellows intermingled into a mandala-like pattern.

"He is an intriguing man," she shared, refraining from mentioning the details of their personal connection. She was still sorting it out, trying to make sense of their chance meeting.

"I suspect he feels the same about you." Kate set the bowl on the table and wiped her hands on her apron.

"It's a moot point anyway. I leave in three days, and it's doubtful our paths will ever cross again."

"Not unless it's meant to be." Kate glanced out the window.

"You believe in destiny?" Ali raised a brow as she glanced at Kate.

Kate nodded. "I don't always like it, but I do believe there is a plan, with a capital P." She joined Ali at the table with a mug of coffee. "Our job is to rise to the test, respond with our hearts open, and our fears locked in a little box, so they don't get in the way."

"Is that the way you live your life?"

Kate peered out the window. "Not as much as I'd like."

"Why not?"

Kate sighed, "I guess I'm not as brave as I'd like to think I am."

"How do you get over the fear?"

"Go to the edge and leap, I guess." Kate sipped her coffee. "I just haven't found the edge. Life is easy here for me, just as it is. No reason to change it."

Ali thought of Gus. "Maybe you're at the edge and just don't know it."

Kate flashed her a startled look. "You'd better eat up. Jack just pulled up." She rose from the table and returned to the kitchen.

Moments later, Jack bounded up the slope, with Lily at his heels. He swished through the kitchen door. "Ready for your first redfish?"

"I've been ready. They just haven't been willing." Ali smiled, realizing she could have easily been describing her love life.

He sat down beside her at the table. "I have a deal for you. You catch your first redfish, and I'll take you to Mexico. The sooner you catch it, the sooner we get off the water. Then you can get some late afternoon pictures of the streets like you mentioned."

Ali sensed Kate's gaze on the both of them, and she glanced briefly in her direction before turning back to answer Jack. "That sounds like a nice proposition." She rose to put her dishes in the sink. "I hope I can perform under that pressure."

"I think you're up for it." He smiled at her and nodded.

"I believe I am," A boost of confidence welled up inside of her. Not only did she think she could, she knew it.

Kate handed Jack a cup of coffee. "Did you bring extra clothes with you?"

"Sure did. Lily, too."

"I see that." Kate looked at Max and Lily, romping through the backyard. "I'll make up the room for you. No sense in you going back across the bay tonight."

"I knew you would." He picked up his coffee and glanced at Ali. "Meet you at the dock in five minutes."

Kate watched him leave and then turned to Ali. "Look's like you're the one at the edge."

Ali cocked her head. "Maybe so."

✳ ✳ ✳

The sun's rays beat down on Ali as she knelt in the water. It was hot, and with only trickle of a breeze, the heat was stifling. Her shirt clung to her, drenched with perspiration. The water, as warm as a bath, didn't provide much relief.

"Time's awastin', Ali," Jack coached.

"I can't find him." She frantically scanned the water, searching for the redfish.

"Fifty feet, moving to the right."

Ali clenched her rod. "I could use a little help here," she whispered, with a quick glance toward the sky.

"Thirty-five, coming straight at us."

"Got him." Ali raised the rod for her first false cast.

"Thirty feet." Jack pointed. "Take your shot, now."

Ali sent the line shooting through the guides.

"He sees it. Strip, strip."

Ali stripped the line feverishly and then felt an intense tug. "Whoa! He's on!"

"Strip set the hook, then raise the rod tip." Jack walked toward her. "Let him run."

"Oh, my God, this is incredible." Ali beamed as the fish darted away from her, the sound of the reel marking his retreat. "This is no Shenandoah bass."

"Not at all." He raised the camera and focused, first on her face, and then changed the setting for a wide-angle shot, capturing every movement of Ali playing the fish.

"When he slows down, start reeling him in."

She turned the reel, noting the power in the resistance. She was also very aware of Jack observing her every move. She wasn't sure which made her more nervous. "He wants no part of this."

"He's coming in. Keep tight to him."

Ali watched as the copper-colored body trailed through the water.

"When he sees us, he'll run again."

The fish darted to the left. "There he goes again! Man, he's a fighter!" She laughed as the fish took another run.

Jack stayed close. "You'll probably be able to bring him in this time."

Ali exerted some pressure on the fish. The muscles in her arms burned from the exertion. "I need to work out more for this kind of fishing." She took a step backward as the fish zig-zagged on the flats. The butt of the rod firmly planted in her abdomen.

"Don't step back. Stingrays may be in your mud trail," he cautioned.

Moments later, Ali had the fish at her feet. She tucked the rod under her arm and reached into the water.

"Don't lip him. Those teeth are sharp." Jack leaned down beside her. "Put one hand under his head, and then wrap the other around his tail."

Ali followed his instructions while marveling at the beauty of the fish. His gold and copper scales glistened in the sunlight, and a light blue tint outlined his tail. Jack snapped photos of her holding the redfish, which measured about twenty-four inches.

"He's beautiful." Ali held him up and kissed the top of his head.

"Probably a girl. Boys drum," Jack said as he removed the shrimp-like fly from its mouth.

"Drum?"

"They make a grunting noise. It's used to warn the other fish of danger and also to attract their mates." Jack made a grunting noise.

"Cute." Ali studied his expression. His face was growing softer as the hours passed.

"Better let her go." Jack stepped back. "Let's get a release shot." The camera made two audible clicking noises, and then the redfish swam away unharmed and eager to join her clan.

"Well, you've met your challenge."

"But, I haven't caught my trophy trout."

He regarded her for a moment. "There will be time for that."

"I hope so."

Jack touched her shoulder. "You've done well."

She liked the sensation of his hand on her shoulder. "You've been a great guide."

"We worked well together..." he smiled, "after we got a few things straight." He moved toward the boat. "Time to head to port and head out for a night on the little town of Nuevo Progresso."

Ali followed a couple of steps behind, watching him stride through the water with ease. He was different from the other men, more contemplative, albeit a bit dark at times. Her imagination unveiled the possibility of a simpler life, living close to the waters of the Mother Lagoon. She quickly dismissed the fantasy. Even though her life had become rather rote, she had no inclination to change a thing.

# Chapter Five

Gus glanced up from the crossword puzzle as Jack rounded the corner into the living room. He was wearing a tropical print button-down shirt and sage green shorts. "I ain't seen you dressed like that before, Jack."

Kate came around from the kitchen carrying a tray of iced tea. "Ali caught her first red today, and Jack promised he'd take her to Mexico."

"Sounds like you got a keeper there." Gus tapped his pencil against the palm of his weathered hand. "Catches her first red third day out. Now all you have to do is figure out how to get her back here."

"It's all catch and release, my friend." Jack sat next to Gus and sipped his tea, wondering if his attraction to Ali was obvious.

Kate chuckled. "You talk a good line."

"Don't give me that evil eye of yours." Jack fidgeted in his chair.

"Suit yourself. I could save you some trouble." Kate winked at Gus and leaned toward Jack. "I'm going to tell you anyway. You'd be a fool to let this one slip away. Ain't no fun living alone till you're old and decrepit."

Gus flashed her a look, arching the silvery brow over his right eye.

A broad grin swept across Kate's face as she peered into the living room. Jack whirled around, his mouth slightly agape as he caught his first glimpse of Ali, wearing a gold tank dress and celadon sandals. A blue paisley pashmina was draped over one arm, and her hair flowed past her shoulders, free from the ponytail that had held it in place for the last few days.

Ali squirmed as three pairs of eyes fell upon her. "Is this alright?" She raised her arms slightly and looked down at her dress.

"You look great." Jack stepped toward her. "Ready to go."

"Wait," Kate approached Ali holding a small woven drawstring bag that she'd taken from her apron pocket. "You'll need these for the kids."

Ali peered inside the bag. "Coins?"

"The beggar children," Kate explained. "I know you won't be able to turn away."

✳ ✳ ✳

A two-lane bridge lay before them as they approached the border. Cars and trucks crept through the checkpoint, those leaving the states paying the tolls, those returning declaring their citizenship and purchases. Pedestrians made their way along a covered sidewalk on either side of the traffic lanes. "We'll park here and walk across." Jack pointed to a parking lot that was brimming with cars.

The sun was resting low on the horizon as Ali eased into a parking place. Tourists dressed in khaki shorts, colorful tops, or t-shirts sporting their favorite beer or vacation spot, wandered to and from the bridge. After fetching her pashmina and bag from the back seat, Ali stepped out of the car. Once again, the grackles serenaded her, only this time she wasn't alone. Jack gently touched her elbow to show her the way.

"You're about to get your first glimpse of a Mexican border town," Jack said as they neared the center of the bridge that crossed the Rio Grande.

Beyond lay a congested street, with cars and people for as far as the eye could see, and signs in all shapes, sizes, and colors announcing the services of dentists, pharmacies, and restaurants. Below them, the muddy Rio Grande meandered toward the Gulf of Mexico. Several boys swung from a tree branch on a rope swing, plunging into the water with no concern for the clarity of the river. Further along the bank, a man dressed in an off-white tunic and matching pants led a horse to the edge of the river. The horse lowered its head and quenched its thirst before taking a step into the water, following his owner deeper into the muddy waters. Ali savored the sights and sounds as they kept a leisurely pace over the arc of the bridge.

The Mexican border check lay before them. Armed guards watched as Jack and Ali passed through yet another turnstile. Halfway through the first congested block, several children approached, with their heads cocked to one side and their dark brown eyes wide with expectation.

"Lady, Lady," they cried as they tugged at her dress.

"Careful," Jack cautioned. "They'll take every last dime you have. It's a racket. They're working for someone else and get a small cut in the action."

"At least they get something." Ali pulled the bag of coins from her purse.

The older kids shoved their way to the front of the pack, lunging their soiled hands toward her. While Ali gave each child one coin, her eyes rested on one little girl standing in the back, her two tiny hands cupped, as she quietly waited her turn.

Ali stepped forward and knelt before the little girl. She put three coins in her hands and then closed them. "Go to your mama."

The little girl's face brightened, and she whispered, *"gracias,"* before scampering down the street yelling for her mother. Ali watched as the little girl faded into the crowd, and a wave of sadness passed through her.

Feeling a hand on her shoulder, she turned to see Jack's questioning eyes. Averting his gaze, she said, "I'd better take some photos." For the next hour, Ali distanced herself from Jack and the children. She focused on the merchants whose wares of silver jewelry, leather belts, baskets, and linens captured the more pleasant aspects of the environment. After walking both sides of the street for several blocks with Jack following closely, she put the camera away and turned to him. "Thanks for giving me the space to focus. I'm ready to shop now."

"How about a drink first?" Jack said, checking his watch. "We can slip over to Arturo's for a margarita and some nachos and then shop before dinner."

"I'd like that." She took a deep breath, bringing herself back to the present. The encounter with the little girl was now safely behind her.

Squeezing between bumper-to-bumper traffic crawling down the street, Jack held Ali's hand and reluctantly released it as they approached the dingy white stucco building with a clay tile roof. "The oldest restaurant in town, I believe," he said, opening the door. "I used to come here as a kid with my grandfather."

"It must have looked very different back then," said Ali, as they entered the building.

"Not by much." Jack led her into a dark, smoky room and gestured to a waiter as they made their way to a table in the corner, just opposite the piano player. Jack held the red vinyl cushioned chair for her before taking his seat. With his hands folded around his pad, the waiter waited to be acknowledged by Jack. A flurry of Spanish followed as Jack gave the man their order.

"You're quite fluent."

"I spent many summers in my youth fishing in Mexico."

Ali chuckled. "You've led an interesting life."

"I'm trying to capture some of those earlier memories on paper."

"A book?"

He nodded. "Isn't that what everyone does in their midlife, as they're staring at the end of their life...go back and write their memories?"

"Not all, but it's a nice way to leave a legacy."

"For whom?" His words hung heavy between them, as the waiter placed the margaritas on the table. The brief pause allowed the crispness of Jack's last remark to soften.

"Writing helps me weather the dark nights and make sense of things that often perplex me in the daylight hours." He squirmed in his seat, seemingly uncomfortable with his revelation. Shaking off his uneasiness, he raised his glass. "To Ali and her first redfish."

"May there be many more." She sipped the drink and coughed. "Oooh, that's strong!"

Chuckles erupted from behind the bar, and Jack glanced in their direction, before leaning both elbows on the table, looking at her intently. "So, is there a Mr. Stephenson?" He reached out and touched her hand. "Or does the absence of a ring denote someone of equal importance but without the formal commitment?"

Ali studied his face before opting for as much transparency as she could muster. "I've recently ended a relationship."

He raised his eyebrows. "How long ago?"

"It's been a process. But I think he finally got the message the day before I left."

His gaze intensified. "Was there a particular reason?"

She met it equally. "Because he wasn't the person I wanted to spend the rest of my life with."

Jack took a nacho from the plate and bit into it. Ali did the same and casually glanced around the room. Tourists, some their age, others older, chatted loudly and sipped their drinks. Smoke hovered like clouds near the ceiling. The piano player switched to a love song.

"How did you know?"

Ali smiled, "He didn't like fly fishing."

He chuckled, "That's a good reason."

✳ ✳ ✳

The colors and sweet aromas of Mexico were neatly stashed in the back seat of the rental car as Jack and Ali traveled back to Mama Kate's. Their conversation was sparse since they'd covered a lot in the hours during dinner and shopping. Instead, they listened to instrumental music playing on the stereo, occasionally commenting on the brightness of a constellation. But for most of the hour-plus drive, they were content in their own thoughts.

"I think I've done all of my Christmas shopping." Ali gestured at the bags in the back seat of the car as she pulled into Mama Kate's driveway.

"You could always come back if you've forgotten anyone," Jack chanced a look in her direction. "Fishing is great in December."

"That might be something to think about." She smiled and met his gaze.

He reached across the console and touched her cheek. Ali closed her eyes. He leaned toward her and gently brushed his lips on hers. "I'm not looking forward to you leaving."

Ali opened her eyes and stared into his. "Neither am I."

They exited the car and walked toward the house, with their arms around one another. The door opened quietly, and Max looked up from his post in the hallway, his tail thumping against the floor. Lily jumped to attention and greeted her master. Ali first scratched her ears and then did the same for Max. "Night, Max. Night, Lily."

She entered the stairway first, with Jack behind her. She reached for his hand and gently led him up the stairs and down the hall to her room. The door was closed, and for a moment, they both hesitated. She turned. "I don't make a habit of inviting men into my bedroom so soon after meeting them."

Jack kissed her. "I know." With one hand around her waist, he quietly opened the door and guided her inside. Candles illuminated the room. A flower arrangement with roses from the garden graced the nightstand, evidence that Mama Kate sensed where the night would end. Ali kicked her shoes off and guided Jack to the bed. They sat on the edge, gazing into each other's eyes. Many emotions surfaced within her, but none of them was doubt. She didn't know why, but she knew making love with this man was completely right. She unbuttoned his shirt, taking in every inch of his muscular chest with her hands and eyes. He watched her intently, touching her cheek and running his fingers across her lips and through her hair. With the last button undone, she removed his shirt slowly and then rose to place it neatly on the back of the chair. She slipped out of her dress and felt his eyes fall upon her.

Crossing the room, Jack embraced her from behind, leaving a trail of soft kisses along her neck. His hands gently caressed her hips and her abdomen. She turned around, and they kissed passionately. Jack freed her breasts from the confines of the silky beige bra. He then slipped his fingers in the top of her lace panties and gently lowered them to her ankles, kissing her as he descended to his knees, lingering long enough to send shivers of delight through her body.

Rising to embrace her, Ali rested her face in the crook of Jack's neck, savoring the blend of soap and the smell of his skin. She knew she'd remember it forever, even if they never saw one another again. Then she took a step backward, so she could loosen his belt and lower the zipper on his shorts. Soon he was standing naked before her, and they moved toward the bed.

Their kisses and gentle caresses escorted them deeper into ecstasy. Jack gently rolled Ali to her back, kissing her as she parted her legs. They moved rhythmically, without hurry or words, eyes locked. Time stood still, and the world fell away as she surrendered to Jack's gentleness.

For a moment, he stopped thrusting and looked upon her. "You're a special woman." A tear slipped from the corner of his eye, and she reached up to brush it away. He kissed her, and again, their bodies moved in unison. Then the moment they both wanted—and yet didn't—arrived, and they clung to each other, allowing their passion to rise and subside gently and naturally.

Intertwined, sleep approached. Ali turned her head to look into Jack's eyes, but they were closed. She touched his cheek, memorizing the expression on his face. Gone was that driven, pained look that was often present. The peace on his face mirrored what Ali felt in her soul. "Thank you, Jack Cooper," she whispered before drifting off into her own deep sleep.

✳ ✳ ✳

Ali woke to the smell of coffee wafting up the stairs. She rolled over, expecting to find Jack lying next to her, but instead, she discovered an empty space where he had slept. She rose and put on her fishing clothes, eager to join him on the boat. Although she knew that Kate foresaw the evening's events, she wondered how she would meet with Kate's questioning eye.

Descending the stairs, she kept her ears perked for Jack's voice. Disappointment settled in as she rounded the corner, seeing only Kate standing at the stove. "Good morning."

"Morning," Kate looked up from the pan of scrambled eggs. "Sleep well?"

"Very." She took a sip of her coffee. "Where's Jack?"

"Down at the dock." Kate scooped the eggs into a bowl. "Said he wasn't very hungry this morning."

"We had a big dinner last night."

"Good time?" Kate sat down at the table.

Ali poured some juice into a glass. "Festive."

"Maybe it was the margaritas then," Kate offered. "He looks in a foul mood this morning, more so than usual."

Ali felt the color wash from her face. She swallowed a couple of bites of egg and skipped the toast. "I'd better get going. It's my last day of fishing."

"Hope it's a good one," Kate said, with a hint of doubt hanging in the air.

Ali carried her dishes to the sink. "Me, too."

✳ ✳ ✳

She moved in slow motion, painfully aware of the sinking feeling in her stomach, mirroring her first day of fishing, as she stepped out onto the covered porch and peered at the dock. Jack was sitting on the seat behind the console, his arms crossed and a mug of coffee in one hand. Lily sat by his feet. Taking a deep breath, Ali made her way down the path, pausing momentarily when she reached the dock.

"Missed you at breakfast," she said with feigned confidence. Lily jumped off the boat, wagging her tail at Ali's appearance.

"Wasn't hungry." His dark eyes appeared even darker than the first day they met, almost vacant of a living soul.

"So I heard." She held out her rod, and he reluctantly reached for it.

Anger bubbled in her veins. "Look, I'm not asking for a lifetime commitment. A little civility would be nice, however."

Jack met her eyes. "What happened last night shouldn't have."

Ali dropped to the pier and sat cross-legged before him. "Jack, it did, and it was beautiful... at least I thought so, and I thought you did, too."

"What were we thinking?" His face flushed with frustration. "We didn't even use a condom!" He turned away from her, sipping his coffee.

Tears welled in her eyes. "God, if that's all you're worried about, then don't. Karma demerits. A chance in a million that I would get pregnant," she choked. "And I'm clean."

He gazed out over the water. "When two people open up like that only to go their separate ways..." he hesitated. "Nothing good can come of it."

Her voice quivered. "All I know was that last night was meant to happen."

"It happened because we chose it. Not because of predestination. That's Kate's line." Anger shrouded his words, and he banged his hand on the console. "Do you ever stop to consider how your choices might affect your future?"

Ali struggled to keep the voices from her past at bay as she got to her feet. "I'm not a child, and I most certainly am quite capable of taking responsibility for my choices." She stormed off toward the house.

"We're scheduled to fish." He jumped up on the pier. "Kate will wonder what's going on."

Ali whirled around, glaring at him. "Like she doesn't already know? She doesn't have to witness this scene to figure out that you're being a jerk. Or have you, in all your intellectual wisdom, overlooked that?" Ali stomped up the slope of the yard. When she reached the porch, she plopped down in the chair to pull off her flats booties. "Consider it a day off with pay."

"Ali, I'm sorry." Jack stood in the center of the lawn, suddenly looking confused.

Without looking up, she whispered. "So am I." And then she burst into the lodge, heading straight to her room. *Good move, Ali Mae. When will I ever learn!*

✳ ✳ ✳

Bracing herself for Kate's scrutiny, Ali reappeared after a couple of hours. Kate was cutting vegetables and tossing them in a large white bowl, etched with blue fish dancing on the edges. "What happened to the fishing today?"

"I have a lot to do before I leave." She leafed through her notebook, avoiding eye contact with Kate. "I need to go to the island, get information on other places to stay, guides. The usual. And more photos."

"Uh, uh." Kate eyed her suspiciously.

Ali checked the battery supply on her camera. "And I'm interviewing another guide later this afternoon, the head of the guides' association."

"Skipper?" Kate tossed the salad and carried it to the table. "Just remember, his bark's worse than his bite." She pulled a chair out for Ali at the table and nodded for her to sit. "You have to eat first."

Ali willingly obeyed and sunk into the chair. "Wanna come along?"

"I have another group arriving in a couple of hours."

"Will Jack be guiding them?" Despite her best efforts, the color rose to her cheeks.

"He canceled." Kate took a thick slice of homemade oat bread from the round wicker basket. "Lucky for him, I found a replacement."

Ali stuffed her mouth with a forkful of lettuce. She chewed slowly, keeping her eyes on the Arroyo. The last thing she wanted to do was eat, but she also knew Mama Kate wouldn't let her get away otherwise. A white tug ambled by, pushing two barges side by side. The gray containers ladened with cargo sat low to the water. "Don't set a place for me tonight." She put her fork on her plate. "I'll pick up something while I'm out."

"Get Skipper to buy you supper." Kate took a sip of her tea. "He's 'bout the only one that can get close to Jack."

"Last night was a big mistake. I let my guard down. It certainly wasn't very professional of me." The words stung like a hornet.

"Now, whose opinion was that?" Kate chided.

Ali ran her hand through her hair, vaguely aware of the return of her headache. She sighed audibly.

"He'll come around," Kate shared.

Rising from her seat at the table, she grabbed her satchel from the chair next to her. "I'm not about to set myself up for repeat rejection from Captain Cooper."

"We all have to take chances."

Ali sighed. "Been there, done that, far too many times."

Kate glanced out at the water. Squawking gulls dipped into the frothy water, searching for pieces of mullet, which had been processed by the tug's propellers. "I can understand that." She rose from her chair and put her arms around Ali. "But you're strong, and you shouldn't let a little bump on the shin hold you back."

"I've had more than my share of bumps," Ali quipped. "I'd better go."

In the refuge of the car, as she drove down the long straight section of FM 1847, the dam finally burst. Tears that she had choked back all morning streamed down her face. She pounded the steering wheel. "You are such a fool, Ali Mae." She wiped her nose with a tissue. "Just a Blue Ridge hick, like your mama." Unlike her mother, though, Ali kicked in her steely resolve, determined to forget the one-night stand as quickly as possible. She drove for miles reviewing all of the mistakes she had made with men, oblivious to the solace that nature was offering along the road.

Crossing the bridge to South Padre Island, Ali forcefully shifted her attention to the water and the birds, noting the numerable boats below, including a speed boat with parasailers dangling from the sky. The parking gods were shining on her, and she pulled into a spot just as she entered South Padre proper. The sites and sounds of the restaurants and shops, steered her editor's eye to her assigned task, and she snapped photographs as she sauntered through the main street, bypassing most of the beach shops, and stepping into one that offered more than the usual bathing suits and t-shirts.

After meandering around the island taking photos, Ali traveled back across the bridge, this time far more attentive to the pink and blue hues highlighting the afternoon sky. Just over the bridge, she spotted Pirates, the restaurant that was her next destination. Port Isabel was also busy with ambling tourists; however, here, the shops sported more of unique offerings, including antiques, original art, and handmade furniture. She parked on the one-way street about a block away from the restaurant to take in the scene. She was immediately greeted with the aroma of frying fish and became aware of her increasing hunger.

Inhaling deeply, she squared her shoulders and adjusted her salmon linen tank over the waist of her white linen pants. She scanned her surroundings and set her sights on the restaurant. Gulls rested on trash cans, and cars maneuvered the narrow street, dodging tourists now and again. Ali ambled along the shop-lined sidewalk, capturing a few photos of the shells, wood-carved birds, and brightly colored fish-framed mirrors. She glanced at the men passing by for anyone who might resemble Jack. She knew that despite her ability to focus on her work, he would be a distraction for some time. She closed her eyes, feeling his arms around her and smelling the scent of his skin. Shaking her head to clear her thoughts, she sat down on a bench outside of Pirates and began reviewing the questions she prepared for the interview with Skipper.

"You must be the reporter from up north." A voice boomed over her.

She looked up and saw a tall, deeply tanned man with a bushy silver mustache and close-cut silver hair peeking out from under his cap, sporting the logo with his name. She rose.

"You must be Skipper." She noted his freshly washed sage guide shirt and khaki shorts.

"The very one." He waved a large, tanned hand toward the building. "C'mon in. I'll buy you supper."

"There's no need."

He grinned. "It's on the association. Couldn't afford to wine and dine you otherwise."

She eyed him suspiciously, wondering if he was kidding.

They entered the restaurant with wood-planked floors and ship relics on the walls. A life-sized, carved pirate stood near the hostess podium. A waitress in her early thirties appeared from the lower deck. Wearing a denim skirt and a white polo top, her short-blonde hair made her look like a pixie. She smiled widely as she approached. "Hey, Skipper."

"Hi there, Ginny. Got my table ready?"

She whirled around. "Best one." She led them through the crowded room and out onto the deck overlooking the Laguna Madre. The balmy afternoon breeze immediately refreshed Ali's spirits. The waitress motioned for them to be seated. "I'll be your waitress."

Skipper held the chair for Ali and then took his seat opposite her. Ali briefly surveyed the area and then turned back to Skipper, whose eyes were squarely upon her. "Ginny, this here is Ali Stephenson. She's the reporter from the magazine Jack's been guiding for the last few days."

Ali extended her hand to Ginny. "Nice to meet you."

The two eyed each other warily as Skipper continued, "Ginny and Jack have been an item for a few months."

Ali withdrew her hand, her mind searching for a proper comment. "You're a lucky lady. He's a very nice man."

Ginny rolled her eyes. "So I thought."

Skipper jumped in. "You two have a spat?"

"He ain't called me all week." She flashed a look at Ali. "Guess he's been too busy." She pulled her pad from the black apron tied around her waist. "Get you something to drink?"

"The Bread & Butter Pinot Noir, please." Ali's voice sounded strong, despite her inner misgivings.

"The usual." Skipper added.

Ginny whirled around and hastily strode out of the room.

"Don't mind her. She's a bit of a polecat, if you know what I mean."

Ali disregarded the comment by studying her notes. "You said that you had a list of guides for the area."

"I sent you an email about an hour ago. I highlighted the fly guides."

She opened her phone and scanned the list.

"Jack is our best. He only does fly."

"And the others?"

"Like me, they do what they can to get by—chunking hardware or live bait. It's all in a day's work," Skipper offered his explanation with a sense of resolve in his voice. "It's a tough way to make a living, but I'm not sure I'd do anything but this."

Ali raised a brow. "Jack says you're the best fly rodder in the area."

"Won a tournament or two."

"Beat out the bait and spin fisherman in the TIFT?" She twirled her pen while trying to size up the man across the table. The words "shit eatin'," crossed Ali's mind as he broke into a toothy grin.

"That I did."

"Perhaps I should have gone out with you."

He shook his head. "You couldn't have picked any better guide than Jack."

Ginny returned, placing their drinks in front of them. She hesitated for a moment, with her pad held high and her pen poised. She glanced at Ali. "I'm sorry I was a little short with you earlier. You understand, being a girl and all. Some guys can be so exasperatin'."

"I do know what you mean." Ali lowered her eyes to her menu, wishing she was any place but on the deck at Pirates.

* * *

The morning sunlight was a welcome friend, sending away the long dark hours of the night. Parting the curtains, Ali looked down at the Arroyo. Several boats passed, making her heart leap. She sighed loudly, startling herself. Turning away from the window, she resumed her packing. Kate had washed and folded her fishing attire, which now lay neatly stacked alongside her luggage. She placed the pile inside the suitcase before returning to the closet for the remaining pieces of clothing. As she folded the dress she had worn to Mexico, her thoughts once again turned to Jack. Another face flashed beside his—the pixie blonde waitress that had rattled Ali's core. Her stomach turned, and she threw the dress into the suitcase before closing it. She was tired of attracting unavailable men.

She opened her brown leather satchel and thumbed through its contents. Her research was complete, and photographs were taken. The camera tucked away, as was her computer. The fly rod was propped against the door, discarded like an old toy on Christmas day. She turned away. It only reminded her of Jack. She'd tormented herself repeatedly during her long drive on the Valley roads thinking of him, going over their night together, and coming up with only one conclusion. He may have been right.

A light rap on the door saved her from further contemplation. "You all packed?" Kate entered the room tentatively and sat in the chair with a light "harumph" escaping her lips.

Ali surveyed the room. "Just about. I'll be ready to leave soon."

"You going to tell me what happened?" Kate looked intently at Ali. "Jack hasn't even come back for his check."

"You tell me, Kate." Ali sat on the bed.

"I'd rather hear it from you."

Ali stared out the window. Two hummingbirds flitted around a feeder, which hung from the eave of the roof. "I was drawn to him, very much like those hummingbirds are to that feeder."

"It was the same for him," Kate offered. "You scared him. That's all." Kate patted her hand. "You reminded him of something he has locked away deep inside of him." She gazed out the window at the hummingbirds. "Soon, those hummingbirds will leave and journey to their homes in Mexico. But by Valentine's Day, they'll be back through here." She turned her attention back to Ali. "My prediction is that you'll be back here before long, as well."

"Highly improbable."

"It don't seem possible for those tiny birds out there to fly hundreds of miles, but they do." Kate rose from the chair. "There are no accidents, Ali."

Joe's face flashed across Ali's mind. "I've heard that before."

She patted Ali's shoulder. "Come down soon. I've made a special breakfast."

Ali conjured up a weak smile. "I can see why people want to be here." She clasped Kate's hand. "Thank you."

# Chapter Six

Ali stared at the computer screen, reviewing her story. Everything was there. She recounted the highlights of her stay at Mama Kate's, described the local flora and fauna and presented a detailed accounting of her experience on the bay with the local fly fishing guru Jack Cooper. No one would guess her true feelings. Her journalistic style and integrity were firmly in place. But as her mind wandered back to her week in the South Texas paradise, her heart ached in such a way that she thought she would surely die. She closed her eyes and fought back the tears. The source of her sadness was more than Jack. The culmination of life events was catching up with her.

Breaking free of her mindful meanderings, she stood before the window of her office, watching the traffic buzzing along the highway that paralleled the beach. But the view that she missed the most was the boats motoring by Mama Kate's, the egrets and the herons vying for territorial rights of the dock, and Max's tail thumping on the peach tile. She missed Kate and Gus—and she missed standing knee-deep in the warm waters of the Laguna Madre.

A knock on the door swept Ali out of her reverie. "Come in."

She glanced over her shoulder to see Sam enter. His white starched shirt matched his skin tone, something she hadn't noticed before. "Welcome back."

"Thank you." She turned her gaze back toward the ocean's horizon and heard him shuffle his feet.

"I thought we'd make amends, go to the mountains this weekend, like old times."

Her energy seeped through the soles of her feet, at the thought of spending time with him. "It's over, Sam."

He walked up behind her, putting his hand on her waist. "Ali, please."

She whirled around with a fiery expression on her face. "Don't touch me. I told you before I left that I didn't want to see you anymore, and I meant it."

He pounded his fist on the desk. "Another one of your whims."

"Our relationship might have been a whim," she spat. "But ending it was not." She sat in her chair. "Now, if you'll excuse me, I have a piece to finish, and I'm sure you have work to tend to as well." She sat in front of the computer and feigned reading the words on the screen.

Sam slammed the door, alerting their coworkers to their less than amicable discussion. Ali knew it would be hours before she dared venture out. She hated confrontations and loathed being embarrassed even more. She leaned back in her chair, with her heart pounding and hands shaking, taking several deep breaths to calm herself. Slowly, she recovered. She repeated a mantra, and soon, a blanket of peace soothed her shattered nerves.

✳ ✳ ✳

The afternoon arrived, and Ali hadn't yet left her office. Rereading the story, she made a few changes and had to admit it was good. As 2:00 rolled around, a light tap disrupted her focus.

"Ali," Bleu tentatively poked her head in the door. "You okay?"

"Yeah."

"We heard Sam all the way in production." Bleu, with her flaming red hair and flowing cobalt blue dress, sat down across from Ali. She leaned on the desk and propped her head in her hand. "What happened? And I'm not talking about Sam."

"Long story." Ali rubbed her temples and tousled her hair, massaging her scalp. "I'm not sure who I am anymore or if I even belong here."

"I'm not surprised." Bleu leaned against the back of her chair. "I've had the image of you being a trotter in a harness, just doing your job, staying on the track."

"Done it well, though." Ali quipped.

"What fun is that!" Bleu was a bit exasperated.

Ali paused for a moment. "Not much." She choked on the words and looked at Bleu for some encouragement.

Silence fell between the women as they both stared out the window.

"Gonna tell me about it sometime?" Bleu asked in a soft voice.

"Maybe." Ali glanced at her friend, her eyes moist from held-back tears.

Bleu got up to leave. "Rob has selected his favorite photos, but he still needs a draft of the story."

"It's more than a draft." Ali stood up. "I'll email it over in a few minutes."

"That was quick!" Bleu was a bit surprised. "Although it does fit your MO. Get the work done, no matter what."

"I wanted to write while all of it was still fresh in my mind." She closed her eyes and inhaled gently.

"What do you smell?" Bleu inquired.

"The salty flats, a sweet, pungent aroma." *And Jack's warm skin against mine.* "Makes my heart sing."

Bleu studied her friend's expression. "You sure that's all?"

"Positive." Taking a stack of paper from the tray, Ali methodically sorted the sheets and then tapped them on the desk before clipping the sheets together and putting them in the file folder.

Bleu leaned over. "I've never seen anyone look like that over salt flats before."

Ali raised her eyes to Bleu's. "You have now."

"Whatever you say." Bleu arched her eyebrow. "I've known you long enough to see you're hiding from something. You may be trying to fool yourself, but you're not fooling me."

Rubbing her brow, Ali sighed. "I've got the career thing down, but the man thing—it totally eludes me. And I'm tired."

Bleu smiled. "I have faith in you."

"It's nice to know somebody does." Ali strode toward the door, draping her arm across Bleu's shoulder. "Let's see what kind of magic our creative director can do with this piece."

Ali paused at the women's restroom. "Go on ahead. I'll meet you there," she said to Bleu. Stepping inside, she looked at herself in the mirror. "Just put it to rest, Ali Mae. The best place for you to be right now is right here in this office and tending to your job. Everything else can wait—forever if need be." She took a deep breath and set her jaw before turning to leave the room.

Rob Hansen was absorbed in his computer, when Ali swept determinedly into the room. In her beige pinstriped skirt and purple draped neck blouse, no one would ever know the demons she wrestled inside of her, except maybe Bleu. She learned to dissociate from her mistakes well, tucking them into the far corner of her heart.

"Hey, there's the redfish mama." Rob stood up and gave her a big hug. "Glad you're back. It's hell around here with Sam acting like he's at the helm." He returned to his chair. "Heard you demoted him."

"Let's talk shop, okay?" She flashed him a look of warning.

"Not until you give me my present." Rob diffused the look that would have made anyone else crawl under their desks.

Ali shook her head, smiling at Rob. He was the young spirit in the office, like the little brother she never had. "You are impossible."

"I know, and I like it that way." Rob flashed her a toothy grin. His expression, coupled with his vibrant green tie and bright buttercup shirt, made him look like a living cartoon character.

She held out her hand and dropped a South Texas magnet into his hand. "It's the best I could do. They don't have one for Arroyo City."

"Tiny, huh?" He examined the palm trees and the kiskadee on the magnet.

"Not even on the map." She turned to the computer. "Not yet, anyway."

They turned their collective attention to digital images. "You got some great shots," Rob pointed to each of his favorites. "Mama Kate is a charmer. Reminds me of my grandmother."

Ali's heart thumped wildly. "Mine, too."

"And the vistas. Fantastic." He crossed his arms and let Ali move in closer. "Those sunrises are awesome. Makes me want to be there."

"That's the idea," Ali said.

Bleu squeezed in between them. "Who is that? My God! He was worth the assignment in and of itself, fish or no fish." Bleu patted her chest. "Salt flats, huh?" She squeezed Ali's upper arm.

"God, what a specimen," Rob gasped.

Ali commented, cooly. "Jack Cooper, my guide."

Bleu searched Ali's face. "Available?"

"Do I ever attract available men into my life?" Ali chuckled. "I emailed the file to you, Rob. Now let's see a layout."

"Yes, ma'am." Rob saluted.

Ali turned to leave the room. Bleu called after her, "How about dinner at Bubba's tonight?"

She shook her head. "I'll pass. I feel like having a nice quiet evening on my patio."

Bleu chuckled. "Don't be a recluse."

"Never," Ali shot back, fighting off the urge to immediately flee the premises and hide in her cocoon, someplace where anonymity would be her best friend.

✳ ✳ ✳

"Haven't seen much of Jack lately," Gus commented as he ambled into the kitchen carrying a sack of groceries.

"Sulking, no doubt." Kate took the bag from Gus and began unloading it.

Gus nodded. "Think she'll be back?"

Kate moved to the sink and began cutting sweet potatoes into quarters. She put the potatoes in a pan and coated them with oil. "Her soul belongs here. Plain as the nose on her face."

"Maybe she's got ties up north, you know, romantic ones."

"Didn't mention it," Kate whirled around with the pan of potatoes and opened the oven.

"Maybe her kin then."

"What might be right for our kin might not be right for us."

"Have you ever figured out what's right for you?"

"What's got into you!" Kate squawked. But before he could answer, Kate handed him a stack of dinner plates. "Help me set the table. Those fishermen will be back to port anytime now and hungry, no doubt. Gotta at least have chips, salsa, and beer ready for 'em."

✳ ✳ ✳

Jack pulled up to his dock and tied his boat into the slip. Lily pranced around, barking at him, but he ignored her attempts to coax him into playing fetch. "Not now, girl." He moved like a beaten-down old man. He unloaded his gear from the boat, placing it on the lawn, and began washing his rod. Lily pranced around, biting at the stream of water coming from the hose.

A boat slowed behind him. "Hey, Jack, wanna go to Pirate's for a beer?"

He turned to see his friend pulling up to the dock. "Not today, Skipper," he said as he tied the boat to the cleat. "Too many early mornings this week."

Skipper put his feet up on the console of his boat and crossed his arms. "Ginny's been asking 'bout you. Thinks you've done drowned or somethin'."

"Or something." Jack continued cleaning his boat. "Need some rest, that's all." His voice trailed off.

"Hell, Jack. We ain't seen nothing of you since that reporter gal was around." Skipper chewed his toothpick, and a devilish smile crossed his face. "She had a nice cast. Looked like someone you might want to take up with."

"Go to hell." Jack glared at his friend as if he'd betrayed him in some way.

"I done found the Lord, so that ain't gonna happen." Skipper removed his sunglasses. "So why are you so darn heated up?"

"I'm tired." Jack pushed Skipper's boat from the dock. "I'll see you out there tomorrow."

"Aye, aye, captain." Skipper saluted as Jack strutted up the path to his cottage. Lily followed reluctantly, her head hanging low. She paused once to take a look back at Skipper before continuing in her master's path.

The screen door opened with a creak as Jack entered the dimly lit enclosed porch. He spent hours here in the evenings, pounding the keys of his laptop or tying flies, serenaded by the cicadas and the din of boats making their way back to port. Tonight, he didn't feel like writing or tying. Skipper's words were like painful swords penetrating his gut. Sinking into his rocking chair, he let his thoughts rest on Ali and the last time he'd seen her. He cringed. He'd been a jerk.

Frightened of the feelings she unleashed within him, he retreated to the safety of his self-made exile. He was beginning to see the danger in that.

Abruptly, Jack rose and went into the kitchen. He opened the refrigerator door and took out a Bucklers. He was leery of drinking alone. But he liked the taste of a cold beer, especially after a long day on the water. He closed the door, opened the bottle, and took a swig. Then with determination, he strode across the room and into the den, aiming for the desk on the far wall beneath the window overlooking the bay. His eyes fell to the blotter. Slowly, with his shaking hand, he reached for a business card tucked into the left-hand corner of the leather frame.

Like many times before, he ran his fingers along the edge. This time, he sat down at the desk and dialed the number. He sank into the chair as the phone on the other end rang four times. It was after hours, a safe time to call. She wouldn't answer. But this time, he'd leave her a message. Six rings. He took a deep breath, waiting for her voicemail. "Hi, this is Ali Stephenson. I'm sorry I missed your call. Leave your name and number after the beep, and I'll get back to you as soon as possible. Thanks. Have a great day."

At the sound of the beep, he hesitated and then said, "Hi. I just thought I'd...." A thousand things came to mind, but nothing that made much sense. He ended the call. Sweat beaded upon his forehead. "I just can't do it," he whispered aloud, cradling his cell phone in one hand and his beer in another. Lily eased up to him and laid her head on his lap. He ignored her, too. He just didn't have the energy to reach out to anyone.

\* \* \*

Ali strolled up the path to her office building. Her energy was waning much like the moon's, so her pace was slow, and her shoulders slightly slumped.

"Hey, Ali, wait up." Bleu crossed the parking lot, with her neon green and yellow-striped scarf waving out behind her. "Called you last night."

"Went to bed early."

Bleu held the door to the building and let Ali step inside. "You okay?"

"Just haven't been up for much lately."

"Let's go dancing tonight."

Ali groaned. "The last thing I want to do is be out with a bunch of lecherous flyboys, and I'm not talking about the ones with fly rods—even if we invoke our safety mantra. It didn't work last time."

Bleu shrugged. "You have to admit it was fun."

"Oh yeah. The guy with the tongue piercing young enough to be my son wanting show me his tricks." Ali chuckled. "No, thank you."

"Then yoga in the morning?" Bleu pleaded. "We haven't done a class in ages."

Ali ran her hand through her hair. The idea appealed to her. "That might help."

"Maybe something is going around in the building."

Ali cocked her head to the side, inviting an explanation.

"Joe hasn't looked too great lately, either." Bleu's concern hung heavily between them. "He's awfully pale."

"I hadn't noticed." Ali cringed at her admission as she pushed the button on the elevator.

"What about using the stairs?" Bleu's astonished expression peered at Ali from the matte steel surface of the elevator doors.

"I'm saving my energy for yoga," Ali quipped. The doors opened, and Ali stepped inside alone.

Bleu shook her head. "I'll see you up there. I'm going to take the stairs like we always do."

The doors closed, and Ali erased the worried look on Bleu's face from her mind, and in doing so, tried to erase her own worry. Something was terribly wrong, and she feared whatever was plaguing her had sent her into an abyss that she'd been running from her entire life. The elevator chimed the arrival to the tenth floor. Ali donned a perky expression. Fake it until you make it had gotten her a long way, so far. She waved to a couple of other staffers as they readied for the day inside their cubicles. At the end of the hall, she paused and glanced toward Joe's office. She thought of ducking in but hesitated. Joe liked his mornings.

She placed her satchel on the chair and hung her jacket on the coat rack. Then she opened the blinds. She paused to remember how lucky she was to have a great job, a beautiful townhouse, and a few good friends. The only thing she lacked was a good man. *Maybe I'll always be alone.* It was a hard thought to digest.

Whirling around, she stood before her desk and adjusted the braided indigo belt on her burnt sienna dress. Out of the corner of her eye, she saw the voice mail light flashing. She sunk into the chair and reached for the phone, sweeping a pencil into her hand before dialing her access code. "One new message." The mechanical female voice greeted her. Ali cut her off and hit "1." An odd silence came across the line, followed by a man's voice. "Hi." More silence followed before she heard, "I just thought I'd...." A loud click ended the call. Ali fell back in her chair; the receiver pressed to her ear. Her mind whirled with possibilities. Leaning forward, she repeated the message.

Closing her eyes, she knew who she wanted it to be. Tempted to erase it, Ali paused with her hand over the keys as the mechanical voice returned. "Hit two to save. Three to erase." Her index finger pressed "2," and she gently replaced the receiver to the cradle. Jack Cooper was going to make her crazy. She covered her eyes with her hands. "But so have all the rest," she said aloud. "And I've gotten over them." She rose from the chair and headed for the door, determined to put the call out of her mind.

Joe was behind his desk, dressed as always in his white starched shirt with the monogrammed pocket and dark trousers. He looked relaxed, his long legs outstretched. In his hands was a stack of white paper that he had been reading. When he saw her enter the room, he pushed his glasses on top of his head.

"Have a seat." His eyes brushed over her features. "You're looking a might pale, my dear."

She avoided his comment. "Heard you've been under the weather."

He shrugged. "When you get older, sleep becomes elusive, and as the good doctor always says, a good night's sleep is worth all the pills in China, or some such thing."

"Troubles?" She furrowed her brow. Joe was far more than her boss, and concern rippled through her.

"Nothing that I can't figure out on my own." He pointed to the stack that he had since laid on his desk. "I was rereading your story. Sounds like a nice place for a vacation."

Ali took a deep breath. "Rob's got the layout just about finished." She rubbed the palms of her hands together. "I want it to be good, Joe, so if you see anything that needs polishing, just let me know. We're ahead of schedule on this, so there's plenty of time." Disappointing him was the last thing she ever wanted to do.

"It's great." He leaned on the desk. "Let me just ask you this..."

Ali braced herself for a difficult question.

"Would you go back?" He raised his eyebrow.

"In a heartbeat." The words slipped out as if someone else said them for her.

He nodded. "I thought so."

She glanced away. *It was easy to imagine living there, but doing what? Selling bait, mowing lawns?*

"You seem torn." Joe prodded.

She raised her eyes to meet his.

"I guess it's my midlife crisis settling in," she chuckled. "Isn't it about time I had one?"

"I've had a few." He smiled.

"So I'm due."

"Are you happy here?" He wrinkled his forehead.

"I'm very grateful for all the opportunities you've given me."

"That didn't answer my question." He sat back in his chair. "All of this can be yours one day."

"That's what you've said before."

"It bears repeating now and again."

Suddenly, she felt tears welling up. It wasn't every day that someone was handed a publishing empire, but she wanted more, and her dream continued to slip from her grasp.

"What's up, my dear?"

She shook her head, clenching her jaw to regain her composure. "If only I could get the guy thing figured out, I'd be on my way to really having it all. Add a baby to the mix, and I'd be one step closer to heaven."

"It's time for you to stop settling." He urged lovingly, without judgment or expectation.

"I've tried, but failed just about every time."

Joe rolled his eyes. "Oh, how I know. You've got one hell of a bad picker!"

His reaction brought a smile to her face.

"You'll find your partner."

She wanted to find reassurance in his words. "Think so?" Silence hung between them for a moment, and then she leaned forward. "Have you?"

He nodded. "Indeed, I have." His voice was barely above a whisper. "Not in the biblical sense." He rose from his chair and took his sports jacket from the back of his chair. "My timing's a bit off, and she's otherwise occupied." He took two steps toward the door with his long legs. "I'm off to a meeting. Hold down the fort."

Kate retreated to the porch, after serving two fishermen breakfast, and making a casserole for dinner. She had the day ahead of her to do as she pleased. She propped her feet up on a wicker chair and sipped her tea while watching the mullet jumping on the Arroyo. She scanned her yard. Four gobblers preened themselves under the mesquite, and Max charged the dock to protest a pelican landing too close to his territory.

It was a quiet morning, with only a few boats making the run to the Laguna Madre. Summer was coming to a close, according to the calendar, and most of the fishermen had turned their attention to hunting. Dove season had just opened, turkey and deer to follow. Birders would soon appear. They posed even less trouble than the fishermen. They rose even earlier than Kate as they headed out into the dark of the night in hopes of catching a glimpse of some elusive bird. She hardly saw them, except when they stumbled bleary-eyed into the lodge to pay their bills.

A slight chill was in the air, foreshadowing cooler weather. Fall was around the corner. She liked this time of year. If she had someplace to go in August, she'd leave. But this was the only thing she knew. Life on the Arroyo. Forty years now. It was a long time. Twenty without Cy. It just wasn't the same without him, but it was all she knew—all she cared to know. She never chanced to love again. It hurt so much when he passed. She considered joining him but stopped only because she imagined him meeting her at the pearly gates and saying, "Now Kate, what did you go and do a foolish thing like that for?" But the thought had crossed her mind more than a time or two. Life wasn't bad. It was just lonely. She missed his body in bed next to hers. They were good together. She could never imagine another in his place.

The clanging of the Nepalese yak bells that hung from the knob of the back door alerted her to Gus's arrival. An old friend from an earlier time in her life had sent them to Kate. She was a globetrotter, just the opposite of Kate, who preferred her hearth.

Moments later, the patio door opened, and he stepped onto the porch, carrying a mug of coffee. Kate had made it fresh before coming outside, knowing he'd soon join her. It had been like this for years, and she had to admit she enjoyed this time of day with him.

"Morning, Gus."

"How ya doing this morning, Kate? Sleep well?"

She shook her head. "Nasty dreams." Cy was a familiar force in her dreams. But he didn't visit her last night. It was a dark shadow that loomed over her with a menacing grin. As she recounted the dream to herself, a pack of coyotes howled on the far bank of the Arroyo, sending a chill up her spine.

"Maybe you need a change of scenery." Gus said as he took a sip of his coffee. "Want to go to the markets?"

She shrugged.

"I want to buy some more plants."

"Ain't you got enough?" She eyed him, and a soft smile took hold of her thin lips. She enjoyed their banter.

"Never can have enough." Gus choked on the next sip of coffee, and an alarm went off inside of Kate.

"Put your hands over your head." She bounded from her chair and stood behind him, holding his arms up. He stopped coughing, and she released her hold on him, allowing her hands to rest upon his shoulders. It was hard to admit, but she'd miss him if he ever left. Their friendship was good. Gus was always there when she needed him. She sometimes felt that she hadn't returned the favor. She did what she could, what was safe.

"I'll go change and grab my purse." She paused at the door. "You're right about the plants. I'd like to get more flowers."

"Thought so." Gus smiled knowingly.

Nearly two thousand miles away, Ali was experiencing a replay of her own fitful night. Something or someone was tugging at her consciousness, demanding attention. Even as morning approached and she knew she should rise, but she resisted opening her eyes, hoping to stay in the dream realm and find some answers. As daylight began filtering into her room, she drifted off into a dreamless sleep. She awakened to a loud pounding on her door, followed by the repeated chime of the doorbell. She scrambled from the bed, disoriented and unsteady on her feet. A wave of nausea grabbed her, and she stopped midway in the hallway and braced herself against the wall. She shook her head. She didn't have time to be sick.

"You ready?" Bleu pounded on the door for the second time.

Ali unlocked the door and headed back to the bedroom, "I overslept. Pour me some juice."

"No coffee for the java queen?" Bleu prodded as Ali scurried to the bathroom.

When she spied her reflection, the word "gaunt" crossed her mind.

Bleu rounded the corner and handed Ali the juice. "You okay?"

Ali opened her medicine chest and took out a multivitamin. She popped it along with a vitamin C tablet and headed toward the door. "I didn't sleep for shit last night."

"What's the matter?" Bleu tugged at Ali's sleeve with a look of concern.

"Weird dreams," Ali said as she pushed past Bleu toward the door, hoping the fresh air would soothe her queasiness. She stepped outside, and a cool breeze wafted across her face. It was refreshing. She liked the fall, always had. It reminded her of raking leaves, drinking apple cider, and curling up next to the woodstove at night. For just a moment, she allowed herself to miss the farm. It had been a while since she could think about her childhood home with any fondness. She glanced at Bleu. "I'll be okay."

"I'll drive," said Bleu as she unlocked her orange Subaru CrossTrek.

\* \* \*

Ali and Bleu walked into the yoga studio just minutes before the class began. Sunlight danced on the floor as they arranged their colorful yoga mats, hers in teal, Bleu's in orange. The instructor, a tall thin woman, with long dark hair streaked with gray, stood at the center of the room. They began with the Salutation to the Sun, stretching their hands high above their heads, then down to their toes. The flow began.

A wave of nausea rippled through Ali again, and this time it was accompanied by dizziness. What is wrong with me? Steeling herself against the physical sensations, she moved through the asanas willfully for the next forty minutes.

"Okay, let's do some work on the floor for rejuvenation," Hedda instructed as she moved about the room carrying blankets. "We'll end with *Savasana* for a well-deserved rest."

Ali stretched out on the floor, and the woman gently touched her shoulders. "Relax."

Another wave of nausea descended upon her, and she grimaced.

Hedda closed her eyes and then returned her attention to Ali. Ask your body what message it's trying to send to you."

Ali knew prayer worked. Her difficulty was in following the direction she received. Her head always got in the way. Her mother had just the opposite problem. Her heart was her downfall. Taking a deep breath, Ali formed the words silently upon her lips. "I'll listen this time. I promise. What's going on with me?" Instantly a baby's torso and face appeared in her mind's eye, the skin pale and yet glowing. The baby smiled at her. Ali opened her eyes and stared at the ceiling, slowly moving her hand to her lower abdomen. *The scar tissue will make it virtually impossible for you to bear children.* The words had haunted her. And yet, now they seemed to make no sense.

Hedda came around to her again. "Did you get an answer?"

Ali now sitting cross-legged, nodded. Hedda smiled.

"Come back. Yoga will help you during this time."

✳ ✳ ✳

Three weeks passed before Ali mustered the courage to make a doctor's appointment. Her period had yet to arrive. As much as she tried to doubt her guidance, her symptoms were increasing with each passing day. And now, the moment of truth was upon her. She was either pregnant or dying.

With perspiration dripping down her side, Ali tapped her fingers on the exam table, took a deep breath, and tried to slow her racing heart. When the door opened, she jumped.

"Ali, relax." A tall, middle-aged man touched her shoulder.

With his dark hair and blue eyes, he could have been her brother, if she'd had one. The resemblance always startled her and also reminded her that she was truly alone. Her friends were the only family she had.

He studied her chart. "You had your annual just six months ago."

"I know."

He raised an eyebrow. "How are you feeling?"

"Exhausted."

"Appetite." He took out his stethoscope and placed it on her back. "Scanty at best."

"Take a deep breath." He put the cold instrument over her heart. "Nausea?"

She nodded. "Every day for the past couple of weeks."

"Let's get the nurse in here so we can do an exam." Dr. Cap strode to the door, and moments later, a woman with short dark hair, dressed in pink scrubs, entered the room. "Did we run a urine sample?"

"The results will be ready shortly," she said matter-of-factly as she put on her rubber gloves.

With her feet firmly planted in the stirrups, Ali closed her eyes as the doctor gently examined her uterus and ovaries. "Is this menopause or something?"

Dr. Cap stepped back and removed the plastic gloves, dropping them into the trash can. "I'm betting on the 'or something'."

Ali stared at him with wide eyes as she raised herself into a seated position. A knock came at the door, and the nurse retrieved the lab report, handing it to the doctor. Ali waited anxiously, watching his face intently for any sign. A wide grin swept from one ear to the other.

"Congratulations, Ali."

"What do you mean?"

"You're pregnant. About eight weeks is my guess." He seemed genuinely pleased to give her the news. There was nothing matter-of-fact in his voice.

Her mouth dropped open. "But you said it would never happen."

"I said there'd be little chance." He grinned.

She laughed and cried at the same time. "This is unbelievable."

"I'd call it a miracle." Then he jotted a few notes on the computer. "You'll have to make an appointment for some blood work. Other than that, we'll see you back in a month. Now go share the news with the proud papa."

"This is a solo adventure."

Dr. Cap closed the door. "Another unwilling partner?" He peered at her intently, waiting for the answer.

"More or less." Ali looked him straight in the eye. "The father hasn't got a clue and never will." She scooted off the table. "This is what happens when you give your heart away for one night."

He paused, holding his hand lightly on the doorknob. He nodded ever so slightly before looking at Ali with a soft gaze, sending a shiver up her spine. "No, this is what happens when grace enters your life."

# Chapter Seven

Sitting at her kitchen table, Ali's eyes wandered to the yoga calendar hanging from a magnet on her refrigerator. She was now two weeks closer to her due date, and she hadn't told a soul, not even Bleu. It seemed too special. At the same time, she didn't want to be forced into answering the inevitable questions, like the identity of the father and what her plans were. She knew who the father was. There was no question. She hadn't slept with Sam for several weeks before leaving for Texas. It was the other question that bothered her. What was she to do? Stay under the watchful eye of the entire staff and have the baby? Move back to the farm and telecommute, resurfacing only after the baby was born? Look for another job elsewhere? Or be brave and tell Jack Cooper that he was about to be a father and hope that he'd make an honest woman of her? Sometimes Cinderella was far more real to her than she wanted to admit.

She grabbed her car keys from the table and headed out the door. For now, she'd go through her days as if nothing had changed. All things considered, she'd have a couple of months or more before she'd start showing. That was plenty of time to devise a plan for this next stage in her life.

All this ran through her head as she drove several blocks to the office, pulled into the parking lot, and pranced across the blacktop sprinkled with ice crystals. Fall was definitely here. She'd be a mother in the spring. Her heart leapt, not with anxiety, but with joy as she confidently strode up the six steps and entered the double glass doors that encased all she'd known as a professional for the last fifteen years. She really owed a lot of her success to Joe, and that thought made her anxious. *How could I ever think of leaving him?* She pondered that thought as she bypassed her office and headed to his.

Standing outside Joe's office, Ali took a deep breath. She toyed with the idea of sharing her news as she rapped on the door.

"Come in." His voice filtered weakly through the thick wooden doors.

Ali entered the room, and Joe motioned for her to sit down. He looked unusually tired, and the lines in his forehead were deeply etched.

"Is everything all right?" She sensed something troubling him and realized her news would have to wait.

He leaned back in his chair and studied Ali, his hands folded, with his thumbs rotating forward and backward. She squirmed under the scrutiny as her mind whirled with possibilities as to why he called her to his office so early in the day. Suddenly, his demeanor changed, and a twinkle appeared in his eyes. Ali relaxed, sinking back in her chair in response to his change.

"I've decided to retire in the spring. I want you to take my position."

"Joe, I'm flattered..."

"I know it's a big decision. I'm not asking you to make it in this instant. We'll all be out of here in a few hours for the holiday. Take the time to think it over." He inched forward in his chair. "It'll double your salary, and you'll be a part-owner in the company as well." He smiled at her in a fatherly way. "You'd be great for the job, Ali."

He paused for a moment. His face softened. "It's what I've always wanted for you. You're the only one I trust to take over this illustrious empire that I built so long ago." His voice trailed off as he surveyed his office, pausing on the power wall, lined with awards and photos with famous personalities.

Ali reflected upon his words in silence. His expectations, especially now, complicated matters. She rose from her chair. "I appreciate your confidence. I'll give it great consideration over the break." She stepped toward the door, her mind whirling with this latest development.

"There's no one else but you." He stood up behind his desk. "The farm might be a good place to think things over."

"Bleu and I are going to do a quiet dinner at her place."

Joe gazed out the window. "It's important to revisit our past, especially if it reminds us of who we truly are."

"And what are your plans? Care for a textured vegetable protein turkey breast?" Ali asked as she rose from her chair.

He rolled his eyes. "Thank you, but I'm visiting some friends."

"Good. You look like you need a little break." Ali put her hand on the doorknob. "And Joe," she paused, regarding him closely. She cared for him far more than she ever thought she could care for a friend. "Thanks for the vote of confidence."

"You earned it." He shooed her out the door. "Get out of here. And I mean out of the building. There's nothing here that can't wait until Monday."

As the door closed behind Ali, Joe lowered his gaze. The admissions papers from the hospital had arrived just that morning by FedEx. The doctor outlined the experimental procedure in detail. If all went well, it would buy him a few more years. He sighed and briefly glanced at his watch. He had just a few hours before he had to leave for the airport.

Ali woke early to a foggy Thanksgiving morning. She stretched like a cat, tousled her hair, and sat up to look out the window. Despite the gray sky, the urge to take a walk on the beach drove her from the warmth of her bed. Flinging back the puffy white down comforter, she sunk her toes into the beige Berber carpet and then padded across the carpet to her oak dresser, one that she carried with her from the farm. She let her eyes rest upon the photos neatly arranged on the lace doily that her grandmother had made. One of the photos was of her mother, holding her as an infant, and another of her grandparents, both in silver frames. *Maybe Joe is right.*

She pushed the thought aside as she continued to dress, donning a pair of black fleece pants, green flecked wool-blend socks and her green fleece top. She suddenly wished she had a dog and fondly remembered Max walking beside her at Mama Kate's. She pondered what Kate and Gus were doing to celebrate the day. She placed her hand on her abdomen, allowing her mind to wander to Jack. Her mood dipped until she consciously turned her attention to preparing her morning tonic—half a glass of orange juice, topped off with purified water and three teaspoons of a green vegetable powder. She took a couple of sips and then slipped out the door.

Climbing over the dunes, Ali inhaled the crisp air. A rush of excitement coursed through her veins. Gulls cried overhead, and the salty aroma of the morning air mingled with that of decaying fish. To some, it would be repulsive, but not to Ali. It was life and death all mixed together, and the mystery was alluring.

She veered to the right and slowed her pace, taking the time to listen to the waves lap at the beach. The Chesapeake Bay was docile, and the waves were barely a foot high. She was assured passage as far as she wanted on the narrow beach, with no danger of being trapped by the incoming tide. She was grateful that there was no need to hurry. She wanted to just *be*—Bleu's favorite admonition for Ali.

Walking for a few hundred yards, she perched on a mound far enough from the water line to keep the rising tide from meeting her. It was a luxury to sit, something she had little time to do on her early morning walks before work. She was alone, except for one man walking his dog a few yards down the beach. She focused on the water lapping the shore.

Mesmerized by the sound, her breath synchronized with the rise and fall of the waves. Soon Ali was unaware of her surroundings, and for the first time, she sensed the soul of her child. A wave of peace enveloped her, reminding her of the comfort of her childhood home with her grandparents. She wanted to provide that for her child—no tension, no harried lifestyle, just good old-fashioned simplicity. Life was too short for anything other than that.

A chill shot through her, which was more an emotional sensation than physical. It was hard to admit, but she'd been frittering away too much of her life on busyness. Resting her hand on her belly, Ali realized that this child would bring her more than the experience of motherhood. The baby would provide Ali with the reason to slow down.

Ali rose and continued her walk through the ever-thickening fog, pondering how to bring simplicity into her life. Unable to see more than a few feet around her, she had no idea how far she had gone, despite her efforts to distinguish the familiar roof lines of the houses along the dunes. She took a deep breath, not out of fear or confusion, but to savor the morning air once more. On her exhale, her attention was drawn downward. There, resting between her feet, was a seahorse, an unusual find for this area. She bent down to pick it up and nestled the stiff body in the cup of her hand. In an instant, she was back on the white-sand flats of the Laguna Madre, with Jack by her side as they watched a seahorse floating by as it clung to a piece of grass. She closed her eyes and imagined him holding her. It was the first time she allowed herself to savor the memory of his embrace in quite some time.

Tucking the seahorse in the pocket of her windbreaker, Ali turned to go back to her home. Kate and Gus popped into her mind, and she longed to be with them. Sadness seeped into Ali's heart. *That's home.* She paused and looked out over the water. "The question is," she said aloud. "How do I find my way there again?"

She continued her walk, weighing the longing to be nestled in the embrace of the Mother Lagoon against the opportunity Joe had presented to her. They were on opposite ends of the spectrum. One provided her with adventure and an entirely new path, something she hadn't experienced since leaving the mountains to go to college in the city. The other provided her with comfort and security, just like staying near her grandparents in Shayville. It was all very confusing, for she could see the pros and cons in both and wasn't sure which one outweighed the other. Those thoughts followed her back to her condo.

✳ ✳ ✳

"Happy Thanksgiving," Ali shouted as she opened Bleu's door, carrying a silver platter with her homemade vegan cheesecake appropriately adorned for their holiday.

"I'm in here. Happy Thanksgiving to you, too." Bleu was bent over the stove, testing a broth as Ali entered the room. "Mmm. Mmmm. I should have been a chef."

"Still time to make a career change." Ali eyed her friend as she set the cheesecake on the counter.

"The same can be said of you."

Ali removed her coat and tossed it on the cushioned window seat. "That may happen."

"Yeah, right." Bleu turned the heat on the burner down. "We're both waiting for some sign from God to prod us in another direction."

Ali pushed up the sleeves of her olive green sweater. It was big and bulky, providing her both warmth and a sense of protection for her secret. She sighed and then looked at Bleu. "I've got mine."

"Your sign?" Bleu removed her apron, revealing a bright red fleece sweatshirt over a pair of black tights. She motioned toward the futon in the living room. "Mimosas await."

"I'll pass."

"On the meaningful conversation with your friend or the mimosas?"

Ali grinned. "The mimosas. Water will be fine." She took a blue-rimmed hand-blown glass from the shelf above the sink and then opened the spigot of the spring water dispenser. Bleu settled onto the deep mauve sofa and propped herself up on a bright yellow overstuffed pillow. Ali joined her, aware that her heart was beating with excitement.

"You're taking Joe's job," Bleu blurted.

"So much for confidentiality." She sipped her water.

Bleu pulled softly at her hair, making the short strands stand upright on top of her head. "He offered it, right?"

Ali nodded. "Keep this between us..."

Bleu swatted Ali's knee. "Fess up."

"I'm pregnant, Bleu." Tears came to her eyes. Not tears of sadness or fear, but of joy.

"That's some sign." Bleu flopped back on her pillow. "Sam?"

Ali shook her head.

"Thank God." Bleu sipped her drink, her eyes darting back and forth as if she were reading the page of a book. "Then, who?" Her voice trailed off as if she were waiting for an answer from someone other than Ali.

Ali set her glass on the coffee table and drew her knees toward her chest. She looked into Bleu's eyes and softly said his name. "Jack Cooper."

"You've been holding out on me. I knew it. I could feel it. You've been one changed chic since coming back from that assignment. Now, I know why."

Settling back against the pillow, Ali allowed Bleu to continue her contemplative babble. She closed her eyes and conjured up Jack's face the night he made love to her. The tears flowed more earnestly and were decidedly bittersweet.

"So, when are you joining the proud papa?" Bleu inquired.

"He doesn't know." Ali reached for a tissue and blew her nose. "We had one night together, and in the morning, he unilaterally decided that our act was irresponsible, and we were better off forgetting it ever happened."

"Fuck." Bleu poured herself another drink. "Nothing since, no text even?"

Ali shrugged. "I had a strange call a couple of weeks ago." She shook her head. "Probably just my wishful thinking."

"Why not call him?"

"I can't. He was so adamant about how wrong it was for us to be together the last time I saw him." Ali ran her hand through her hair. "He sent me on my way, making me feel like a chastised, starry-eyed schoolgirl. I'm not sure I can get beyond that."

"Too bad you can't partake in this to wash down some of that bull-shit." Bleu sipped her drink. "Ali, I hate to say it, but you attract some real winners."

"Joe says I have a bad picker," Ali chuckled. "It was the best week of my life, and quite possibly the worst. I fell in love with Kate, Gus, the water, the birds, the expansive sky, the fishing—and then got pregnant." She reached over to the table and lifted her glass of water.

Bleu regarded Ali and then stared off at the space above her head. "What are you going to do?"

"Haven't figured that out yet." Ali rose from the sofa. "I have time. But right now, I need some food."

Bleu followed her into the kitchen. She went to the oven and pulled out a sweet potato casserole and vegetarian turkey loaf. "You're not going to have an abortion, are you?"

Ali shook her head. "Never. I'm going to have a healthy baby and spoil her rotten." She smiled wistfully. "I've seen her in my dreams." Ali carried the casserole to the table. "But I do need to figure out my next step."

Ali's cell phone rang, and she picked it up out of her purse. Looking down at the caller ID, she tensed. "Sam."

"Creep." Bleu rolled her eyes. "You need to get away from here. He'll haunt you forever."

Ali nodded. "You may be right."

✳ ✳ ✳

"Kate, I got those sweet potatoes, like you asked." Gus set the bag on the counter. "Kate, where are you?" He walked from the kitchen into the dining area and looked out the patio door. There was no sign of Kate on the dock, at the bird feeders, or even by the fence, chatting with the neighbors. And no turkey roasting in the oven. "Kate! Doggamit." He took his hat off and tossed it onto the coffee table. "Where is she?"

*Whuff.*

"Max, where are you?" Gus headed toward Kate's bedroom door, hurrying his step in response to Max's desperate scratching. He put his hand on the knob and then knocked. "Kate...." Waiting for only an instant, he opened the door and peered in. It took a moment for his eyes to adjust to the darkened room. The shades had yet to be drawn. Max pawed at Gus's leg and turned circles in front of him. Then he trotted toward the bathroom, barking wildly.

Gus followed and pushed the door open tentatively. He spotted Kate lying naked on the floor. Blood oozed from her head, pooling into a crimson puddle on the peach tile. Her leg twisted beneath her. He knelt down and touched her cheek. "Kate, Kate, can you hear me?" With shaking hands, he detected a slight pulse on her wrist. "Oh, thank God." He scrambled to his feet. "Don't worry, Kate. I'll get you to a doctor."

He took the cell phone from his pocket and dialed 9-1-1. With a crackling voice, he spewed out the address and requested the emergency crew to hurry. Ending the call, he scanned the bedroom for a throw. Seeing none, he grabbed the quilt from Kate's bed and hurried back to the bathroom to cover her. He wanted to hold her but feared moving her. Instead, he paced back and forth from the room to the front door, leaving Max to stand guard over Kate. With each step, Gus, wide-eyed in shock, tried desperately to keep his mind from imagining the worst. *Not yet, Dear Lord. Please, not yet.*

He opened the front door and checked his watch. Fifteen minutes had passed since his call. God only knew how long Kate had lain on the floor. In the distance, he could hear the sirens, and he hurried to the end of the driveway. Gus spotted the ambulance rounding the bend, and he frantically waved his arms. "Here, here."

Two young Latinos sprinted from the vehicle. "Hurry, she's in the bathroom. " Gus scampered ahead of the crew, leading them to the bathroom.

"Max, come here, boy. Let the good men help Kate." He pulled the dog aside and sat on the commode as the EMTs assessed Kate's condition.

"Pulse is slight but steady." The youngest man said. He glanced up at Gus, his dark brown eyes showing a great deal of concern. "How long has she been here?"

Gus shook his head. "Not sure. Had to happen somewhere after 6:00 this morning. We talked on the phone 'bout that time." Gus looked at his watch. Six hours. She could have lain here alone and dying for six hours. "I got here 'bout a half hour ago with the sweet potatoes... for dinner." He choked back emotions he had long thought he'd put to rest. "Is she going to be all right?"

"We'll do everything we can, sir."

Another man piped in. "Her BP is critically low. Set up an IV." He reached for his radio and called in a report. "We have a female, approximately 70 years old...."

"Seventy-two." Gus offered.

"BP is 80/50, pulse 55 and weak. Appears to have a broken leg, possible fractured pelvis, and a large gash on her head. ETA thirty minutes."

"I'm going with you." His voice echoed with determination and fear.

"Sir, it would be best if you drove behind us. It'll give us room in the ambulance to tend to her while we're en route."

Gus watched them gingerly lift Kate's near lifeless body onto the stretcher. A slight moan escaped from her pale lips. Max cocked his head and whimpered as he watched his mistress being wheeled from the room.

"Keep care of her," Gus hollered as they closed the door to the ambulance. "She's all we've got."

# Chapter Eight

Ali followed the winding dirt road past the familiar landmarks, until she reached the small cemetery at the four-way stop. Benign neglect described it best. Her eyes rested upon her grandparents' graves, beside them, her mother's. The family gravestone stood majestically above the nominal granite blocks marking the others. Ali spared no expense on the rose granite stone that stood over the remains of her family.

The smell of pine sap and dried leaves welcomed her to her childhood hometown. She adjusted her felt hat and then wound the scarf around her neck, tucking it inside the collar of her brown fleece jacket. Slowly, she entered the cemetery through the creaky metal gate. It was white once, but now it was fashionably distressed with patches of rust intermingled with green moss. Keeping her eyes on the stone which glistened in the sun, Ali's mind ran over the scenes from her past, including the one that haunted her regularly.

She cringed as the scene replayed in her mind as she followed the path to the gravesite. The sound of her mother's wails echoed in her ears. The cold linoleum seeped into the palms of her hands. The black and green swirls on the dingy white background appeared before her eyes. These images were always followed by her mother's body, still warm, with a trickle of blood seeping from her mouth, a pool of crimson cradling her head.

Ali looked down at her hands. Shaking her head to dismiss the memory, she let her gaze fall upon her mother's grave. The anger had long disappeared. For a time, she hated her mother for dying, for leaving her alone in the world. Her explosive tantrums as a child troubled her grandparents. They'd done the best they could, grieving their only child while raising Ali as their very own. But after a while, the knowledge that her life had been spared, and by the man that was her father, seeped into her heart. It was then that Ali vowed to avenge her mother's death by being successful, not relying on any man for her security, and choosing better partners. She'd gotten all but one right.

"Miss Ali, is that you?" A man with shaggy brown hair and a dingy baseball cap leaned out of the window of a battered blue pickup truck.

Ali whirled around. "Mike!" She crossed the cemetery and went to the side of the road to greet him.

"Shoot, you shudda told me you were comin'." He grinned widely. "I wudda started you a fire in the woodstove."

Ali shrugged. "Last minute decision."

"I'll go on up ahead and fix up a fire while you visit with your kinfolks." He motioned in the direction of the gravestone.

"Thanks." She put her hand on his arm, feeling the tattered red plaid wool jacket beneath her fingers. "I'll be along in a little bit."

"She'll be toasty warm by the time you get there." With a nod Mike took off, grinding a couple of gears in the process.

Sighing, Ali looked around. The trees were bare, and a carpet of leaves crunched beneath her feet as she walked back to her family's grave. Part of her knew it was silly, but she had to talk to them. She came here often as a child, playing at the foot of the gravestone. She would tell her mother all her deepest secrets, those things she thought her grandmother would never understand. And when her friend, Jenna, pierced her ear, she put a hat over her head and visited the grave just to show off her new earring. The thought of her old friend made her sad—and a tad guilty.

Kneeling next to the gravestone, Ali placed her forehead against it. "Grandma, Mama, looks like we'll have another girl in the Stephenson family. Watch out for us, will ya?" A hint of her past floated over her lips. "Grandpa, you get that shotgun out. She's gotta make better of things with the men in her life than me and Mama." Ali rose and then kissed the top of the gravestone. "Love ya." Her voice cracked as she fought off the loneliness that smothered her from time to time. She turned with determination to ward off any of those feelings. She hadn't yet realized that she was no longer alone.

Ali returned to the car and completed the last two miles of her drive to the place she once knew as home. She didn't know what she was looking for, only that the desire to be here was something she couldn't ignore. Driving up the sloped gravel driveway, she parked the car at the foot of the stone pathway that led to the front door of the simple structure that still hinted at her grandparents' lives. Gone, however, were the magnificent flower beds that her grandmother tended to on a daily basis during the growing season.

Crumpled leaves hung limply on dried stalks in the bed along the base of the porch. A shriveled potted plant swung in the slight breeze from one end of the porch roof. It once contained purple pansies that Ali brought with her the last time she visited, which she hoped would be a celebratory occasion, but Nigel decided otherwise. He wasn't ready to leave his wife and three children for a family of their own, no matter how miserable he said he was. Instead of a commitment for the future, Ali received a check to cover her medical expenses. She did as he demanded, hiding the evidence of their time together.

Carrying her suitcase and her brown leather satchel, Ali firmly placed her feet on each step. She reached the porch and examined the door. The brass knocker needed polishing, as did the door handle and lock. The faded green paint on the trim was flaking, and the white clapboards demanded a fresh whitewash as well.

Her grandmother would never let such things go. As Ali peered into the tarnished brass, her grandmother's gnarled hand came into view. *"Grandma, you work too hard."*

*"Ali Mae, we may not be rich like some of our neighbors, but you'll never see the Stephenson farm look unkempt, not as long as I'm alive."*

Ali's stomach turned at the recollection of those words. Pushing away the memories, she stepped inside. The furniture was covered with sheets, and layers of dust covered everything. The sight was overwhelming, and she suddenly needed fresh air. Dropping her bags to the floor, she fled from the house, quickly stepping along a familiar path around the back of the house and then up over the hill.

She followed a stone fence, continuing her ascent. After she'd walked for about fifteen minutes, she veered off the path, climbing over the fence and entering the forest. Birch trees intermingled with oaks and elms. The floor of the forest was carpeted with a fresh layer of leaves, some still holding hues of golds and oranges. An occasional bird called out, causing her to pause and listen intently to the chirps and shrills. She identified a cardinal and a chickadee before continuing her journey.

Then she came upon the gurgling stream that her grandfather held dearest to his heart. A short distance upstream, a deer was taking a long drink from a deep pool, unaware of Ali's presence. She remained still, not wanting to disturb it. The young doe raised her head, peered at Ali, and then turned nonchalantly, continuing up the hill.

A large boulder held forth on the side of the stream. Ali continued toward it, climbing carefully over the smaller ones that provided her passage. Sitting cross-legged atop her perch, she peered into the water, studying the riffles and eddies. She'd forgotten how nice it was to just sit next to the stream. It was the one special thing she shared with her grandfather. She sighed, reflecting on the similarities between her grandfather and Gus.

She dipped her hand into a pocket of calm water. It was cold, but she lingered, enjoying the dramatic sensation. Out of the corner of her eye, she detected movement. A brook trout about a foot long with a hooked mouth stared at her. It appeared undisturbed by her presence, mainly curious. Ali studied the trout's dark body, which was covered with lighter spots, in the center of which was a red dot. The fish's belly was a bright red, almost crimson. She'd forgotten how spectacular the hues were on this ancient fish whose roots traced back to the ice ages.

Slowly, she inched her hand toward it. The fish stood her ground, her mouth opening and closing. Her eyes fixed on Ali's. *Be true to your heart,* Ali heard the fish whisper as the two regarded one another.

Then the fish turned, brushing her tail against Ali's fingers. She sat back, still feeling the sensations of the fish's tail on her fingers.

*Be true to your heart.* The whisper of the trout was undeniable.

"How do I do that?" Ali asked as she peered back into the water searching for a clue.

\* \* \*

The morning light shone brightly through the bare windows, awakening Ali from a deep slumber. She rolled over and moaned. Every muscle in her body ached from the hours she spent cleaning the house. Only the two small bedrooms on the second floor remained untouched. The bottom floor, however, had been scoured from ceiling to floor. She sat up in bed and surveyed the room. It looked better than she had remembered. The homemade quilt on the bed smelled like lavender, as did the sheets. The oak dresser sparkled with a fresh coat of lemon oil. Only the lace curtains had to be rehung. Satisfied with her accomplishments, she swung her feet to the floor and ventured into the living room, stopping at the woodstove to stoke the fire before making her way to the kitchen. There, she unpacked her groceries and put them in the cupboards, while waiting for the water in the teapot to boil.

Sinking into the sofa with her cup of tea, she silently said her morning prayers. Ali had just two days to make her decision about Joe's offer, so prayer for guidance was utmost on her mind. Something about the offer just didn't feel right. *Is this why the trout whispered, "Be true to your heart?"*

During her zen-like approach to cleaning her family home, she realized the last few years at the magazine had been more a distraction from her disastrous love life than a true work of the heart. She reached for the journal on the coffee table and began free-writing the thoughts flitting around in her mind. The question: *What is it that you want?* came to her repeatedly. She tapped her pen against her lips as she stared out the window. Creative fulfillment, with the freedom to set her own schedule. She frowned, unsure of how to accomplish that goal without playing the starving artist. She no longer had herself to think of. She put her hand on her belly and closed her eyes. With her journal laying open on her lap, she lapsed into a deep meditation. An hour later, she rose from the sofa to unpack her computer.

\* \* \*

It was well past noon before Ali closed the lid to her laptop. The proposal flowed effortlessly from her mind to the computer screen. It was a compromise between what she desired and what Joe expected of her. Most importantly, it provided her with the freedom to have her baby away from the scornful watch of her former lover and with the financial security that she needed for her peace of mind.

Stretching into an upright position, Ali stepped into the middle of the room and proceeded to do yoga. Sanskrit chants echoed from the small Bluetooth speaker on the coffee table as she focused on each element of the Sun Salutation. The stretch refreshed her, and Ali was ready for lunch when she finished. She stopped by the window on the way to the kitchen. The sun was high in the sky, and the grounds beckoned for her attention. Her fingers twitched, signaling her desire to dig in the earth. It had been too long.

Donning jacket and hiking boots, Ali stepped out into the cool afternoon air. She took the three porch steps with care, holding onto the railing as she surveyed the yard. The bed in front of the porch demanded the most attention. With a lightness in her step, Ali crossed the yard to the far side of the garden, once vibrantly rich with squash, tomatoes, and green beans, now lost in a mass of dead vines. Opening the door to the garden shed, she was greeted first by the creak of the hinges and then by the tiny squeals of mice running for cover. Careful in her reach, she retrieved a trowel and a three-pronged weeder from a thick encasement of spider webs.

She sauntered back to the porch, focusing not on the ground beneath her feet but upon the ragged peak of Old Ragg Mountain standing high above the house. The majestic stance of the rocky mountain reminded her of how much she missed being on the farm, living by the rhythm of the natural surroundings as she once did with her grandparents. But as much as she longed to stay indefinitely, there was a mandate behind the proposal, and she knew her only hope for lasting peace of mind for herself and her child was to follow through with the plan.

On her hands and knees, Ali began cultivating the dirt and pulling the dried plants out of the ground in front of the porch. She was lost in thought and nearly two thousand miles away when she was startled by the sound of a stone rolling across the driveway.

"Ali, is that you?"

She turned toward the voice that commanded her attention. "Mr. & Mrs. Wilson?"

"I told Bill I thought I saw someone over here last night. You were up late," Olive's snow-white curls bounced beneath her red beret as she spoke.

Ali rose to her feet. "There was a lot to clean before I could even go to bed."

"You should have called. I would have helped Mike get the place ready," Olive said.

Bill Wilson stepped forward, his round belly protruding from beneath his tan barn coat. He wore a brown plaid hat with a small brim, and a pipe hung from his lips. "How's the magazine business?"

"Busy."

"Will you be staying long?" He raised an eyebrow as he posed the question.

Ali shook her head. "I have to be back at the office on Monday."

"Well, we will be seeing more of you again, won't we?"

Ali sighed. "I'm not sure." Affirming her proposal, she added. "I've written a proposal for a South Texas travel book. As soon as it's approved, I'll be spending a few months there."

Olive glanced at Bill. "That's where Jack lives."

Ali's head swirled at the mention of his name. She glanced at the couple. "He was my fly fishing guide for a few days." She paused. "I'm sorry about Jenna."

Silence shrouded them.

"How is he?" Bill now held the pipe in his hand.

"Sad." It was the only word that Ali could come up with.

Olive shook her head. "Gave up his career and just ran away, like that would solve anything." She wrung her hands. "We haven't seen him since the memorial service."

"He seems to be coping in his own way." Ali looked deeply into Olive's eyes and then Bill's. "He's a great guide. He knows a lot about the area and the fishery."

"We not only lost Jenna, but we lost Jack, too." His voice trailed off, and he put the pipe up to his lips. "Hate to see him waste away." A puff of smoke circled his head.

"Is he seeing anyone?" Olive inquired, touching Ali's arm with her gloved hand.

"I don't think so," Ali offered.

"He shouldn't be alone." Olive sighed and then glanced at the house. "Come over for supper tonight, would you? We can catch up more then."

Ali smiled. "I'd like that."

# Chapter Nine

G us rubbed the bill of his cap first one way and then another, his tanned leathery hands shaking. The room smelled of furniture polish and antiseptic. "I hate hospitals," he muttered. At that instant, the door opened behind him. A man in his forties, dressed in a long white coat and green scrubs, entered hastily.

"Mr. Lammons, I'm sorry to keep you waiting." The man with tender green eyes extended his hand. "I'm Dr. Lopez. I understand Kate McGregor has no relatives and that you are the closest friend."

"That's right." He clasped the arm of the chair tightly and studied the doctor's expression.

Dr. Lopez sat behind his desk, reviewing a medical chart. "Mrs. McGregor is in recovery now. We've had to do extensive surgery to her pelvis and her leg."

"Is she al right?"

The doctor removed his scrub cap and peered intently at Gus. "Her condition is stable for now. But I'm not going to lie to you. It's touch and go. We had to resuscitate her on the table. Her condition is far more complicated than her injuries."

Gus shook his head in disbelief and then raised his eyes to search the doctor's face. "What's wrong?"

"We won't know for sure until we run some more tests, but her heart seems to be the real concern. We've called in a cardiologist."

Gus took a white handkerchief from his pocket and dabbed his nose. "Can I see her?"

"When she's back in her room." The doctor glanced at his watch. "Go have some lunch. She should be ready for your visit in a couple of hours."

Gus studied the young man's face and didn't like what he saw. The doctor's eyes were filled with compassion and very little confidence. He stood up to leave, mumbling his thanks, and then headed out of the building. It was hard to think of eating with Kate lying so close to death. The thought of being without her terrified him.

After sitting by the two-story fountain in the Spanish-style courtyard outside the hospital for more than an hour, Gus entered Kate's room tentatively, no longer willing to wait to see her. From the doorway, he could hear the steady beep of a machine that monitored her heartbeat. He rounded the corner and peered behind the curtain. There, lie Kate, pale, with tubes in her nose and an IV running into her arm. His knees grew weak, and he stumbled into the chair by the side of the bed. "Kate…," he whispered her name as he reached for her hand. "Good to see you. Doctor says you're going to be fine. Good as new in no time."

Kate moved her head slightly. "Cy?"

Gus's heart sank. "No, it's me, Gus." He leaned closer so she could see him.

She appeared to be looking through him. "I saw him."

"Saw who?"

"I was surrounded by light, and there he was."

"Kate, you're still sedated from the operation." He squeezed her hand. "You rest. We'll talk more tomorrow."

"He sent me back." Kate's lips formed a slight smile. "Didn't want to leave. I felt such peace." Her voice trailed off, and she closed her eyes again. "I didn't want to disappoint him."

A tear slid down Gus's cheek as he bent over to kiss her. "Rest now. I'm here for you. Always have been."

* * *

The double mahogany doors loomed before Ali, and she paused for a moment to remember the words that the trout whispered—*Be true to your heart*. Her courage rose to the task before her. She raised her hand, formed a fist, and swiftly rapped on the door.

"Come in," Joe peeked over the top of his glasses as Ali entered. "Nice holiday?" He motioned for her to sit in the large burgundy leather chair opposite his desk.

"Very nice." She studied his face, attempting to read his disposition. "And yours?"

"Exquisite." He leaned back and took off his glasses, still holding them in his right hand. "Have you made a decision?"

Glancing down at the folder on her lap. "I can't accept the offer." Disappointing him weighed heavily upon her, but her self-preservation had taken on greater importance. She chanced a look at him, biting her lower lip.

Joe studied her. "Any particular reason?"

"Just one."

He tossed his glasses on the desk and folded his hands in his lap. "And it is?"

Ali took a deep breath and looked him squarely in the eye. "Do you believe in miracles?"

His expression softened. "More and more."

"I'm bearing witness to one."

"Do tell."

"I need absolute confidentiality."

"Scout's honor." Leaning forward, he raised his fingers in the salute.

"I'm pregnant," She said, barely above a whisper.

"Sam?" There was hope in Joe's voice that this was not the case.

"No," she replied flatly.

"Thank God." His relief was palpable.

Ali wondered if she should tell him the whole truth. But before she reached a conclusion, a broad grin swept across Joe's face. "The fly fisher."

She nodded.

"I detected a mystery between the lines of your prose." His eyes twinkled. "Does he know?"

"No, and I won't tell him." Ali ran her hands through her hair. "I don't want anyone else to know. It's just you and Bleu."

"How long do you think you can conceal your secret around here?"

"If I'm lucky, until the end of December."

Joe rubbed his eyes. "Then what?"

Ali put the folder on the desk. Joe eyed it and then glanced at her.

"It's a proposal for a Leisure Time Travel Guide for the Rio Grande Valley." She looked at him with pleading eyes. "I need your help getting the powers that be to accept it. I'm hoping to get a healthy advance, plus my medical coverage and a year's leave in order to do this book—and have the baby."

Time passed slowly as Joe skimmed through the proposal, occasionally nodding and scribbling notes. Ali's heart beat wildly, wondering what she would do if he wouldn't support her in this.

After turning the last page, he closed the folder and leaned back in the chair. "Then what?"

"Not sure." Ali looked out the window at the swaying pines. The sky threatened rain, if not snow.

"Would you consider accepting my proposal at the end of the year?"

"Joe, don't wait for me to retire."

"I didn't say I would." He looked at her with genuine concern in his eyes. "I just want to preserve your options. You'll have a child to consider, and I'd hate to see you *both* left out in the cold."

Ali closed her eyes, looking inside for an answer. "Yes, I'd consider it," she said as she met his gaze.

Relief once again swept over Joe's expression as he reached for his phone. "Philip, Joe here. How's your schedule look right now? I have a pressing matter to discuss with you." He glanced at Ali and winked. "Wonderful. See you in a few."

Ali prepared to leave. "Thanks, Joe."

He adjusted his tie as he strode around his desk. "Don't thank me yet, my dear." He reached for his sport coat and flung it over his arm. "I still have to sell the idea to our cohorts in the book world. Hard to know what they'll think."

# Chapter Ten

Jack rushed in the door of Pirates with cold air blasting in from behind him. "Damn norther! Blew us out again. Ten storms, and it's not even January."

He nervously searched the crowded room for Skipper, trying to identify him amongst a group of tanned, disgruntled men and a few early Winter Texans—all who looked at him with a bit of disgust for making such a scene. Jack spotted him sitting at a table in the corner, reading a paper.

"I've counted eleven." Skipper's deep voice boomed over the table toward Jack. "I ordered you a coffee."

Ginny sauntered over to the table. "Missed you, Jack." She placed two cups of coffee in front of the men and then rested her hand on Jack's shoulder. "Been a while."

Jack glanced at her briefly, long enough to notice the sadness in her eyes. "I know." His response was uninviting.

"I think it's time for us to order now." Skipper's voice broke the thickening chill.

"I'll have the Mexican plate." Jack closed the menu and pushed it to the edge of the table.

"The same." Skipper added. She turned abruptly and walked away. "Kinda hard on her."

"I made no commitments."

Skipper chuckled. "No, but you were pounding a steady trail to her door up till a few months ago."

"I'm not cut out for relationships." There was no remorse other than shame for initiating the relationship in the first place. "She can do better."

"She don't want better. She wants you."

"It's not her call."

Ginny returned to the table and placed the food, first in front of Skipper and then Jack. She leaned forward and looked him square in the eye. "You can just go to hell, Jack. You're nothing but a cold-hearted son-of-a-bitch." Her voice was loud enough for everyone to hear. She twirled around angrily and stormed through the swinging door into the kitchen area.

"Better eat before she comes back and dumps that plate on your lap." Skipper picked up a tortilla. "Can't say as I blame her."

"You don't know the whole story, Skipper." Jack looked up at his friend and studied his lined face.

"That's 'cause you haven't let on to what you've been stewing about." Skipper took a bite of beans. "Been holed up in that place of yours when you ain't been on the water."

Jack pushed a pile of rice around with his fork. "Had a lot on my mind."

"Sorrows shared are sorrows halved."

Jack shook his head. "Not now."

"I'll wait for your word, my friend."

✳ ✳ ✳

The offices of *Southern Style* magazine were adorned with gold and silver snowflakes. A Christmas tree stood in the corner of the art room, with handmade ornaments made from old magazine covers decorating every branch. Ali paused and inhaled the scent of warm cider, popcorn, and chocolate. The buzz of voices swarmed around her as she made her way to the tree, carrying a large bag filled with gifts. The mood was festive. For the first time since the magazine's inception, the office would be closed for ten days, allowing for redecorating.

Joe sauntered around the room, wearing an elf's cap and carrying a cup of cider. He belted Christmas carols with a slight hint of his gentlemanly Southern drawl. Ali retreated to a far corner where she could safely observe the festivities. This had been her family for the last fifteen years, and while some of the faces and names changed now and again, the magazine provided her with more security than she'd known for much of her adult life. Yet, she knew it was impossible to stay. Sam would be aggressively invasive. Not only did she not want to go through the emotionally intense experience, but above all, she needed to that her baby was brought into a peaceful environment.

"Come on, Ali." Bleu plopped down next to her. "Joe's giving out the presents."

"I can see from here just fine."

"You're a party pooper." Bleu put her arm around Ali. "I want to see you smile." She reached up and touched Ali's cheek. "You look so sad."

"I'm that transparent?" She adjusted her teal and blue paisley pashmina and folded her arms in front of her.

Bleu shrugged her right shoulder and tipped her head. "Everybody's wondering what's going on with you."

"They'll find out soon enough," Ali said softly.

The merrymaking unfolded. Presents were distributed, and words of thanks were shouted across the room. Laughter filled the air and whirled around her. Ali felt so different from everyone in the room and always had, no matter how hard she tried to fit in. There was always something that made her stand apart. *Or perhaps it's the way I've kept myself safe from connecting too deeply, only to be hurt again and again?* A fluttering rippled through her womb. She lowered her hand to her abdomen. *Would the baby separate me even more or teach me how to really love, to trust in love?* Her reverie came to a halt with Joe's voice booming over the din of conversation.

"Ladies and Gentlemen." A hush fell across the room as Joe raised his hand. "In addition to wishing you all a very happy holiday, I have a few announcements to make."

The celebratory mood flattened, and several people exchanged worried glances.

"When we come back in the new year, there will be some changes in our staffing and our operations. Everyone will be affected in one way or another."

Whispers erupted. "Relax. No one is losing their job." Joe glanced at Ali and motioned for her to join him.

All eyes were upon her as she crossed the room to take her place beside him. She surveyed the faces in the crowd stopping briefly to catch Bleu's eye for support. She gave Ali the thumbs-up.

Joe reached for Ali's hand. "Our magnificent managing editor has been awarded a contract for one of our Leisure Time books."

Applause erupted. Joe signaled for silence after joining in momentarily himself. "Which means that Ms. Stephenson will not be in our office on a daily basis for the next year. She will, however, act as a field editor, submitting stories from afar, and also have a part-time commitment to the production of the magazine. She'll be telecommuting in the true sense of the word from her base in deep South Texas."

Her eyes were met by Sam's. His mouth was firmly set, and he clenched his jaw. She knew the look well. She averted her gaze, refusing to be emotionally sidelined by him.

"Clark Lewis from the Leisure Time staff will be joining us and taking over Ali's position in the interim." Joe glanced at Ali, giving her silent permission to say a few words.

"This is an exciting opportunity for me to see how our sister publications are birthed," she said confidently. "And it allows me to explore an area that deeply touched my heart during the assignment late last summer."

Several people applauded again.

"Thank you," she paused and looked at Joe. "I assure you that I am available to answer any of your questions, and I will be back, perhaps with more fervor and creativity than I now have at the end of next year."

Slowly, she stepped aside and ducked out of the room. Back in her office, she collapsed in the chair and stared out the window. Deep in thought, she didn't hear the door open.

"So you're going back to be with him." Sam leaned against the door jam, arms crossed.

She didn't turn but lowered her gaze at her clasped hands. "I'm going to do an assignment."

"Where will you be staying?" Sam asked snidely.

She whirled around and met his gaze. "Like everyone else, you'll receive a memo on how to reach me."

"So why aren't you being replaced?" He glared at her.

She fiddled with papers on her desk. "I'll be back."

"I suppose you're the top candidate for Joe's job?"

She returned his glare. "That's none of your concern."

"Pardon me, Sam." Joe appeared in the doorway. He gave Sam a stern look. "The party's still going strong in there, and I have a few things to discuss with Ali. If you'll excuse us."

Sam clenched his jaw. "Sure." He turned abruptly, but not before shooting Ali a disturbing parting glance.

"Thank you." Ali leaned back in her chair.

"The spark is still there, I see."

Ali sighed. "He's having a hard time believing he got dumped."

Joe chuckled as he sat down across from Ali. He reached into the pocket of his jacket. "A Christmas present for you."

Ali held her breath as she reached across the desk for the envelope.

"Your advance, your contract for the coming year, which includes full-time health benefits, part-time compensation for your twenty-hour work week, and a paid eight-week vacation, which I assume you'll take somewhere around the time of the birth of your baby, and…." He paused, taking a moment to look at the envelope and then at Ali. "The contract for my position, signed in advance by the illustrious president of the magazine division of the company, that would be me, of course."

Ali was unable to speak. Her hands shook as she opened the envelope. "Why that contract now?"

Joe squirmed in his chair. "It was the only way the board would agree to keep you on the payroll."

She peered into his eyes. "I guess I have no choice." She reviewed the contract, making sure there were no surprises, and then picked up the blue Mont Blanc pen that Joe had given her when he promoted her to managing editor. Taking a deep breath, she signed her name with her signature flair.

"Looks like we have a deal," she said, handing the contract to Joe.

For a moment, sadness crossed his face, and then he clasped her hands in his. "I look forward to your return, my dear, when the golden leaves fall to the ground and the wind rushes in from the north. But until then, you are to take the utmost care of yourself and that baby of yours."

"Thank you, Joe." Tears welled up in her eyes. She now couldn't imagine not seeing him every day. Leaving was becoming harder than she thought.

"I will accept your thanks now." He rose from his chair, stretching his tall thin frame in a stately way. "I will miss you around here. You've been good for this place." Ali ventured from behind her desk to stand next to him as he looked out the window.

In a fatherly way, he put his arm around her shoulder and in a voice barely above a whisper, he added. "It's just not going to be the same without you." He kissed the top of her head before striding out the door. When the door closed behind him, Ali buried her face in her hands, allowing the sobs she'd been so good at holding back to now come to the surface.

# Chapter Eleven

Gus waltzed through the door of Kate's room at the rehab center, carrying a bouquet of flowers and several presents. "Merry Christmas!"

"You old fool," Kate chided. Her face was no longer gaunt and pale. A faint tint of pink washed her cheekbones, as well as her lips. "I've got more flowers in this room than a daggum dead person."

"Nice to see you're feeling better." He placed the presents on the table near her and tossed his cap alongside them. He wandered to the window and opened the shades. "Beautiful day. Birds are singing up a storm."

"Good for them."

"Kate, you'll be out of here in a few days." He went back to her bedside and handed her a gift. "Here, Santa's been good to you this year. Although I'm not sure why."

Kate studied her old friend for a moment. "I'm sorry, Gus."

He patted her hand. "I'd probably be crotchety, too."

"Worse." She smiled faintly at him.

"No doubt," he agreed.

She held the gift close to her heart. "I dreamt of Ali last night." She peered at Gus. "I miss that girl."

Gus noticed the sparkle in her eyes for the first time. "Well, you may not have to." He grinned. "She called awhile back. Told her 'bout your condition."

Kate peered at him with interest.

"She needs a place to stay for a few months. Said something about writing a travel book on the area."

"What did you tell her?"

"That I'd get her room ready."

Kate fiddled with the bow on the present. "Mama Kate's is closed until further notice."

"We've been 'round this before. I can help you run the place."

"You can't cook."

"I can learn," Gus tapped his foot impatiently. "And Ali can help. You can't afford *not* to stay open, Kate. I've seen your bills—and your bank account."

A pained expression crossed her face. The truth of Gus's words stung. "Maybe I'll just sell the place and move into one of those RVs like the Winter Texans."

"Oh, sure. You'll be happy as a lark in one of them tin cans." Gus shook his head. "Why are you so darned stubborn about accepting my help? Ali's help?"

"You said she has a book to write." Kate's stubbornness was rising to the surface.

"We've already worked out the details," He said confidently.

"Sounds like you two had a lengthy conversation." Kate's curiosity was beginning to overshadow her inflexibility.

"Two or three." Gus's face flushed.

Kate stared out the window and slowly nodded. "Fly fishers are only occasional visitors this time of year. Birders, they're easy. Maybe some Winter Texans would stay on in the units in the guest house for a month or so. I could handle that."

Gus beamed. "That's the Kate I know."

She reached under a magazine on the table. "I couldn't get you a cactus." She handed him the card. "Best I could do." She put her hand on top of his. "You sure been through a lot with me."

"What are friends for?" Gus said as he put his shaking hand on top of hers and grinned.

\* \* \*

Ali pulled into Arroyo City at dusk four days after leaving Virginia. She deliberately took a slow route, frequently stopping to preserve her energy. Her emotions were mixed. She was sad to have left Bleu and Joe. But beneath that was an overriding sense of relief. She was ready for the slower pace that the Valley afforded. And more so, going to Mama Kate's was like going home.

Slowing the car, Ali surveyed the area for any apparent changes. The water tower appeared, with freshly painted letters towering high above the small market that supplied the sleepy town's residents with the basic necessities. Winter Texans, referred to as snowbirds in other parts, strolled along the road, some couples hand in hand. The RV parks were packed to the gills and much more active than in the summer months when most were little more than abandoned parking lots. A few trucks with empty boat trailers were parked at Sanchez's Bait Stand.

She rolled down the window and took her first deep breath of the salty air. A couple of gulls laughed, and across the Arroyo, several cattle stood along the bank, and a deep bellow from a massive bull echoed through the air. Then Ali glanced ahead and saw the sign to Mama Kate's. Her heart leapt with excitement.

\* \* \*

The curtains parted in the front room as Ali pulled into the driveway. She saw Kate wave as she stepped from the car. Gus flung the door open, and Max bounded out, with his tail wagging frantically.

Gus hugged her. "It's sure good to see you again."

Ali choked up. "You, too, Gus."

"C'mon in. Kate's inside. Brought her home a week or so ago." He stepped back to let Ali pass through the doorway. "Not quite up to par yet."

Ali entered the room where Kate sat on the sofa. Her legs were covered with a blue and yellow Mexican blanket. "You sure are a sight for sore eyes." Kate smiled broadly, a hint of a tear glistening in her eyes.

"Hi, Kate." Ali studied the older woman's face. It was hard to miss the sunken cheeks and the dark circles under her eyes. "Looks like we have some healing to do."

Kate let her gaze fall to her lap for a moment. "There's no better place to do that than close to the Mother Lagoon." She patted the sofa. "Come, give me a hug."

The two women embraced. "I'm glad you're back. I dreamt about you."

"I'm delighted to be back."

Kate wiped her eyes and then nodded toward the kitchen. "Gus made split pea soup. Some cornbread, too."

"Can I get your bags?" Gus ambled into the room, carrying two cups of tea. "I bought some of that herb stuff, without caffeine. Doc says coffee's not good for Kate no more."

Ali reached for the cups and handed one to Kate. "I'll just bring in my overnight bag tonight and the brown satchel with my laptop." She yawned, stretching while holding the small of her back. "The rest can wait until morning."

"Go on, fetch Ali's bags, and then get things ready in the kitchen. We'll be there in a bit." Kate shooed him from the room.

He frowned, grumbling about being outnumbered as he turned to return to the kitchen. Ali removed her shoes, then pulled her hair out of the ponytail she'd been wearing all day. Kate watched her with interest. "So how far along are you?"

Ali didn't miss a beat. "Five months."

"Gus may have his hands full with the both of us." Then she peered at Ali. "He may need some back-up."

Ali shook her head. "I'm in this on my own, Kate."

"You didn't get this way on your own."

"I've had no contact with Jack since I left."

"He's had none with us either," Kate offered. "Word has it he fishes and then hides in that cottage of his on the edge of the lagoon."

Carrying her white teacup embossed with purple pansies, Ali went to the window. She watched the tiny Inca doves scurrying along the grass, searching for any hidden seed. "I'm not here for a reunion." She glanced at Kate. "I just couldn't think of anyplace else I wanted to be in the next few months."

Kate joined Ali at the window and placed her hand on Ali's belly. Kate closed her eyes as she let her hand rest against Ali's womb. "I best get out my knitting needles again and lots of pink yarn."

Ali leaned her head against Kate's. "This is going to be some adventure," she chuckled.

"Ladies, supper's on." Gus's voice wafted through the doorway.

"Be right there." Kate looked intently at Ali. "Word may get around that you're here."

"I doubt he'll come looking for me." Ali reached for Kate's elbow, and the two wandered into the dining room. Pausing at the table, Ali added, "And I trust that you won't let on that I'm here either."

Kate refrained from answering. Instead, she glanced at Gus, poised in the kitchen with a serving bowl of soup in his hands. His only response was the shrug of his shoulders.

# Chapter Twelve

The morning fog hung close to the surface of the Laguna Madre, shrouding the bay with an expectant silence. Jack stood on the bow of the boat and let it slowly drift toward the dock. He could barely make out the grayed pilings that supported the wooden structure, nor Skipper's skiff, which was rocking from the wake of a departing boat. Tying off on a cleat, Jack jumped up and headed for the gas pump. He waved to the attendant inside the white stucco building, and the pump made a clicking noise, announcing that it had been activated.

The morning air held a chill. But these conditions barely registered in his psyche as he filled the tank. His mind was troubled by a dream that left him with a deep desire to crawl into a hole and die. Jack closed his eyes, and it all came back to him. First, Jenna's face, then Ali's. More salt in his deeply festering wounds. He shook his head, hoping to clear the images and the emotions they stirred. Sadness crept into his bones, like the morning chill, and thicker than the fog over the bay. The same dismal cloud that drove him south threatened to smother him in the place he sought sanctuary. The Mother Lagoon wasn't so comforting now. She was taunting him with images from his past, one not so distant.

"Morning, Jack." Skipper came up behind him and patted him on the back. "So, are you still going to speak to me now that you're famous?"

Jack returned the nozzle to the pump. "What the hell are you talking about?" He frowned as he turned to look at Skipper.

"What makes you so sour this morning? You need an attitude adjustment." Skipper gnawed on his toothpick. "You alr ight?"

"Didn't sleep well last night." Jack rubbed his forehead. "So, are you going to explain what you were referring to?"

"The magazine, *Southern Style*." Skipper pointed toward the building. "They've got a whole stack."

The color drained from his face. "Haven't seen it."

"It ought to help your business." Skipper patted Jack's shoulder. "Call me if you need someone to cover for you."

Jack headed toward the building.

"And don't be wasting time giving autographs. Looks like your clients are heading this way."

Jack glanced in the direction of Skipper's gaze. A couple in their thirties, dressed like models from a SIMMS catalog, emerged from their car. Jack turned away and stepped inside the store, sincerely hoping they would disappear while he was paying for the gas.

"There's the man!" A stout bristly man with a salt and pepper beard approached the register waving a magazine. "You're doing centerfolds now, I see. " He opened the magazine, and there was Jack holding a twenty-two-inch trout, one that Ali had caught. "Couldn't you have caught a bigger fish?"

Jack ignored the comment as he reached for the magazine with a shaking hand and turned the page. Ali appeared before him, her bright smile about as wide as the redfish she held. The room faded from his consciousness. Flashbacks from his dream crowded his thoughts.

"What'd you do to get that coverage?" A hoarse drawl shook him from his reverie. "I bet you showed her a *real* good time."

Jack whirled around. His steely gaze pierced through the young guide known more for his after-hours adventures than his angling experience.

"Mind your own business." Jack sneered through a clenched jaw.

"Had to do something to get coverage like that." The younger man grabbed the magazine and stared at Ali. "Hell, I'd jump that anytime."

Jack stepped forward, closing the distance between them.

The younger man, standing several inches shorter than Jack, pointed a pudgy finger in Jack's face. "Things like that just don't happen without paying favors of some kind or another." The man jeered. "And I'm betting on the other, especially the way you two were cavorting in Mexico."

Jack shoved the guide. The young man's face flushed with anger. The tips of his shaggy blond hair quivered. Then, he raised his fist. "You son-of-a-bitch."

Skipper's quick response thwarted his blow. "Seems like you two need a time-out." He nodded toward Jack. "Your charter's looking for you out on the dock."

Jack abruptly left the room, and his departure was followed by chuckles from onlookers. He paused just outside the door. Skipper's voice boomed over the rest. "Knock it off. That article is not just about him, you dummies. It's about all of us, the whole dang bay. So leave him alone."

Jack braced himself against the torrent of emotions and forged onward. With a quick nod and a handshake, he escorted the young couple onto his boat, noting the woman's features as she climbed aboard. For a brief moment, their eyes met, and he was instantly reminded of Ali. As he untied the boat from the dock, he vowed to bar her from his thoughts forever.

✳ ✳ ✳

Gus burst into the room, excitement written all over his face. "Ali, it's here. The magazine."

He waved the copy in the air. "Kate, lookie here. There we are, Proprietor Mama Kate and her sidekick Gus whip up a hearty meal in Mama Kate's kitchen."

"Gus, settle down. Ali's sleeping."

"Is she okay?"

Kate reached for the magazine. "Did you open her mail?"

Gus shrugged. "Knew it was the magazine. We got a whole pile of them."

Kate glared at him. "She's fine. She needs her rest."

"So do you."

Kate flipped open the magazine, ignoring his last comment. She studied the image of Jack holding the trout. "Wonder if he's seen it yet."

"No doubt." Gus settled into a chair opposite Kate. "He got into a tussle this morning down at the docks with some punk guide. Seems he made some snide remark about Ali. Jack 'bout decked him."

"Good," Kate said matter-of-factly.

Gus winced.

A whimsical expression danced on her face. "Captain Cooper was more affected by our dear Ali than he lets on."

"What good's that gonna do if we can't get those two together?" Gus said with obvious impatience.

"It's out of our hands." Kate wanted to sound more confident than she was, but even her faith was wavering.

"That's what you always say. Sometimes you gotta take action." He pounded his fist into the palm of his hands.

Kate shot him a glance that warned him not to get carried away, before continuing to read the article. Comfortable silence infused the room.

"Before I forget, I put fresh snapper in the refrigerator. Thought I might grill them for us tonight," Gus spoke reverently as if he knew Kate was doing more than reading the magazine.

"Not too spicy. It'll upset the baby." A puzzled look crossed Gus's face. Kate shook her head. "Men don't know nothing about having a baby. What upsets mama, upsets baby."

"How do you know all that? You ain't never had a baby."

Kate gestured toward a stack of books. "I've been reading Ali's books. I'm going to be her birth coach."

"Her what?"

"I'm going to be with her when she has the baby." Kate looked proud. "We'll be going to class in a few weeks."

"Why do you need to take classes?" Gus scratched his head. "I thought it just happened."

"It does. But learning about it makes it easier on the mother—and the baby."

"And what are you going to do as her coach?"

Kate squared her shoulders. "I'm going to remind her to breathe, and give her ice chips, and hold her hand."

"Sounds like an important job." Gus rolled his eyes.

Kate yanked on his sleeve. "Listen to me." She glanced toward Ali's bedroom door. "See what you can find out." Kate pointed at the magazine. "See if anyone's caught on that she's here, especially Jack. And don't let on to Ali about it."

Gus's eye glimmered. "Reckon we can get these two together?"

"Most likely. Just not sure how to do it yet." She stared toward the dock, her eyes falling on her boat. "Something will come to me. I have to ask for a little help, that's all." She rose from the table. "I'm going to go have me a little chat with Mary." She plucked her rosary from her pocket and headed out the door toward her wicker chair near the shrine under the mesquite.

# Chapter Thirteen

Ali swished around the corner, carrying her fly rod, with her backpack slung over her shoulder. Walking into the kitchen, she snatched an apple from the basket and placed it in her bag. "Kate, I'm leaving."

"You picked a bad time to go to the Island. It's spring break. No one in their right mind goes near there if they don't have to."

"Well, I have to. It's part of my assignment to capture the flavor of the Island with all of its offerings. And spring break happens to be one of them—a big one."

"When will you be back?"

"Sometime this evening. I'm interviewing the director of the chamber; then I have a break until late afternoon, at which time I'll have an interview with the promotions director, and then there's a concert on the beach."

Kate looked up from her recipe book. "What are you doing with your rod?"

"I thought I'd drive up the beach on the bayside and do a little wading." She wrinkled her nose and grinned impishly. "The weather is just too beautiful...." As she glanced out the window, a brief look of sadness crossed her face. "It's still cold up north."

"Miss it?"

"Sometimes. Especially Bleu and Joe." Ali ran her fingers through her chestnut locks. "Maybe it's the structure. Here my day just flows. Back there, I knew exactly what I'd be doing from eight in the morning until at least six at night."

"That don't sound like much fun to me." Kate poured a cup of flour into the bowl. "Gluten-free. Don't worry."

Ali glanced at the bag of flour. "I guess it wasn't. But it helped keep my mind off of things that weren't going so well."

"Around here, nature shows the way. When it's nice, you fish, watch the birds flit around in the feeders, tend to the plants, and smell the roses in bloom." Kate measured a teaspoon of cinnamon. "When it's not, you curl up and retreat to your cave, contemplating life and all its richness. It's the way God intended it to be."

"I'm beginning to understand that." Ali hugged Kate. "Now, take some of your own advice. Go outside and get some sun on your bones. And take a walk."

"Yes, mother." Kate chuckled. "Have fun."

✳ ✳ ✳

Ali left the South Padre Island Tourist Bureau and stepped into the sunshine carrying a stack of brochures and file folders containing all the demographic material she needed for the southernmost tip of the Rio Grande Valley. It had all gone so smoothly. And now her grumbling stomach told her it was time to grab some lunch before heading to the sand to wet her line.

Maneuvering through the throngs of cars with partially clad young men and women hanging out of convertibles and pickup trucks, she ducked into the Psyche Deli. She ordered an avocado salad and vegetable soup. Carrying her meal to the Spanish-style courtyard, Ali took a seat at one of the bistro tables. Above her, a fantail palm about thirty feet high provided the shade she desired. Gulls eyed her hopefully from the stucco wall surrounding the dining area. She ignored them as she closed her eyes and held her hands over her food, whispering a blessing for the nourishment and asking for goodness to come to all those who made the meal possible.

A wave of energy washed through her, and the baby kicked a few times, startling her from her prayer. With a smile on her face, she inhaled and mentally embraced her surroundings. The energy of the Island pulsed around her, and for a moment, she let her mind wander to Jack, musing over his whereabouts. She sighed, knowing she could not dwell on things from the past nor fantasize about some unlikely future. She reigned her thoughts in and focused on the food before her.

Her cell phone rang, and she pulled it from her backpack. "Hey, boss."

"Working hard, are you?" Joe's voice beamed through the phone.

"Very. Listen to this." She held her cell phone at arm's length, pointing it toward the street. Jeers and car horns, along with cackling seagulls, serenaded her.

"Where are you?"

"Spring Break at South Padre Island."

"Aren't you too old for that nonsense?"

"Heck, Joe, I thought I'd take my top off and show off my round belly. Who knows? Might just get the attention of some fine young stud that I can whip into shape as a suitable partner."

"Spare me more concern, my dear."

She chuckled. "How about you?"

"Wonderful." There was a brief pause. "We just sent the proofs of the current issue and design sheets for the next issue. We need them back by Monday."

"No worries." Ali took a sip of her mineral water. "I'll call you tomorrow. My soup's getting cold, and I want to go fishing."

"Enjoy yourself!" Enthusiasm for her adventures hung on the wings of his words.

✳ ✳ ✳

Joe placed the phone back on the receiver and then stood before the window in his office. Gulls and terns soared on wind currents as they hovered above the parking lot. In the distance, he watched the waves lapping at the shore. It was a crisp day, but he suddenly had the urge to go for a stroll on the boardwalk. He donned his black wool coat and left the office without saying a word to anyone. His mind was miles away, considering Ali and the life she was now leading.

Crossing the street, he walked down a path between two hotels. The beach was sleepy, except for a handful of pedestrians walking into a hotel restaurant, a lone biker pedaling southward, and a homeless man with a ragged overcoat picking through the garbage. It did little to bring ease to his mind.

He paused, leaning against the railing which separated the concrete boardwalk from the beach. The breeze brushed over his face. It was invigorating, but at the same time, sent a chill through him. As he continued his walk, his thoughts returned to Ali, hidden away in her subtropical paradise. There was something in her voice that was different. She actually laughed. He paused, considering the last time he had seen her smile naturally, let alone have a good laugh.

Her writing now sparkled, and her editing was flawless. He had to look hard to change even one word. Their weekly conference calls were infused with new life. He sighed. *So what right do I have to insist that she come back?* His head hurt from thinking about it. Shoving his hands into his pocket, he turned to go back to the office. He knew he should let her go. He pursed his lips and shook his head. He just wasn't ready.

Driving past the South Padre Island Convention Center, Ali signaled a left turn into a well-packed section of sand, which led to the bay. The sun glistened upon the water, stirring excitement within her. The baby once again reacted to the emotion. Veering to the right and passing a line of windsurfers, she drove along the water's edge, searching for a section that beckoned her.

About two miles north, she brought her Audi to a halt and took the keys from the ignition. Resting her hand on the steering wheel, she studied the water. Several mullet broke the surface with their airborne acrobats. It was the sign Ali needed to leave her SUV and enter the water. She removed her shoes and then rolled up her khakis.

Adopting a lean approach, she stuffed her fly box in her pants pocket and hung the nippers from a lanyard around her neck. Then she reached for her rod, which was on the back seat. Removing it from the case, she carefully joined the sections and then threaded the line through the guides. She tied a subsurface fly, resembling a shrimp, to the end of the tippet. When finished, she took a swig of water and headed for the water's edge.

Taking a moment to adjust to the slightly cool temperature, Ali realized it had been seven months since she last felt the waters of the Mother Lagoon. So much change in so little time. It was head-spinning and wonderful all at once. Stripping out some line, she made a few casts to test her timing. She'd been practicing on the dock at Mama Kate's, so she didn't feel the least bit rusty. In fact, she enjoyed the dance with her rod much more than she ever had on the corporate pond.

She adjusted her sunglasses and began her wade, watching intently for any sign of a gamefish. She'd yet to learn the subtle nuances of identifying a trout in the water, but she quickly spotted redfish. Her heart beat rapidly as one approached from about eighty feet away. She crouched low to the water and waited until the fish was within distance of her cast. After one false cast, she freed the line on her forward cast, and the fly landed with precision before the oncoming fish. The fish caught sight of the fly and darted at it like it was its last meal.

Within moments, Ali was hooked up, and her reel was singing. "Oh man, it just doesn't get any better than this. Yeehaw." She laughed aloud as the play continued, with her rod bent and the fish intent on freeing himself from her clutches.

✳ ✳ ✳

Two hundred yards from shore, a shallow water skiff was staked. Two occupants lounged against the console, both sipping a beer.

"You got binoculars aboard." Skipper peered over at Jack.

"Why would I have those?" Sarcasm slipped from Jack's lips.

"Something interesting going on near the shore. I think that's a fly fisher hooked up. And if so, that's our cue to move to where the action is."

Jack rolled off the cushioned cooler and then lifted the top of the seat behind the console. He hastily pawed through its unorganized contents, including boxes of flies, tippet, and a faded ball cap, until he found the binoculars wrapped up in the sleeve of a well-worn raincoat. He freed them from the entanglement removing a pair of sunglasses, a woolen hat, and a stringer.

"You are some messy," Skipper chided.

"Controlled chaos. I know exactly what's in there."

"Right," Skipper reached over the console for the binoculars. He tilted the brim of his hat high on his forehead and removed his glasses. "My, my."

"You going to let me in on what you see?" Jack squinted, trying to focus on the tiny figure near shore.

"When I'm ready." Skipper continued to peer through the binoculars watching the lone fly fisher bring a large redfish to her feet. "Seems to be a lady. Kinda looks familiar, but I can't quite place her."

Skipper turned to Jack with a Cheshire grin. "Take a look for yourself. She's a fly fisher for sure."

Jack warily took the binoculars and then raised them to his eyes. "I can't believe it...."

\* \* \*

Ali released the fish and stood up, holding the small of her back as she rose. She realized she'd caught her share for the day. Angling lore had it that catching a fish on the first cast was bad luck. Not for Ali. To her, it boded well, as though it was part of the divine plan. She sensed that somehow she'd been in the right place at the right time. It left her with a warm feeling coursing through her veins from head to toe.

As the fish swam away, she headed toward shore. Slowly wading along, she cast freely in the open space. She paused, practicing several forward casts and an equal number of backhand casts. Closing her eyes and taking a deep breath, she followed the dance of the rod with her body, delighting in the graceful motion. Tilting her head skyward, she whispered, "Thank you." Then she reeled in her line and attached the fly to her rod.

\* \* \*

"Let's head in." Jack abruptly placed the binoculars back in the console seat.

"What's got into you?"

"Nothing." Jack started the motor and cranked the wheel hard to the right. He jammed the throttle forward, and the boat spun in a semicircle before jumping up on plane, spewing a rooster tail of water behind it.

"You gonna tell me what happened between you two?" Skipper yelled over the drone of the motor.

Jack stared ahead, jaw clenched.

"You and I both know that was her. I've seen her cast." Skipper said.

"So what if it was?" Jack slung his exasperation in Skipper's direction.

Skipper shook his head. "You ain't been right since she left." He waited a few moments for some response and then reached down and pulled the kill switch. The motor died, and the boat came to an abrupt halt.

"What the fuck are you doing?" Jack banged his fist on the console.

"I could ask you the same." Skipper regarded Jack with concern. "You've never let on what brought you here in the first place. But by the way you're acting, my guess is that that woman reminds you of something you once had in your life."

Jack nodded his head ever so slightly and gazed out over the horizon as if he were searching for an answer.

"You act like a dead man." Skipper put his hand on his friend's shoulder. "Look at me."

Jack slowly raised his eyes to meet his friend's.

"You're pushing everyone out of your life. Good golly guy, even the big trout are shying from your path. You're barely catching more than schoolies."

Jack smiled. "So, it's not my fly."

"Those sows haven't even seen your fly yet." Skipper sighed, adjusted his hat, and glanced toward the shore. Then he turned and looked squarely at Jack. "You're scaring me, man."

Jack flashed a look over his shoulder at the shore and then turned to Skipper. "I'm scaring myself."

* * *

The cottage grew dim as Jack sat silently on the sofa. The expression on his face conveyed a pain so deep that even Lily knew enough to stay away. Abruptly, he rose and headed to the corner of the room. He loomed over a small domed trunk momentarily and then removed an antique Navajo blanket, whose reds and browns had faded far more than the memories they protected. Taking a deep breath, he squatted in front of the trunk and methodically unlatched two brass hooks. He raised the lid and closed his eyes, tilting his head back as if pleading for mercy. As he lowered his gaze to the contents, a tear slipped down his cheeks.

Inside was an elegantly framed photograph of a couple, dressed in wedding finery; she in a floor-length white gown trimmed in lace, he in a dark tux. The dark-haired woman embraced by Jack had a broad smile and kind eyes. Beneath the photo lay the wedding album. Sitting cross-legged on the floor, Jack began leafing through it, studying each image carefully.

Closing it with a sigh, he held it to his lips as he surveyed the remaining contents of the trunk. He set the album on the floor near the framed photo and reached inside the trunk once again. This time he removed a small wooden box. He opened it with great reverence until the contents were exposed. He held two simple gold bands before removing a yellowed newspaper clipping. His lips moved as he read it silently.

"Dr. Jenna Cooper lost her battle to cancer, leaving behind her husband Dr. Jack Cooper and her parents Dr. and Mrs. William Wilson. Dr. Cooper was a professor of anthropology at the University of Virginia at Charlottesville...."

Jack put his hands to his face and sobbed. His shoulders shook violently as he let the pain resurface without restraint. Lily wandered over to her master and lay her head on his lap. After a time, Jack's sobs quieted, and he stroked her head. He looked deeply into her eyes. "What do I do, Lily?" She pawed at his hand. He wrapped his arms around her and held her closely. "I suppose it's time we went for our evening walk."

Reverently, he placed the memorabilia in the chest. "Come on, girl." She bounced toward him, looking up expectantly as she paused at the door for his command to pass. Together, they walked into the balmy evening air. Lily bounded around the yard, nose to the ground as Jack sauntered through the patchy lawn, a mix of grass and gravel, with hands in his pockets. He paused at the waterside and raised his eyes to the sky.

He located the Pleiades. "Speak to me, Jenna. Help me." He was met with silence. He lowered his eyes and kicked at a clump of grass. Returning his gaze skyward, he waited again for a response, but there wasn't any.

He scanned his surroundings. In the east, several miles across the bay, South Padre Island lit up the night. He could hear the sounds of laughter and horns. It all seemed so meaningless, like his life. When Jenna died, he turned away from everything—his work, his writing, and his spiritual practice, and only of late found the courage to begin chronicling his thoughts to try to make sense of his life. They'd done much of it together, meditating each morning before work and going to the ashram several times a year for a retreat. He turned instead to fishing, tying flies, and watching TV. Even his forays with Ginny were nothing more than a distraction from the errant energy that was slowly driving him into madness.

He cautiously let his mind wander back to that night with Ali. It was different. Sacred, as it had been with Jenna, perhaps more so. That's what frightened him. He couldn't conjure Jenna up that evening. He didn't need to. He rubbed his forehead, hoping to erase the guilt. Turning toward the Seven Sisters once again, he whispered aloud. "I'm sorry, Jenna."

Jack meandered around the yard. *Don't be.* The familiar voice stopped him in his tracks, and he whirled around. Only Lily approached him.

Jenna had given him the message he needed, and with those words, the shackles on his heart began to loosen. His step was a little lighter as he made his way up the crushed stone path that led to the door.

# Chapter Fourteen

The morning light was warm and comforting as Ali strode down the road. Her pace was quick, and she swung her hands in time with her steps. Max stayed close at her heels, occasionally venturing off to visit a bush or two along the way. The outline of her book filtered through her mind, and before long, her pace had slowed.

Only a short trip to the far end of the Valley remained for her fact collecting tasks. Soon she'd be able to focus on finalizing the draft until the baby's arrival, with the revisions scheduled for the months before returning to Virginia. She brushed away the thought of leaving and turned her attention to the *esperanza,* with blooms brighter than the sun and the bougainvillea whose crimson blossoms were vibrantly set against the deep green blanket of leaves. The heavenly aroma of the citrus blossoms mesmerized her, and she paused, closing her eyes, and inhaled deeply. The effect was as comforting as her mantra.

As she continued her stroll, she came upon a blanket of bluebonnets along the road. Max traipsed through them, spreading an aroma of grape candy wafting in the air from the tiny bluish-purple blossoms perched on long stems. On the opposite side, an orange and red carpet of Indian blankets sprawled beneath the mesquite tree. Her senses had become heightened in the last few months and triggered memories of her when, in her teens, she had learned to listen to the whispers of the plants and animals, and even the rocks. They always held answers to her most pressing questions.

Ali's eyes wandered toward the one-story weathered structure, fifty feet from the roadside. Her gaze rested upon a cactus garden to the left of the door. A prickly pear cactus, whose main stem measured about a foot around, stood in the center and surrounded by several low-growing species of cacti, including a crown of thorns. "Morning, Gus," she called as he emerged from the house, with the screen door banging behind him.

She entered the yard and hugged the man. "So is this what you do on your day off?" She waved her hand around the yard. Max had settled himself in the shade of the carport.

"Keeps my mind off my troubles." He beckoned her to follow him to a partially enclosed greenhouse. "How you feeling this morning?"

"Restless." She touched the tiny plants in pots all lined up neatly on two potting benches. Beneath both were stacks of pots and bags of soil.

"Makes two of us. Must be in the air," Gus quipped as he pinched a dead leaf off one of the pink geraniums. "What's on your mind?"

"An urgency to finish my book before the baby arrives. And you?" From his tightly knit brow, she sensed that she might be treading in dangerous territory.

"Unrequited love." He cocked a brow, then set about putting soil in a pot. He sprinkled some seeds into the pot and then patted them lightly with his gnarled fingers.

"Why haven't you and Kate ever gotten together?" She asked, testing the waters for a deeper conversation.

"Same reason lots of people don't." He focused on the task of watering the newly planted seeds. "Ain't in the cards."

"Do you really believe that?" Ali watched the water sprinkling from the can.

"I do." He set the watering can down on the table with more force than expected, startling both of them.

"Or is it that you haven't had the courage to reach out to her?" Ali asked, with a hint of sadness in her voice.

"Maybe you should try asking yourself the same question about the father of your baby."

Ali quivered at the harshness of his voice, which had rendered her silent.

Gus shook his head. "Enough of this nonsense. I got work to do." Gus stormed away.

Retreating to the path along the road, Ali stung from his comments. She pressed too hard. She'd walked about ten steps when Gus called out.

"Wait up, Ali." He joined her under the canopy of a papaya tree and looked down at the ground, kicking a stone with his worn work boot. "I'm too afraid of hearing Kate say 'no.' Partly because all she ever talked about for years was Cy." He took his hat off and wiped his brow with a red handkerchief. "He was my friend, too. Didn't ever want to do anything to disrespect his memory. He was like a brother to me."

He hated to admit it, but Jack and Ali's predicament shattered the container where he stashed his disappointment about his relationship with Kate.

"She never talks about anyone but you."

Gus met her gaze. There was a spark of hope in his eyes. "That's nice to hear."

"So you see," she touched his arm. "It's not too late."

"Then it's not too late for you either."

"I don't think that man even thinks about me."

"I'd bet otherwise."

Ali glanced at the ground as a dozen large red ants scurried by carrying small bits of greenery on their backs. "How is he?"

"Haven't seen him. But I hear he's not doing so good." He pointed toward the ground. "Cutter ants. Nasty little things. Love my tomatoes. Eat 'em all if I let them." He studied Ali, who continued to observe the ants, and then he cleared his throat. "Bout all he does is fish. He hasn't gone to a fly club meeting in ages."

"Then how do you know he's not doing well?" She eyed him suspiciously.

"Got my sources. Just like you journalists." He put his arm around her. Max eyed them from his spot in the shade. "The way I figure it, the tide's got to turn for the likes of us some time or another. Either that or we gotta stop letting life cut away the best of us."

"So, you haven't given up hope?"

Gus shrugged. "I'm a romantic at heart." He chuckled and pointed his finger at her. "I know what's wrong with you! You ain't been out on the flats in a while."

She rubbed her belly. "It's gonna be a bit before I can hop in a boat, I'm afraid."

"Well, as soon as that baby's born, we'll get Kate to babysit, and me and you, we are going after big trout." He paused by a rosebush laden with large pink blossoms. Retrieving a knife from his pocket, he cut one full in bloom and two buds. He twirled it in his hands.

"Big trout, the magic elixir." She smiled. "C'mon, Max. Let's finish our walk."

Gus handed her the roses. "Would you give these to Kate for me?"

"Sure." She examined the delicate petals. "I'll see what I can do to plead your case."

"Much obliged." Gus waved as Ali and Max headed back to Mama Kate's.

Now all he had to do was convince Jack to come out of hiding.

✳ ✳ ✳

Staring at the computer screen, Ali could make no sense of the jumble of words before her. She rubbed her forehead and scrolled down the text. It was garbage. "Ugh!" She slammed her pencil on the desk. "I gotta get out of here."

Spying her rod in the corner near the closet, she decided that fishing might be the cure. Quickly changing into shorts and a large fishing shirt that would cover her baby bump, she headed down the stairs. "Kate, I'm out of here. Want to go for a ride?"

Kate peered up from her knitting. "Where ya going?"

"The Island." Ali walked around the kitchen, gathering snacks and drinks for her afternoon trek. "Fishing, the health food store, maybe the bookstore."

"I'll pass. Gotta fix dinner before long. Making a roast." She set her knitting needles down, the pink yarn draping across her lap. "You okay?"

"Just antsy."

"Well, be careful."

"Call me if you need anything from the store." With that, Ali headed out the door and hopped in her Audi. Despite the heat, she opened the window and relished the grain-scented afternoon air. By the time she reached Port Isabel, her agitation was but a mere memory, and she was planning her strategy for fishing the sand.

She crossed the causeway, taking in the view of the aquamarine water below. The hotels towering ahead on the Gulf side of the island triggered a moment of homesickness as she remembered similar sights in Virginia Beach. *Life is about choices, Ali Mae. You can't have everything.* Her grandmother's voice echoed in her head.

Sitting at the stoplight at the end of the causeway, Ali said aloud, "Well, Grandma, I don't want everything. But I do want what is right for me." She flashed a defiant look toward the sky, just as the light turned green, and she continued her journey northward along Padre Boulevard.

Soon, her attention was on the water, as she traveled along the packed-sand road to the bay, north of the convention center. Ali focused on the water, hoping to get a sense of where to stop and fish. She came to a halt about three miles up the island and surveyed the water. It looked like all the rest to her, but she was tired of driving. She grabbed her gear and headed to the water.

After wading westward about a hundred yards, she veered to the north and began looking for fish. For twenty minutes, she saw only mullet, and so she turned to the west again, her mind more on Jack than fishing. Every boat that went by, she inspected closely, hoping to get a glimpse of him. All stayed a fair distance away from her, preventing a positive ID.

Out of the corner of her eye, she spotted the flash of sunlight on a gamefish. She turned toward it and watched as it cruised along. She raised her rod and made one false cast. The fish caught sight of her and darted away. With a hand on her hip, she surveyed the surface of the water for more fish. Then she glanced toward the island. She had walked a long way and knew she better head back to shore. Her legs had begun to feel wobbly. Checking her watch, she noticed that she'd been in the water for more than two hours. It seemed more like minutes.

Ali trudged through the water and then across the sand. Her hands and legs were shaking with fatigue as she crawled into the SUV and opened the small cooler on the passenger seat. She took a hefty swig of water and leaned her head against the steering wheel. A wave of loneliness wrapped itself around her like a boa constrictor, and she began to cry. Everything in the moment looked bleak: her temporary stay at Mama Kate's seemed foolish; the book wasn't coming together as quickly as she hoped, and her thoughts about Jack were just plain stupid.

As she wiped the tears from her eyes, two guys in a raised red pickup truck, sporting shiny chrome wheels, stared as they passed by, making her feel even more uncomfortable. "What am I doing here?" She looked up at the sky. *Just hang in there.*

"Does it look like I've been doing anything but that—for my entire fucking life?"

Shaking her head, hoping to dam the tears that continued to trail down her cheeks, she started the engine and back-tracked along the sand-packed road to the main highway.

Glancing at her gas gauge as she crossed the causeway, she knew she had barely enough gas to make it to Mama Kate's. She pulled into the first gas station and mindlessly went through the motions of swiping her credit card and putting the nozzle into the tank. She kept her head low, hoping no one would notice her blotchy face. Staring off into space, she prayed for the strength to put Jack from her mind once and for all.

"You're nothing but a lousy, two-timing son-of-a-bitch!"

The shrill of the woman's voice rattled Ali out of her prayers. She turned in the direction of the angry woman's voice. Standing next to his truck was Jack Cooper, with Ginny standing in front of him, her face flushed and her hands moving frantically as she continued her rampage. He was pinned against the truck, trying to open the door to escape. Then Ginny raised her hand. *Smack!* The sound reverberated in the air. Jack held his cheek, stunned by the sudden assault. The screaming continued as a tall Latino, with his dark hair pulled back in a long braid, darted from the store, grabbed Ginny, and forced her inside.

Jack leaned against his truck momentarily and scanned the parking lot of the small store. Ali bent her head to keep him from noticing her, chancing a glance only after she was sure that he had entered traffic, noted by the squeal of tires as he escaped. Returning the nozzle to the pump, she glanced toward the store and then at the back of Jack's truck as he made his way down the road. A fleeting thought of following him passed through her mind.

*He'll be back.* The voice returned.

"That's hard to believe." She said as she climbed back into her SUV. "And why would I want that chaos in my life!"

# Chapter Fifteen

Ali and Kate sat on the porch overlooking the Arroyo. Both had their feet propped up on footstools, and Max lay between them, his dark body still except for the rise and fall of his ribcage with each breath. Ali rubbed circles around her belly, and Kate held her rosary as she gazed at the water.

"You'll be back on Friday?"

"Uh, uh. My doctor's appointment is at 3:00, so I'll drive straight there from the Upper Valley."

Kate shook her head. "I don't like you traipsing around the countryside by yourself."

Ali leaned forward, placed her feet on the ground, and peered at Kate. "Listen, my deadline for the book is looming. And the baby is due in three weeks. I have to make this trip now. When it's over, my research will be complete, and I'll be able to finish my first draft."

"I should go with you."

"No, you shouldn't. You need to stay here and take care of business and yourself."

Kate sighed. "Who appointed you my keeper?"

"That's part of my renter's clause. I get my room, board, and a say about major decisions in your life—like staying alive." She reached over the mosaic table and touched Kate's arm. "My baby needs a grandma in her life."

Kate pinched her lips together, and her eyes moistened. "I hear yah," she said, barely above a whisper.

Ali sat back in her chair and returned her feet to the stool. "I'll call you morning, noon, and night."

"I guess I'll have to settle for that." She sipped her iced tea. "You know you can be so stubborn."

"The same can be said about you." Ali glared at her. "You need to stay here. It's settled. No more discussion."

"I just don't see..." Kate's voice trailed off upon noticing Ali's expression.

Ali's eyes were closed, and her fingertips were making the shape of a steeple. "Kate, I'd love to have you along, but I have a sense that you just need to be here."

Kate raised a brow. "Seems like there is something other than a baby growing inside of you. Being closer to nature is having a good effect. It's nice to hear you listening to your wisdom."

✳ ✳ ✳

Gus entered the living room and looked about. "Sure is quiet without Ali around."

Kate glanced up from her knitting, which was slowly turning into a pink baby sweater. "She'll be back tomorrow."

"Has she called?" Max blocked his entry into the living room by rolling over on his back and begging for his belly to be scratched. Gus willingly complied. Then, straightening his body with some effort, he stepped over the dog and approached Kate.

Kate cocked her right brow. "Worried?"

"Dang it, you know I am, just like you."

"She's in Rio Grande City."

"Hot as the dickens there." He scratched his head. "Saw it on the Weather Channel."

"Hotter than that from what she says."

"Is she okay?"

"She's fine." Kate set the knitting down in her lap and glared at Gus. " They do have air conditioning up there, too, you know."

Gus took a couple of steps toward the door and then did an about-face. "Want some tea?"

Kate returned to her knitting. "Sure. But then you need to sit down. Your fidgeting is driving me crazy."

Gus wandered to the kitchen and opened the refrigerator, taking out a glass container filled with tea, infused with fresh mint. He poured the amber liquid into two glasses. Standing by the sink, he peered out the window, and his mouth dropped. "We've got company." He set the glasses on the counter. "And you ain't gonna believe who it is."

Kate gazed out the window. "I'll be. I didn't even feel him coming. Ali said she sensed I needed to be here, and maybe this is why."

"Easy, Kate," Gus warned as he put the tea next to her chair. "Don't want to scare him away."

Dockside, Jack secured the boat to the cleat and then jumped on the dock. He paused, readjusted his cap, and then strode up the path toward the house. Lily ran ahead, eagerness in her stride.

Kate stepped out onto the porch, watching him approach.

Jack came to a halt a few feet from the porch. "Hi, Kate."

"Howdy, Jack."

Max darted by Kate to join his friend, and the two dogs sprinted across the yard, rounding the garden and then circling Jack. He watched them go by and then turned back to Kate.

"I heard that you've been sick." He stuck his hands in the pockets of his shorts and kicked at a stone near his feet. "I'm sorry I haven't come over sooner."

"Damn near died. In fact, I did." She smiled devilishly. "Suppose I haven't finished my work. You know how I love sticking my nose into other people's business. Seems to be my calling."

Jack took a deep breath.

"Want some tea?" She motioned to the door. "Gus is inside, just poured some."

"That would be nice." Jack joined her on the porch and removed his sunglasses.

Kate gazed at him tenderly and patted him on his arm. "C'mon. Been too long."

Jack followed Kate into the house and sheepishly raised his eyes toward the second-floor balcony.

"You take that fake sugar if I remember correctly." Gus handed him a glass of tea and then followed Jack's gaze.

"Yes, sir."

"Don't give me that sir stuff." Gus hugged Jack. "I done lost my best fishing buddy when you disappeared."

"And I lost my best teacher."

"Still haven't caught a big trout, huh?"

Jack shook his head. "I'm trying." He sipped his tea. "I think I'm ready."

Kate peered at Gus, signaling her curiosity with a raised eyebrow. "So what makes you think so?" She asked.

Jack swirled the glass between both hands.

"You might say that I've spent many long nights contemplating Gus' words of wisdom." He cracked a smile. "And maybe some of yours."

Gus flashed Kate a look of caution. Kate shrugged in response.

Jack knitted his brow and slowly scanned the room, letting his eyes wander up the high walls of the vaulted ceiling in the living room once again toward the second floor. His eyes stopped for a long moment on the walkway between the bedrooms. "Is she here?"

"Depends on who you're talking about."

"Kate, please. Don't make this difficult." His voice quivered.

"Seems to me you're the one that's made it difficult, Jack Cooper." She glared at him. "Running out of here like you did."

Jack studied the ice floating in the tea, nodding his silent agreement. "I agree."

She took a deep breath. "Ali is not here." Kate watched as disappointment washed across Jack's face. "Did you expect to find her here?"

Jack stared out the window. "I thought I saw her fishing the sand."

Kate put her elbows on her knees, folding her hands together. "So why do you come round here looking for Ali now?"

"I can't get her out of my mind."

The look on his face made her heart quiver, but she wasn't about to be soft. "You should have thought about that before you hightailed it out of here the morning after you spent the night with her." She shook her head. "Did you expect her to be okay with that kind of behavior?"

"Now, Kate." Gus attempted to soften the harshness of her remarks.

"It's like you touched a hot stove and pulled your hand back so's not to get burned," she continued.

Jack hung his head. "I have been."

"Oh, shoot. We all have at one time or another," Kate spat. "You gonna explain, or will this continue to be a mystery like your disappearance eight months ago." She lifted her glass. "Gus, I think we need refills all around. This may take us some time."

Jack raised his head. "Do you know why I suddenly appeared three years ago?" His face was flushed, and he challenged Kate to rise up against him.

"Haven't a clue." She settled back in her chair, indicating that she was waiting for him to continue. Gus sat off to the side, uneasily watching the exchange between the two.

"I haven't always been a fishing guide." He looked at Gus and at Kate. "My life was very different in Virginia."

"So that's where you come from." Kate peered at him, her green eyes looking like a cat stalking a bird. "Explains a lot."

Gus cleared his throat. "Kate, now hush. Let the man speak." He nodded toward Jack. "Go on, Jack. I'd like to hear your story."

Jack took a big audible breath. "For years, my wife and I tried to have children, and we never could. Finally, she was diagnosed with ovarian cancer." Jack stared at his clenched hands. "She died within six months of the diagnosis." His voice trailed off to a whisper. "My life ended on that day."

He chanced a look at Gus and Kate with tears in his eyes. "I quit my job at the university. I was chair of the archeology department. Jenna was chair of the anthropology department." His voice became reverent at the mention of her name. "We were a team in everything we did." He stood up and stared out the door. "I was born just fifty miles from here. My dad had a cabin five houses down the road from you. We fished every weekend when I was a kid. And I've spent time here every summer since leaving for college."

His eyes followed the current of the Arroyo as it flowed by the dock. "I came back because I didn't know where else to go. And I just couldn't stay there."

Kate pondered Jack's words, and her body relaxed. His loss reminded her of her own. She sighed. His confession made things difficult. It would have been easier if he'd been just plain bullheaded and commitment-shy. Then she could have lied about Ali's whereabouts without compromising her integrity. "Why don't you call her?"

Jack took a sip of his tea as he observed Gus and Kate. Gus squirmed under the scrutiny. "I had to try here first." He placed the glass back on the coffee table. "Thanks for the tea." He headed toward the door, pausing with his hand on the door handle. "Gus, let's go fishing soon."

"How about Tuesday?"

Jack smiled. "I'll be here at dawn."

"I'll come your way. Save you some boat time," Gus offered.

"Sounds good." Jack looked toward Kate. "Glad to have you back in the land of the living."

"Seems we could be saying the same about you." She smiled at him, the fondness she felt toward him growing once again.

# Chapter Sixteen

Gus drove the familiar path to Jack's house in the early morning hours. The horizon barely hinting at the light of the coming day as he traveled the long straight highway out of Arroyo City. *"Now, don't you let on that Ali's here."* Kate's voice echoed in his head. He couldn't see why not, except that he'd have to face the wrath of Kate if he did. She told him to be patient, but the way that he looked at it, patience didn't promise anything more than loneliness. He'd seen it in Jack's eyes and in Ali's. It mirrored his own. He sighed and raised his gaze to the sky. One star shone brightly overhead. "I could use a hint or two on how to figure things out. I hate to see those two kids go the way Kate and I have."

He turned into the dirt driveway that led to Jack's cottage, hoping he'd have an answer and soon.

Lily barked excitedly as Gus pulled his old red pickup to a halt. Jack emerged from the screen door and waved. "Morning, Gus."

"Morning." Gus reached for his rod in the bed of the pickup. "Ready for big trout?"

"As I ever will be." Jack reached for Gus's gear bag. "Boat's ready to go."

Gus beamed, "Well, let's get at 'em."

\* \* \*

As they boated up the channel, both men were content to be with their own thoughts. They turned into a cove after being underway for about twenty minutes, and Jack killed the motor. They surveyed the water for the telltale black triangle tail of a trout or a wake of a cruising fish. The morning was calm, and the surface of the water glassy as a mirror.

"Does she ever call Kate?"

Gus eyed him. "Why are you so interested?"

Jack sighed. "I think about her day and night." He took a swig of coffee from his mug. "Can't seem to get her out of my mind, and God knows I've tried."

"Are you sure you're ready?"

The corners of Jack's mouth turned upward, making him look years younger than he had in quite a while. "As I ever will be."

Gus stood up. "Well, let's see about that." He took his rod from the holder behind the seat. "Big trout await us." He pointed his rod. "That one's yours."

Jack followed the path of the rod and studied the water. Then he slipped off the boat. Gus stayed aboard and watched as Jack approached the fish. Once clear of the skiff, Jack let his line glide through the air, and on the third arc, let the fly fall. The fish boiled beneath it and then made the strike. "I'm on," Jack yelled as the fish jumped out of the water. The yellow membrane of its mouth flashed as it attempted to throw the fly.

"Yeehaw," Gus yelled. "Get her. Don't let her go." His heart beat wildly as he watched Jack skillfully play the fish, letting her run when she wanted and reeling her in only when she stopped to rest. Ten minutes passed, and then Jack had the fish at his knees. "Hey Gus, get the camera."

Gus beamed. "Sure will." He slid into the water, carrying Jack's digital.

Jack held the fish out of the water. "What do you think?"

"Looks like a six-pounder to me." Gus took a couple of pictures and then reverently touched the fish's head. "You done good."

Jack lowered the fish into the water, and Gus snapped a release shot. Together, they watched as she swam off. "Looks like you got the sign that you're ready." Gus gripped Jack's upper arm. "I'll see what I can find out about Ali."

Jack nodded. "Thanks, Gus."

✳ ✳ ✳

Ali took one last bite of her watermelon and then put the rind in the compost. "Kate, we'd better take our walk before it gets too hot."

"Give me a minute to fetch my hat," Kate called from the dining room table, where she had been flipping through an issue of *American Baby* magazine.

As she rinsed her plate, Ali gazed out of the window at the Arroyo. Several boats were streaming by, with passengers donned in orange life preservers, looking eagerly ahead of them. She let her hand rest on her protruding belly. The baby kicked her side, an activity that was now causing her more discomfort than excitement.

"You okay?" Kate entered the kitchen, donning her hat and sunglasses.

"I feel huge," Ali groaned.

"You are," Kate giggled. "And beautiful."

"Love your honesty." Ali smiled at Kate. "One week and counting."

"Scared?"

Ali shook her head as she opened the door. "More eager than anything."

They sauntered across the front grass and passed the cactus patch that had doubled in size since Ali's first visit. Reaching the end of the driveway, they took a left and headed toward the park. Their footsteps had worn a figurative path in the pavement over the last few months. However, the pace was slower than it once had been, more like it had been at the beginning of the year when Kate needed time to regain her strength. Kate now had to slow her steps to keep from getting ahead of Ali, a good indication that her healing had been successful. They walked along in silence for about a half a mile.

"Mama Kate, what ya doing out here?" A truck slowed down beside them, behind it a trailer carrying a blue skiff. Ali's heart skipped a beat. She looked around. There was nowhere to hide. The truck came to a halt next to the sidewalk, and Skipper leaned out of the window. "Miss Ali, is that you?"

"Hi, Skipper." Ali met his gaze directly, while inwardly wishing she could be invisible.

Kate touched her hand lightly and stepped forward. "Aren't you supposed to be out on the water?"

"I will be in about twenty minutes, give or take the time I talk to you beautiful ladies. Headin' for the Bay House for the weekend." He let his eyes fall on Ali's stomach. "Seems congratulations are in order." He chewed on his toothpick and waited for Ali's response.

She eked out a barely audible, "Thank you."

"Who is the lucky man?"

"Ali's a modern lady," Kate chimed in. "She don't need no man to be a mother."

Skipper paused, peering first at Kate and then moving his gaze to Ali. He cleared his throat while checking his rearview mirror. "I'd best be getting along." He turned to Kate and Ali. "You two be careful now."

As Skipper drove away, Ali whirled around and headed back to the house.

"Where are you going?"

"Into seclusion." She set her jaw. "Before anyone else sees me and tells Jack I'm here."

"Is that what you really want? You came here because you hoped Jack would come to his senses."

Ali halted in her tracks, looking like a trapped animal.

"Who you think you're lying to?" Kate stepped in front of Ali and peered at her . "It ain't me."

"I guess this is a part of me that still believes in Cinderella, despite what my past has taught me." Ali took a deep breath. "But, his life's a mess, and I just don't want him making mine any more difficult than it already is."

"What do you mean?"

"I saw him with his waitress friend having a very public lover's spat."

Kate shook her head. "That don't mean nothing. I told you she was a polecat, and nothing more than a convenience." Kate paused. "What do you call them nowadays? Friends with benefits?"

"I'd be better off sticking to those kinds of relationships." Ali began walking back home.

Ali's back faded from sight as Kate stood in the middle of the sidewalk, pondering the situation. Lost in her thoughts, she didn't hear Gus's approach.

"Why you standing out here?"

Kate whirled around, her face etched with worry. "I'm not sure her heart's open to him anymore."

Gus took his hat off and ran his hands through his thick white hair. "Darn, Kate, we got to do something." He sounded alarmed.

Kate eyed him. "Something you're not telling me?"

"He caught his big trout," Gus offered.

"Interesting."

"He's ready."

"May have to wait until after the baby for sure now." Kate motioned to him. "Finish my walk with me."

"She okay?"

"Mighty fidgety."

"What do you make of that?"

Kate shook her head. "Could be time for that baby to arrive."

\* \* \*

The sounds of dishes clattering in the kitchen startled Kate out of a deep sleep, and she bolted up in her bed, worrying that she had overslept. Dressing quickly, she stepped out into the living room. "Ali, is that you?"

"Yep. I started breakfast." Ali stood behind the counter, her large belly covered by Kate's flowered apron.

"You're up awfully early." Kate glanced at the table that had been set.

"Couldn't sleep." Ali opened the oven and touched the center of the loaf of bread. "I made some banana bread and a frittata. Lunches are made. Everything's lined up on the dock for the guides."

Two men sauntered in from the guesthouse. "Morning, gentlemen." Ali whirled around and whisked to the table, carrying a pitcher of orange juice.

"Damn early to be so cheery," The taller of the two quipped. He scratched his two-day-old beard and yawned.

"It's a bit unusual to see her at this time of day," Kate replied as she poured four mugs of coffee as two other fishermen entered the room behind their friends, each sporting five-o'clock shadows.

Ali took the frittata out of the oven and bent back to reach for the banana bread. A gush of water flowed down her legs. "Uh, oh."

Kate flashed her a wide-eyed look.

"Could you hand me a jar of pickles?"

"Cravings, huh." The taller man, the only one seemingly awake enough to banter, called out from the dining room table.

"Not exactly." Ali straightened her back and then peered at the puddle on the floor, before excusing herself from the room.

Kate dished up the bread and the frittata, along with a skillet of sausages, placing the food on the brightly colored platter. Setting it on the table, she said, "Help yourself to more coffee." She nodded toward the pot in the kitchen. "Seems we have a baby about to enter the world," she added as she strode across the room and called Gus.

Gus opened the door for Ali, and she slowly swung her legs out of the car. Kate reached down to help, but Ali held up her hand. "Here comes another one." She stared at a crack in the sidewalk and breathed with the contraction. They were getting stronger and more frequent. When it was over, Gus and Kate helped her to her feet. Kate then reached in the back seat for her suitcase and turned to Gus. "Remember, there's a lasagna in the refrigerator and some rolls. Just make a fresh salad and serve watermelon for dessert."

"I can handle that." The worry, however, was etched in his face. "Think you'll be back by breakfast?"

"She'd better be," Ali chimed. "I'm not sure I can take much more of this."

✳ ✳ ✳

Ali was whisked into the birthing room immediately after her arrival. Wearing the light blue hospital gown, she leaned back on the pillow and stared at the wallpaper covered with prickly pear in full bloom, with blossoms in shades of yellow, salmon, and crimson intermittently mixed with purple sage. Kate sat by her side, holding a stopwatch. "Seems about time for another one," she cautioned. Ali closed her eyes and began taking long deep breaths. Soon, she changed to short rapid ones. Kate wiped her brow. "You're doing good, real good."

A Latina in her fifties, dressed in a white coat and green scrubs, stepped into the room. "How we doing?"

She picked up the chart and checked her watch. "Time for another exam, Ali."

Ali whimpered, "Not again."

"We need to see how far along you are," The doctor said warmly. "On the next contraction, I'll check your dilation." She washed her hands in the nearby sink, before putting on a pair of examination gloves.

It came sooner than she expected, and Ali tensed.

"Take a breath, Ali," Kate coached. "Don't let it get the best of you. We're almost through."

The doctor parted Ali's legs and inserted her gloved hand.

"Get your hands off of me," she spat. Her expression gave Kate a fright.

"That's a good sign." The woman smiled and patted Ali's knee. "Your baby should be here soon." She signaled for the nurses. "Time to get ready for delivery."

"Kate, I can't do this," Ali cried.

"Yes, you can." Kate's words floated on the air offering Ali assurance that her birth journey was about to end.

"Oh, shit. Another one." Ali's damp hair matted against her head as she rolled it from side to side.

"Breathe, Ali," Kate commanded. "Look into my eyes and breathe."

Ali did as she was told, peering into Kate's eyes, holding the gaze until the pressure to push could no longer be ignored. "Ahhh!" She groaned aloud.

The doctor was now accompanied by a young, wide-eyed nurse. "Go ahead and push when you feel the urge."

"UGH!" Ali's face turned bright red as she exerted pressure. Kate held her hand, offering words of encouragement during the next few contractions.

"I see the crown." The doctor glanced at Kate and nodded reassuringly. Two more pushes and the baby's head appeared. "Almost there, Ali."

Kate peered around Ali's legs and glanced at the baby. Her dark hair was plastered to her head. "She's beautiful, Ali. Your little girl is beautiful." Kate teared up as she looked at Ali and brushed her hair from her face. "You're doing fine. You'll be a mama soon."

Ali squeezed Kate's hand, indicating it was time to push again. The baby's shoulder appeared.

"One more, mama, and you'll be just about through with this workout." The doctor's voice was calm amidst the flurry of activity around her.

Ali let out a bellow and then collapsed on the pillow. "It is, indeed, a girl." The doctor placed the baby on Ali's belly, and the nurse cleared her mouth. Ali beamed at the sight of her daughter.

She and Kate laid their hands on the infant's body. The women silently blessed the new life brought into the world. When the umbilical cord stopped pulsing, the doctor gestured for Kate to cut it.

"Remember, we want to keep the placenta," Kate eyed the midwife with authority. "We've got an orchid tree waiting to be planted with the baby's placenta as soon as we get home."

"I won't forget." The doctor affirmed that the nurse understood. "One more push, and we should be about done."

The baby was now at Ali's breast. There was a sense of peace in the air, as mother and baby bonded. Kate beamed. "Welcome to the world, Grace Azalea Stephenson."

Ali beamed. "She's beautiful."

"Just like her mama."

"She's got Jack's nose," Ali whispered.

"Cheeks, too."

"Maybe someday she'll meet her daddy," Ali said, without even a hint of sadness.

There was much to be grateful for. This wasn't the time for regrets. She caressed her daughter's cheek. Grace was no longer a vision, but here in her arms. "Grandma Kate, you better call Grandpa Gus."

# Chapter Seventeen

The sun was shining from high in the sky as Gus approached Ali. She wore a large straw hat and a long-sleeved light shirt as she tended the garden. He stopped for a moment on the path and looked about the yard. It all seemed so different, so full of life. Ali's presence had changed the place, and now little Grace had brought an extra spark to their lives. He heard giggles from the porch and turned to see Kate rocking the baby. The two of them lost in their own world, oblivious to either Gus or Ali.

"Hey, Gus, look at these tomatoes!" Ali held out the basket for him to get a closer look. "I feel like gazpacho for dinner."

"Gaz what!"

"Kinda like cold tomato soup."

"Couldn't you just say that?"

"What fun would that be? Besides, I just taught you something new to share at coffee with the guys."

Gus rolled his eyes. "Oh yeah, like they'd care." He adjusted his ball cap, pulling the brim down to shield his eyes. "Speaking of learning something new." He pointed toward the boat. "It's time you took her out on your own."

Ali shook her head. "Gus, I can't do that. I don't know the bay well enough."

"Nonsense. It's the only way to learn."

"What if I get turned around or stuck on a sandbar?"

"Someone will help you. That's what the radio is for."

Ali stared at the boat, biting her lip. "What's the weather like tomorrow?"

"Virtually no wind first off. Should be tails."

"Less than ten, huh?"

"Blowing at fifteen knots by noon or so." Gus took the basket from her. "Just go south of Bird Island until you see wakes. Shut down and wait it out. The redfish should start feeding in no time. You *know*. We've seen it together."

A sparkle glistened in Ali's eye. "Okay. You talked me into it."

"Now you're talking," he grinned. "Kate and I will watch the baby."

"I had no doubt." She slipped her hand through the crook of his arm as they sauntered toward the porch.

Gus was beginning to believe his plan might just work. He knew that if Ali could become more comfortable with the Mother Lagoon, it would be harder for her to leave.

✳ ✳ ✳

Ali rose before dawn and spent a few moments in meditation. Her routine had become so simple and unpressured. She thought briefly of her life back in Virginia. It seemed like a different lifetime and utterly unnatural. She had no idea how she could go back to her former routine of getting up early and going to the office for eight to ten hours a day. She looked over at the crib where Grace slept, and panic raced through her mind.

Rationally, she had no idea how she'd make a living without going back. Thus far, Ali could see no alternative other than returning to the magazine at the end of the year. She turned inward and began praying for direction. Thoughts of her past and her future drifted away, leaving her with the familiar cloak of peace. Then as if on cue, Grace whimpered, bringing Ali out of her reverie.

Ali rose and picked up Grace. "Good morning, my sweets."

The baby put her fist in her mouth, making loud sucking sounds. Holding her daughter close, Ali felt Grace's essence. Their souls merged, dancing with each other in joy. Awe filled Ali's mind and body. Blessings were all around her, and she savored them. "Let's go see if Mama Kate is up."

Ali strode down the stairs, hearing sounds of rustling in the kitchen. The aroma of apple filled the air.

"Morning, girls."

"Morning," Ali hugged Kate, and in turn, Kate kissed Grace on her forehead.

"I've made our stewed apple, and I'm about to make a shake. Your tea is over on the end table."

Ali sat in the rocker, cradling Grace in her arms. She crossed her legs and propped her elbow on the arm of the chair, before freeing her breast for her daughter. Peering out the window, she said, "Looks like a pretty morning." She settled back into the chair and relished the comfort, not only of nursing her daughter but also of having her breakfast awaiting her.

"Still as can be. Every angler's dream." Kate carried two bowls of apple over to the living room and sat down with Ali. Grace happily suckled her mother's breast while the two women sipped tea. "Gus will be by in about twenty minutes to help you with the boat."

"Feels a little like I'm on a time clock today."

Ignoring Ali's comment, she said, "It will be good for you to know how to run that boat." Kate took a bite of her apple and mashed the rest around in her bowl while she chewed. "Besides, the tournament is just two weeks away, and you need to be in it—no matter what."

"I've already made my commitment to it, Kate."

"I know, but what if Gus breaks his darn leg or something? I can't run the boat for you. I need to be home with the baby."

Kate's comment sent an arrow through Ali's heart. Grace had become such a big part of Kate's life. Ali brushed her daughter's cheek with the back of her index finger, wondering what Grace would miss if they left their idyllic life in their South Texas paradise. She lifted her daughter to her shoulder and began patting her tiny back. A little burp escaped her rosy lips.

"I think she's done. You want to take her while I get ready?"

Kate sat back on the sofa and reached for the baby. "You need to ask?"

"I guess not." Ali stood over the two for a moment. "Thank you."

"Nothing to thank me for. It's you who deserves the thanks." Kate touched the little girl's nose. "I came back for her."

Ali choked at the surge of emotions inside of her. "Gus is gonna be hollering at me to hurry up if I'm not on the dock soon." She rushed from the room, fighting the image of leaving with Grace sometime in the coming months. It wasn't going to be easy.

\* \* \*

Ali sat at the helm of the boat, her fly rod standing upright behind her seat, poised and ready for use. "Go over the roll thing again, Gus," she said.

"Motor tilted in and raised all the way up. Turn the wheel all the way to the left and hit it hard on the throttle. Don't be timid."

"Okay, kind of like entering I-95 on rush hour."

"I guess. Never been on I-95," Gus said.

"You're not missing a thing." Ali tightened her hat so it wouldn't blow off. "I'm ready."

She lowered the motor, tilted it in. She turned the key, and the motor began humming like a sewing machine.

"Back her out slow and keep the wheel straight."

The boat came off the ramp and floated freely in the Arroyo, now pointing toward the east, with the horizon just beginning to glow in yellows and oranges.

"Go gettum, girl."

"Aye, Aye, Captain Gus," she saluted him as she pushed down on the throttle, and the force of the motor brought the boat on plane. She raised the jack plate into cruising position and settled into the early morning ride eastward on the Arroyo. The sun peeked above the horizon, and the seagulls glided toward town, their version of a morning commute. She inhaled deeply and surveyed the shoreline. The neighborhood was awakening, and lights illuminated many of the kitchens. A few televisions flashed their images as she cruised by as well.

Passing the park boat launch and noticing several boats lined up to enter the water, eagerness to be at her destination coursed through her veins, and she exerted more pressure on the throttle. She entered the mouth of the Arroyo and checked for boat traffic. It was a weekday, so few boats were out, except a couple anchored along the channel. She headed south for about a half a mile and then cut to the east, raising the motor as she entered the shallow flats. Mullet scurried in all directions in response to her intrusion.

Soon the depth of the water decreased, and Ali angled in a more southeasterly direction, carefully scanning the water for signs of waking fish and obstacles to avoid. Wakes shot away from the boat like a starburst. It was her cue to stop. She circled around and then pulled back on the throttle, bringing the skiff to a halt. After securing the boat in place, she scanned the horizon, and a flickering tail signaled that it was time to enter the water.

The drone of a motor approached, momentarily sending the tailing fish into hiding. She knew as soon as the boat passed, the fish would resume feeding. The skiff stopped about a quarter of a mile south of her. Two men disembarked quickly, one wielding a fly rod, the other a bait-casting rod. Their voices rose over the quiet of the morning. "Hey Charlie, how about a bet?"

"Sure."

"Twenty bucks says I'll catch twice as many fish with my mullet than you will with that fancy piece of yarn tied to that buggy whip of yours."

"You're on, Bud."

Ali chuckled in response to their conversation before turning her attention back to the horizon. A tail popped up fifty yards to her right. She stepped forward, cautiously testing the firmness of the bottom. Each step sent concentric ripples toward the fish. She knew that this alone would alert the fish to her presence, and so she slowed her pace and became extremely conscious about moving her feet. There was little wind to create a natural ripple on the water, so her steps were broadcast for many yards. Later, as the wind came up, her presence would be more easily camouflaged by the waves on the surface of the water. But for now, the stealth of an experienced huntress was required.

The fish continued his approach, and when he was within a hundred feet, Ali stripped out the line and halted her advance. She waited as the fish came within casting distance, and then she began her cast. Two false casts later, she presented a well-placed orange topwater fly near the fish's head. She saw him come out of the water and suck up the fly. "All right." Her reel whirled feverishly as the fish made his retreat. Then as he slowed, she began reeling him in, expecting him to attempt another escape once he spotted her. He did so twice, each time retreating to a lesser distance. Then she brought him to her knees. Reaching into the water, she tucked the fish into the crook of her arm and released the fly from his lip.

"Thanks for the dance." She kissed the top of the fish's head and placed him back into the water.

After checking her fly and the tippet, Ali surveyed the horizon. A few more tails were coming toward her but still out of reach. Then a flutter caught her eye, and she slowly turned to her right. Every nerve in her body was on high alert. She knew it was Grandmother Trout. She focused on a place in the water where nothing more than a black tip of the trout's tail broke the surface. She took a deep breath and calculated her cast. The fish remained motionless, except for her eye, which was watching Ali's every move. She showed no fear. Instead, she appeared to be waiting for Ali to engage with her.

Ali raised her rod, and after one false cast, sent the fly within inches of the trout's mouth. The trout attacked the topwater fly with wild abandon, and once again, Ali's reel screamed as the fish retreated. She knew the fight would be different than with a redfish. Ali had to take it slow and put gentle pressure on the fish as she reeled it in.

The fish slowly came to her feet, with Ali marveling at her luck. A face-to-face meeting with Grandmother Trout was about to be hers. However, the fish had other ideas. It made one attempt to be free by darting between Ali's legs. Ali reached down and grabbed the tippet. With a nearly audible pop, the fish spewed the fly from its mouth and swam off.

Her presentation was perfect, her play gentle and firm. Her landing needed improvement. *Slow it down, Ali. There's no rush.*

"Daggum bird." The gruff voice pulled Ali out of her reflections. About a hundred yards from her, the man, sporting a blue trucker hat with a cigar hanging out of his mouth, was fending off a Forster's tern. Thirty feet above the man's head, the tern hovered like a kite, obviously tangled in the man's line. Ali reeled in her line and secured the fly to the guide as she waded quickly toward the man.

"Hold on. I'll give you a hand." She picked up her pace while carefully shuffling to ward off any stingray that might lay in her path.

The tern descended closer to the man as she approached. With a swoop of his age-spotted hand, the man grabbed the black and white tern and put him under the water. Ali watched with concern as the man stomped his feet, then reached beneath the surface, and brought up the bird.

"Good fishin'?" The man asked as Ali came near.

"Great!"

The man eyed the rod which Ali had stuck behind her, securing it in her wading belt. "Fly rod, huh. My buddy's a buggy whipper as well. Thinks he can out-fish me. We got a bet."

"I heard."

"Here, hold this." He thrust the rod toward Ali. "Well, I didn't come here to catch no damn bird, that's for sure."

Ali watched as the man took the large hook from the bird's bill. She could feel the bird's fear and see its plea for assistance in his eye.

"This bird's in tough shape." He chuckled.

Ali was perplexed at the comment. The hook came out easily, and Ali was eager to reach over and free the bird from the fishing line. She was about to offer her help but was abruptly halted by the sound of bones cracking as the man wrung the bird's neck. Her mind whirled to comprehend the events that had just unfolded before her eyes. The man tossed the bird's lifeless body into the water. She watched in horror as it began to float downwind. "Take this too since you wanted it so damn bad." He threw the piece of mullet at the bird and glanced at Ali.

"What the hell did you do that for!" Disgust boiled in her belly. She scooped the bird up out of the water. "You had no right to kill this bird."

"I got every right in the world. It's nothin' more than a bird." He waved his cigar at her.

"Not only is it immoral, but it's illegal as well."

"I can tell by your accent that you're some tree-hugging, do goodin' northerner." He bit off the end of the cigar and then spat in the water.

"It's about time you learned to mind your own business. This here's a different country."

Ali glared at him. "It's about time you learned the difference between right and wrong." She wheeled around, carrying the body of the lifeless bird in her arms. "Asshole."

Storming back to the boat, a wave of grief seized her. She looked down at the bird, staring at her with a lifeless eye. She had done nothing to stop the senseless murder of the creature, and it had been within arm's reach of her. Reviewing the scene in her mind, there seemed little that she could have done. It had happened all so quickly. Her reactions had been dulled due to her disbelief that a human being could be capable of such a heartless act, the same disbelief that kept her from accepting the loss of her mother by the hand of her father. Yet, if she honestly looked within, she knew hesitation had been her enemy and her mother's as well. Ali just didn't listen to the whisper of her own wisdom. And now the tern was dead. *When are you every going to trust yourself?*

She reached the boat and reverently placed the bird in the ice chest, sorting through the memories of all the mistakes. There were so many yellow flags ignored, that had created turmoil in her life and fueled the feelings of unworthiness burning deep within her. And now they bubbled to the surface.

After freeing the boat from its anchored position, she prepared to start the motor, tilting it high so the propellor wouldn't graze the bottom of the estuary. There was no more fishing for her that day. She put her hand on the wheel and glanced in the direction of the fisherman. Propriety called for her to get up quickly and exit the area without disturbing the fishing of other anglers. Niceties, however, were the farthest thing from her mind.

She quickly hit the throttle and turned the wheel to the left. The boat jumped on plane but instead of pulling out and heading west, Ali veered southward until she could see the man's face, his eyes wide with fear. Fighting the urge to run him over, she pulled hard to the right, accelerating the throttle hard, sending a two-foot wake from the stern of her boat, and splashing the man with the spray of the motor. She glanced back and waved. His fishing would be over for a while.

✳ ✳ ✳

Pulling into the dock, there wasn't the slightest hint of remorse for disturbing the man's angling area nor soaking him as well. In Ali's mind, it was the least she could do to avenge the bird's life, and yet it did little to soothe her anger. She eased the boat onto the ramp and glanced toward the house. Kate was coming out of the door with Grace in her arms, followed by Gus.

"So how'd you do?" Gus walked on ahead to help Ali winch the boat.

"Fine."

With concern registered on his face, Gus asked, "What happened? Hit something?"

"No, but I would have liked to." Ali dropped to the ground and took off her booties. "Some asshole wrung a bird's neck right in front of my eyes."

"Ali, I ain't never heard you cuss!" Alarm rang through Gus's voice, sending the pitch of his words an octave higher.

She ignored the comment as she bolted back to the boat. Opening the ice chest, she lifted the bird's body and carried it to the lawn. "Kate, can I bury this poor thing someplace?" She glanced around the yard. "How about under the mesquite?"

Kate stood next to her, and Grace was reaching out for her mother. Ali leaned over and kissed her daughter's head. "In a minute, honey."

Ali shook her head, tears welling up in her eyes. "I couldn't do anything about it. He did it right in front of me. I ran over to help him free the bird, not murder it." Inwardly, she was still trying to convince herself that there was nothing she could have done, and it wasn't working. *I knew. Just like I've always known. And I held back. I hesitated, and now it cost a life.*

Shaking her head, Ali stormed off toward the garden shed. She flung open the door and grabbed a shovel from the stack of tools. The image of the bird looking at her right before the man wrung its neck ran through her mind. Anger boiled in her veins, and she slammed the door so hard the shed shook. Standing beneath the mesquite tree, she took a deep breath to calm herself. When she felt less agitated, she silently said a prayer, requesting peace for the bird's spirit and assistance in choosing the best spot for the bird to be laid to rest. Immediately, Ali's eyes were drawn downward and to the right. A fist-sized rock marked the site. She put the bird to the side as she dug the hole, and when it was about the size of a watermelon, Ali reverently placed the bird in its grave and then covered it. She squatted low to the ground and stared at the crude resting place for the tern.

As a final gesture of respect, she placed the rock on top and said another prayer. Finally, she could no longer hold back the flurry of tears that tugged at her heart. She folded her arms and buried her head inside the crook of her elbows and cried, long and hard. It was more than the bird. The bird's death was just a catalyst. She cried for the mother she missed, and for the father she never knew, nor understood. And she cried for Grace, because she too would be missing someone important in her life as well. Her wails, echoing in the midmorning air, silenced the green jays and the kiskadees as they watched with curiosity on the branches above her. This was one of those occasions where the unfairness of life had caught up with Ali, despite her best efforts to see the good around her. Sometimes, it just didn't measure up.

Kate slowly approached Ali and rested a hand on her shoulder. "Something tells me this is about more than the bird." She sat cross-legged next to Ali and waited for the younger woman to acknowledge her presence.

Ali looked up, and Kate handed her a tissue. "You're right."

"He has a right to know."

Ali shook her head. "What am I supposed to do? Knock on his door, and say 'Hi Jack, this is your daughter. We're living at Kate's in case you want to come by for dinner.'"

"Might be a nice start."

Ali took a deep breath. "I can't do it. He made his wishes known, and that's something I have to live with."

"Then, why are you here?"

"The book assignment allowed me to leave the office, maintain a way to make a living, and have my baby in peace."

"Don't give me that crap."

Ali glared at Kate. Rationally, it sounded like a great reason, but in reality, Ali didn't want her daughter to grow up without knowing her father. She'd hoped by just being here that their paths would cross. "Well, God waved his magic wand to bring us together once," she wiped her nose on her sleeve. "He'll have to do it again."

Kate stared at the water. "God can only put the play into motion. We have our roles. We are his hands, his ears, and his heart in the world. We need to take action."

Pushing thoughts of how her inaction likely led to the bird's death, Ali quipped. "Kinda like what you've been doing all these years, Kate?" Ali looked at the older woman. "What about Gus? What role haven't you chosen to play with him?"

"That's different," Kate said flatly.

"If you don't mind me quoting a great sage..." Ali cocked one brow. "Don't give me that crap. You've been waiting for your life to pass you by so that you can be with Cy again."

Pain washed across Kate's face. "Maybe so."

"Well, you came back for a reason, and I have a feeling it's not just because of Grace." Ali rose to her feet and brushed the dirt from her pants. "Maybe you haven't been reading God's script too well."

"We've got free will."

"Well, if you can sit around waiting for some divine intervention, so can I." Ali stomped off toward the house, stopping briefly to take Grace from Gus's arms without saying a word to him. The beautiful morning had just turned to shit, and she was ready for a break from it—from all of it.

Gus heard the conversation, clearly, including Kate's words, "That's different." His heart ached from the sound of them. They echoed in his mind over and over as he washed the boat. It drained him of any enthusiasm he had for the day. He set the hose nozzle back on the hook and then sauntered up the hill, around the side of the house.

"Where you going?" Kate's voice echoed after him.

"Home."

He strode down the sidewalk, counting the cracks along the way. He knew there were fifty of them between his place and Kate's. He'd counted them before. It settled him down after Kate's barbed remarks set him in his place. At least, it usually did. Today was different. He wandered past the cactus garden, barely giving it a glance. He usually stopped and spoke to each one of his plants.

Opening the door to the kitchen, the cool, darkened room greeted him. He paused at the refrigerator to retrieve a Tecate. He shuffled into the living room and sank onto the grey paisley-patterned sofa, avoiding the cushion with the broken spring. He popped the top of the beer can, and it echoed through the room. Only the ticking mantle clock joined the serenade.

The copy of *Southern Style* magazine lay on the coffee table, open to the article that Ali had written. He showed it to everyone who came by, some friends, others who stopped in to buy plants. His life was full, and simple but at times loneliness crept into the walls of his home. He looked down on the page sporting the photos of Ali and Jack. He had folded the page, so they were side by side. They looked good together.

He glanced at the mantle above the fireplace that he barely used. On it was a picture of Kate and him in a gold frame. Skipper had taken it at one of the fly fishing functions a couple of years before. "We look good together, too." He took a swig of his beer and then threw the can at the fireplace. Beer splattered across the room and onto the floor as the can rolled around on the darkened hardwood planks.

Gus held his head in his hands, elbows perched upon his knees. He was a desperate man, with something gnawing ferociously at his heart. The fight between Ali and Kate was not in his plan, and he knew with Ali's stubbornness, no good would come of it. This morning's jaunt to the bay was supposed to cement her into staying. Instead, he sensed she was about to flee. "I could use some help here," he said aloud. His gaze fell once more to the magazine. He picked it up. He opened the magazine to the masthead and dialed the number listed on his flip phone.

"Southern Style, how may I direct your call?"

"Joe Driscoll, please."

# Chapter Eighteen

Conversations from the dining room filtered up to Ali as the fishermen returned from the bay and settled in for their evening meal. A tinge of guilt washed over her as she realized Kate was in the kitchen alone. But it quickly faded when Ali reminded herself that Kate had handled the place without her for years and soon would be doing so again.

The mother and daughter cuddled on the bed for most of the morning and into the afternoon. It had been years since Ali did nothing all day. Not even following Grace's birth did she rest completely. Between naps and feedings, she read her manuscript or peeled potatoes for Kate. Today, she didn't have the energy for anything. Thoughts of Jack filtered through her mind, sending her into a siege of tears each time. Tears that she hadn't finished shedding over the last few months—or even a lifetime. Losses that she had stuffed into the closet of her heart demanded to be acknowledged.

Ali sat up and turned on her light. It was hard to admit, but she had hoped that Jack would discover her at Mama Kate's, take her home with him, and be present for the birth of their baby. But she hadn't been willing to take the risk of yet another rejection to make that even a remote possibility.

Instead, she wished for the stars to align and to bring them together once again. *Fucking Cinderella.* She set her jaw. The anger she felt toward herself mounted.

"Still waiting for the prince, Ali." She shook her head. "Like that's ever worked."

She caught a glimpse of her reflection in the mirror. Her eyes were swollen, and her complexion blotchy. A pile of tissues lay on the nightstand. She surveyed the room. It was in shambles. Soon, it would be nearly impossible for her to share space with the baby and her office equipment in this tiny abode. All signs seemed to be pointing to her departure, now just two months away. *Why should I wait? If I have the strength to fish, then I have the strength to drive back to Virginia.*

Swinging her legs off the bed, she picked up her cell phone. She dialed Joe's number. His voice mail immediately picked up. "This is Ali. Call me when you get this message." She took a deep breath. "I'm coming back sooner than planned."

She took the energy bar and water out of Grace's diaper bag. It would have to sustain her. She resolved not to engage Kate anymore that day, and that meant holing up in her room. She had plans to make. Scanning the room, she mentally began packing.

✳ ✳ ✳

With the last of the dishes put away and the fishermen back in their cottage, Kate left the deathly quiet house and walked to the dock. A coyote howled in the distance, and the mullet jumped and slapped the surface of the water. There were no voices of people fishing off the docks, no boats motoring up the Arroyo. Chilling stillness surrounded her.

Sitting on the bench, Kate reached for the ever-present rosary and held it feebly between her fingers. She didn't have the energy to say her prayers and touch the beads one by one, as was her usual practice. The image of Gus rounding the house, shoulders slumped, burned in her mind. She knew it was the look of rejection, one she'd seen on his face time and time again. Rejection that she caused.

She took a deep breath, and for a moment, wondered if Ali had been right. Maybe she did come back for more than Grace. Her heart ached so sharply at that moment that she feared she was having another heart attack. Squeezing the rosary, she looked to the heavens, feeling the vastness of the sky as the stars sparkled above her. "If God can create this universe," she whispered. "Then certainly, he can bring peace to our lives. All of ours."

Wiping tears from her eyes, she rose and ambled to the statue of Mary, pausing briefly to observe the fresh grave of the bird. She touched the cool concrete statue, and spoke softly, "Mary, fill my heart with your presence. Show me the way. Show us all the way. Please." Her voice cracked, and more tears trickled down her cheeks. A night heron squawked, rousing her from her reverie, and she returned to the house, feeling more weary than she had in months.

Morning came, and Ali could no longer stand the hunger. The smell of fried bacon and eggs wafted up to her room, waking her gently from her fitful sleep. The energy bar and water that she had snacked on the evening before was long gone. She opened the door to the bedroom and listened for any sign of Kate, only to be greeted with silence. The anglers had departed well before dawn.

Wandering down the stairs, carrying Grace on her hip, Ali ran over the words she needed to say to Kate. The first was an apology. The next her plan for leaving.

She rounded the corner from the stairway, and there, Kate sat in her blue chair in the living room. She held her rosary in her hands, and her eyes were closed. She looked ten years older since Ali had last seen her, just hours before. A stab of regret seared through her heart, but she squelched it quickly. It would only interfere with her decision.

"Morning." Ali's voice was barely above a whisper.

Kate opened her eyes and laid her rosary on the table next to the chair. "I'll get you some breakfast. You can starve yourself, but you can't starve that baby. Not on my watch." She rose from the chair, and Ali reached out and touched her forearm.

"I'm sorry. I said some mean things yesterday, and they were really all about me, not you."

Kate eyed her for a moment. "Not entirely." She brushed by, barely glancing at the baby, despite Grace reaching out for her with her tiny hands. Kate dished up a couple of eggs, adding a few slices of bacon and a biscuit. Setting the plate on the table, she said, "I'll get your tea and come back and hold the baby while you eat."

Ali took her place, much like an obedient child. Kate came back to the table with two cups of tea and reached for the baby. She sat down adjacent to Ali and stared out at the water.

"Gus coulda' been my man a long time ago." She brushed the baby's hair with her fingers. "I just couldn't go through another loss. Cy was my heart and soul. When he drowned out there, my world ended. Or at least I hoped it would." She fished for a tissue in her pocket and dabbed her nose. "It didn't, and I got so danged mad at God."

"But you're so faithful," Ali said softly.

"Made my amends awhile back." She shook her head. "Finally had to admit that maybe I didn't know it all." She sipped her tea. "Had a lot of help from Mother Mary."

Grace banged a spoon on the table, made gurgling noises, and then giggled. The two women broke out in smiles.

"It seems a little late for me and Gus now."

Ali touched Kate's hand. "That's not true. He just needs a little encouragement."

Kate blushed and then looked pointedly at Ali. "Then what about you?"

"This isn't my world, Kate." She cupped her hands around her mug of tea. "Everything I know is back in Virginia. My friends, my work. It's time." Ali looked up at Kate with tears in her eyes.

"Is that why Joe's comin'? To take you from here?"

Ali's mouth dropped open. "What?"

"He'll be here the day after tomorrow."

# Chapter Nineteen

Ali whisked into the kitchen with Grace propped on her hip. "Kate, need anything from town?"

Kate emerged from the laundry room, carrying a stack of napkins and several tablecloths. "Laundry detergent." She lay them on the counter and then peered into the refrigerator. "Grace needs apple juice."

Ali added it to the grocery list, and then looked at Kate, whose face was sullen. "Relax, you'll love Joe."

Kate began folding the napkins with a huff. "He's taking you from here."

"I was leaving anyway. Only now, just a little sooner." Ali felt her heart skip a beat.

"You're running out on us, and your commitment to Gus."

"I wouldn't win the tournament anyway," Ali said defensively.

"Winning isn't the issue." Kate glared at her. "It's about testing your abilities, squashing the doubts that keep you from doing things to see what you're made of." She shook her head. "It's about stepping out onto the edge and saying to God, 'Okay show me what else I can do.'"

"We've been over this." Ali whirled around and grabbed a bottle of water from the refrigerator and stuck it in her bag. "It's just a tournament."

"I can't see why staying a couple of more weeks would hurt." Kate watched as Ali danced her way around every excuse she could think of.

"I'm not sure I'm up for it." She picked up a banana and put it in her bag. "Two whole days on the water. I won't be able to nurse Grace, and my boobs are going to be as hard as rocks when I come in."

"You can pump."

She rolled her eyes. "Oh yes. 'Excuse me, Gus, I'm going to ignore those tailing redfish while I milk my boobs.'"

"He's seen you nurse." Kate carried the stack of napkins to the pantry. "Besides, the tailing action is over by midmorning. You can pump while you're taking a break."

Ali glanced at the clock above the sink. Her eyes briefly paused to watch a great blue heron land on the dock. Her mind wandered to the book of animal and bird symbols she referred to when she had a close encounter with a blue heron not too long ago when fishing with Gus. The bird stood alongside her watching her cast and then pounced on the fish as Ali reeled it in. The bird's focus and determination captured her attention more than the fish on the end of the line. The symbology of the bird was described as aggressive self-reliance. *Perhaps that's not a good thing all the time.* She turned away from her thoughts. "I've got to get going."

Kate gave Grace a kiss. The little girl giggled and put her wet fist on Kate's cheek. Ali tried her best not to let the scene get to her, but the pangs in her heart told her that despite her determination to do the smart thing, her emotions were edging into the lead.

She diverted her gaze once again out the window. Two turkeys rested under the mesquite. The hen had one wing spread out beside her. "Do we need chicken scratch?"

"Running low on that, too," Kate replied as she straightened up, holding the crook of her back.

"It's on my list," Ali called over her shoulder as she and Grace headed out the front door.

✳ ✳ ✳

Settling into the Audi, Ali peered into the rearview mirror. "Grace, we're going to Mr. G's to see the animals." The little girl gave her mother a wide-eyed look, her blue eyes sparkling like sapphires in the afternoon light. Picking up chicken scratch at the feed store had become a ritual for Ali, and with Grace in tow, it had become much like a visit to the zoo. It took so little to keep Grace content. She had been an easy baby from the start, as if God doubly rewarded Ali with not only a baby but one who didn't place too many demands on her other than being held, which Ali always gladly did.

Ali started the engine and connected her iPhone to the radio. Soon, sacred chants of Deva Premal filtered through the car, but Ali barely heard them through the conversation with Kate regarding her departure replaying in her mind. Ali's original plan was not to leave until October, making the trip well before the weather turned winter-like. It was only late July, but leaving now seemed like the sensible thing to do. Yet, her stomach somersaulted as she visualized pulling out of Kate's driveway for the last time in just a couple of weeks.

Passing the orange groves, her mind segued to February when the creamy white blossoms appeared, filling the air for miles with a divine aroma, something that Grace would miss experiencing. Ali shook the thought from her mind. She'd have others, like honeysuckle blossoms.

If she had to leave, she might as well do it now before Grace grew even more accustomed to their life along the Arroyo. Not every child had a grandmother and grandfather figure in her life on a daily basis, she reasoned. Besides, Ali had to make a living. She knitted her brow. She'd been through it all before, a thousand times over. It just made sense to leave as soon as possible so they both could acclimate to life alone in her townhouse. Stopping at the intersection of FM 106 and FM 2925, Ali asked Siri to remind her to have the place cleaned before their arrival. She sighed. One foot was raised and about to be placed in the world from which she came. The other was firmly planted on the banks of the Arroyo. It was unsettling, not being fully in either.

As she turned off the main road just outside Rio Hondo, Ali glanced in the rearview mirror at Grace. Dressed in a white dress with pink roses, she was sound asleep, looking her usual angelic self. "Grace, we're at Mr. G's."

Ali pulled into the driveway of the feed store, a ranch-style building with gray barn-board siding. Three cages of chickens stood in the shade. The inhabitants were busy pecking the dirt for feed. Stepping from the vehicle, she watched two kittens playfully chase a piece of hay as she opened the rear door and took Grace from her seat. The child roused and blinked in the bright sunshine. Ali placed Grace's matching wide-brimmed hat on her head, and the two ambled around the parking lot, stopping first at the cage with the chicks.

"Hey, Miss Ali." Mr. G sauntered toward them. He wore a white straw cowboy hat, a red and tan checked shirt with the sleeves rolled up to his elbows, and his customary jeans and boots. His metal belt buckle dazzled in the afternoon light. "How's my Grace doing today?" He chucked her under the chin. The little girl kicked her feet, babbling as she pointed to the cage. "She's getting so big." He nodded toward the back pasture. "We just got a pony this week. Pretty soon she'll be big enough to go for a ride." He grinned. "How's Mama Kate doing today?"

"Great." Ali shielded her eyes as she looked up at the man. His brown skin glistened as beads of perspiration dripped from his forehead.

"She and Gus came in here last week." He grinned again. "Lost some weight. Says she's been walking with you and the baby about every day." He paused. "Said something about yoga, too. Don't know much about that."

Ali's heart did another jig, and she glanced at her watch. "I've got to pick up a friend at the airport."

He opened the door for her. "More chicken scratch?"

"Better make it three bags this time." She placed twenty-one dollars on the counter. Keep the penny." She smiled.

Another broad grin swept across his face. "You're going to make me a millionaire at this rate. If everyone was like you, Miss Ali, I could retire before too long."

"You wouldn't be happy without your animals." She called after him as he walked up a wooden ramp to the storage area.

"You're right." He appeared carrying a fifty-pound blue and white sack of chicken scratch on his shoulder. "I'd miss visiting with you and Miss Grace, too."

Ali bit her lip. She felt assaulted from all angles. Mr. G didn't seem to notice as he disappeared to put the scratch in her SUV, only to reappear moments later, taking long strides back to the storage room.

Ali scanned the walls and display cases around the store. It reminded her of her grandfather's workshop in the barn, with his collection of antique carpentry tools, some of which hung on the walls, others that lay scattered about on workbenches along with fertilizers and more modern gardening tools. The walls of Mr. G's were decorated with bridles and saddles. Birdcages perched on dusty showcases stocked with liniments and other remedies for horses and cattle.

Her eyes fell to the counter, where she noticed a newspaper clipping sporting Mr. G's smiling face. The man definitely seemed happy with his lifestyle. She took a moment to read the profile. The man had followed his heart and created a sanctuary for birds and animals of all shapes and sizes. A peacock screeching in the background was a testimonial to this. Grace cooed and kicked her legs as two kittens followed Mr. G through the door, in his last ascent to the feed storage room. The kittens ran toward them, mewing with ferocity as if they were starving, most likely for attention and not for food. One climbed up Ali's leg, clinging to the green- leafed fabric of her capris. She lifted the kitten for Grace, and the little girl touched the kitten hesitantly and then giggled.

"You want it?" Mr. G nodded to the kitten.

Ali shook her head. "I'm not too sure Kate would appreciate me bringing home a kitten."

"Tell her it's for the baby."

Ali smiled. "That would win her." She placed the kitten on the floor. "I'm afraid I'd better not." She was thinking more of the trip to Virginia than Kate's reaction to a cat at her place. She looked up at Mr. G, and for a moment, wondered if she'd see him again. "Grace, say goodbye to Mr. G." She waved the child's hand as they sauntered to the door. Putting her hand on the doorknob, Ali paused and glanced around the room. She rested her gaze on the man. "You have a real nice place here, Mr. G. I've enjoyed coming here." She turned abruptly and closed the door behind them. The bell on the door echoed in her ears long after she'd climbed into the driver's seat and made her way through town.

\* \* \*

Throngs of people, some dressed in shorts and tank tops, others sporting jeans and cowboy hats, filled the airport lobby. It was a typical scene when flights were due to arrive. In between, it felt more like a sleepy Mexican village, with only the three-tier terracotta fountain in the center of the room commanding attention. Ali stood near the cafe and watched as the passengers rode down the escalator. A few took the stairs, and she alternated her gaze between both. She spotted Joe as he bounded down the stairs, wearing white linen pants, a beige linen shirt, and his blue blazer swung over his shoulder. He carried a shiny silver shopping bag, with a big bow peeking out of the top. She smiled as he caught her eye and came toward them.

"There are my girls." He kissed Ali on the cheek. "And you, young lady, must be Miss Grace." He cupped her cheek in his hand, and she smiled. "Eyes like your mama's. Bound to be a heartbreaker."

He turned his attention to Ali, holding the bag up high. "Gifts for mother and baby, and our hostess."

"Did you get my message?" Ali inquired, curiously.

"Of course." Joe responded as if it was a silly question to ask.

"I could have saved you a trip," Ali said matter-of-factly.

He cocked a brow. "I needed a change of scenery."

"I'm ready to come back," she blurted.

He reached for her elbow. "We'll talk later. It's time to get my bags so you can escort me to your humble abode along the Arroyo."

They strode toward the baggage claim, turning the heads of many people around them. Joe, in his polished attire and his tall, lean stature, made him look like a movie star. Ali could have been his petite, younger wife, equally stunning in a white top and her green-leafed capris and beige sandals. Her hair was shorter, bobbed to about an inch above her shoulders, and highlighted from the sun.

"I like your hair."

"Thank you." She felt self-conscious for a moment. It had been months since she'd taken notice of a man's attention, long before her belly swelled.

"Makes you look younger and wiser at the same time." He smiled at her with a twinkle in his eye. "Must be motherhood. Or perhaps a renewed romance with the father."

She shook her head. "I haven't even seen him."

"Any romantic interests?"

"Life along the Arroyo with Kate and Gus, and my little girl." She smiled. "That's all the romance I need."

"It agrees with you." He paused for a moment and studied her face. "I've never seen you look so relaxed. Perhaps a few days here will do the same for me."

Ali stayed behind with Grace and surveyed the people gathering around the luggage carousel, while Joe retrieved his own. Her eyes settled on two gentlemen in their thirties, dressed in khaki shorts and fishing shirts. Both held fly rod tubes as they peered intently at the luggage on the revolving black belt. For a moment, she wondered if they were fishing with Jack.

\* \* \*

Turning on the radio, Jack waited in the loading zone at the airport for his clients. Security knew him by now and ignored his extended stops at the curb. He watched the people exit the building, looking for the telltale fly rods that would alert him to his quarry.

A tall gentleman with white linen pants caught his eye. He was engaged in an animated conversation with a younger woman walking alongside him. On her hip, perched a baby. Jack's heart skipped a beat. While her head was turned, the woman's small, yet athletic frame reminded him of Ali. He followed them in their path across the parking lot until a tap on the window prevented him from continuing his assessment. "Captain Cooper?" Jack bolted from the truck, briefly taking one last glance over his shoulder, before turning to his clients. He knew that the image of the couple would haunt him for the remainder of the day.

\* \* \*

"Kate, we're here." Ali stepped into the house, laying her keys on the table by the door and dropping her bag to the floor. She held the sleeping Grace in her arms.

"I know. I heard you coming." Kate appeared in the hallway, wiping her hands on her red chef's apron. She extended her hand to Joe. "I'm Kate McGregor. Mama Kate to most folks."

Joe stepped forward, and warmly embraced her hand. "I do hope you don't mind if I call you Kate. It's a beautiful name, and its simplicity becomes you."

Kate's cheeks flushed a light shade of pink. "Not at all." She motioned for them to follow. "Come on in. Supper's in about an hour." She walked to the door and opened it. Taking one step on to the porch, she yelled to Gus, who was fiddling with the boat. "Ali's back with Mr. Driscoll."

"It's Joe."

Kate stepped back into the room and eyed him. "Joe."

"If you'll excuse me, I'm going to put the baby down for a nap." Ali left the room, instantly relieved to be alone if only for a moment.

Kate nodded. "I'll pour us some wine."

Joe interrupted. "If you'll allow me, I brought some along in celebration of the birth of Miss Grace." He ducked into the hallway where he left the suitcase. He returned, carrying two bottles of wine and the large package he held as he descended the airport stairs. "Gifts for my ladies."

"I'll get the glasses and the corkscrew," she offered with enthusiasm.

He followed Kate to the kitchen and ceremoniously opened the wine, taking a whiff of the cork and then pouring just a small amount into the glass. He held it out for Kate. She accepted it and took a sip. Her eyes widened. "That's mighty fine."

"Wonderful." He poured four glasses.

Ali appeared, followed by Gus. He took his hat off and held it in his hands. "Gus Lammons, I'd like you to meet Joe Driscoll." Ali introduced the two, and they shook hands.

"Ali tells me you're a master gardener." Joe handed Kate a glass and then Ali. "I have a collection of orchids."

Gus shook his head. "Never had much luck with them. I prefer bluebonnets and cactus."

"And rightly so." Joe offered Gus the glass. "Should we retire to the parlor?"

The four walked through the dining room and into the living room. "Still a little warm to sit outside," Gus remarked. He took a seat in the green leather recliner, Kate in her blue wing chair, and Ali and Joe settled into the beige brocade sofa. He raised his glass. "A toast to the newest member of the Stephenson family, and likely the apple of everyone's eye who are now gathered in this room."

Ali surveyed the scene, studying the expression on Kate and Gus's faces. While gentle on the exterior, she knew from the look in Kate's eyes that she was sizing up her prey and about to go in for the kill. Gus looked as if he wanted to hide.

Kate cleared her throat. "So, how long do you expect to stay?"

"Long enough to attain an understanding of what lured my friend back here." Joe glanced at Ali and winked. He took a sip and then placed his glass on the table. "And now for the gifts."

He pulled out a brown bear sporting a pink tutu. "For Miss Grace when she awakes." He placed the bear on the sofa between Ali and himself. He then reached into the bag and retrieved a small basket with gold wrapping and a silver bow. "For the new mother."

Ali accepted the package and slowly untied the bow, displaying the contents of the basket. Inside was a journal covered with blue marbleized handmade paper, a burgundy Mont Blanc pen, a candle, and lavender bath salts." She leaned over and kissed his cheek. "Thank you."

"The journal and the pen are for the novel you've been threatening to write all these years." He sipped his wine, momentarily looking pensive. "No time like the present to realize our dreams." He dipped his hand into the bag one last time. "And for our gracious hostess." He handed Kate a small square box, covered with the same wrapping as Ali's gift.

"This isn't necessary," Kate said, slightly uncomfortable.

"It is where I come from," Joe remarked.

Kate loosened the bow and then slipped her finger under the tape, carefully removing the wrapping. Inside the square box was a crystal bust of the Madonna. Her mouth dropped open as she reverently ran her finger over the etched surface of the Holy Mother. The room was silent, broken only by the soft cries of Grace from her room.

Kate set the bust on the table next to her rosary, allowing her fingers to linger on the Madonna's head. "I will treasure her always." She dabbed her mouth with a tissue. "I need to check dinner." She rose from the chair, pausing next to Joe, looking deeply into his eyes. "I can see why Ali thinks so highly of you."

# Chapter Twenty

The next morning Ali awakened before Grace and lay in bed reviewing Joe's arrival, their dinner with Kate and Gus, and her life along the Arroyo. It was so different from the life she lived in Virginia Beach. Her life here was much simpler and yet richer. She sighed, which alerted Grace to her mother's presence.

"Hey, my punkin'." Ali lifted the cooing baby from her crib and kissed her cheek. She relished the smell of baby soap and sweet breast milk on her skin. "Did you sleep well?" She lay the baby on the changing table and removed her soiled diaper. Pausing for a moment, she glanced around the room. It no longer seemed as crowded as it had a week ago. Everything fit neatly into the space. Grace had one half of the room, and she had the other. Outside the window, a mockingbird chirped its melodic song while perched on the neighbor's roof. Ali finished diapering Grace and then lifted the little girl to peer out the window. "Mr. Mockingbird is wishing us a good morning." The little girl pointed and made a few gurgling noises.

Ali carried her back to the bed and began nursing her. It seemed too early to join Kate. Joe was the only guest, and not likely to have risen early, so there was no need to prepare for a big breakfast. Closing her eyes while Grace suckled her breast, Ali concentrated on the sounds of the morning. A boat passed, with the din of the motor rising and then fading as it traveled down the Arroyo. The lapping waves against the sea wall followed. An occasional car could be heard on the road in front of the house.

However, it was the gobbling turkeys and the boisterous kiskadees that captured her attention most. She let her mind rest on their calls until she slipped into meditation. Coming into full consciousness when Grace stopped suckling, Ali opened her eyes and peered down at her daughter. She'd miss these relaxing mornings most of all when she returned to the office. Leaving was going to be more challenging than she thought.

Holding Grace on her hip, Ali descended the stairs to find Kate in her chair, a sight that she'd grown accustomed to. She kissed Kate on the forehead. "Morning, Mama Kate." Kate reached up and took the baby from Ali. "Tea?"

"Love some." Kate kept her attention on Grace as the two played peek-a-boo. "Apple is ready, too. I added some flax and pumpkin seeds."

"Sounds delish!" Ali called from the kitchen. "Joe up yet?"

"Hours ago."

Ali peered from behind a cabinet. "Where is he?"

"He and Gus went fishing."

Ali's wide-eyed expression conveyed her genuine surprise. "Oh." She returned to the room, with a tray ladened with their morning fare.

"He said to let you know that you'll need to fix yourself up for a night on the town."

Ali set tea and a bowl of apple next to Kate, who spooned small amounts into Grace's mouth. The baby smacked her lips, delighting in the sweetness.

"Do you mind?" The thought of dressing up and going out did appeal to her.

Kate rolled her eyes. "Of course not. Gus and I can eat leftovers tonight. There's a bottle in the fridge for Grace, so we'll be just fine." She smacked her own lips as she spooned another helping of apple into Grace's mouth.

* * *

After breakfast, Ali, Kate, and Grace took their morning walk. As they sauntered down the sidewalk, Ali became mindful of the peaceful sounds of early morning. A natural rhythm ruled their days, much like life in the Blue Ridge when she was a child.

"Is Joe married?" Kate broke the silence.

"Several times." Ali sighed. "He's not had much luck at love either." Ali shook her head. "But he's not now."

Kate had her hand on the handles of the stroller as they walked along. Grace, still clothed in her white cotton pajamas with teal bunnies, was equally attentive to her surroundings, her bare feet keeping the beat to her own personal drummer.

"Maybe you two shoulda gotten together." Kate raised an eyebrow.

"It crossed my mind, but I didn't want to risk our friendship. It's too precious."

"I can see he feels the same." They wandered along in silence, admiring Gus's cactus patch as they passed his home, now with freshly painted white clapboards and green trim. It glistened in the morning light. "Hard-working man, that Gus."

"Looks like a good catch to me." Ali smiled.

Kate blushed. "Don't go talking nonsense, Ali Mae." The playful tone in Kate's voice reminded Ali of her grandmother, and homesickness pricked at her heart.

"I couldn't be more serious," Ali's tone overshadowed Kate's dismissive response.

Kate remained silent as she turned to look out at the Arroyo.

Returning home, Kate and Ali settled into their daily routine, attending to the chores of the day. Even with Joe's arrival, Ali had a deadline to meet, so she excused herself, leaving Kate with Grace. Several hours passed before she lay her red pen on her nightstand and stacked the manuscript pages next to it. The final draft of the *Leisure Time Guide to the Lower Rio Grande Valley* was almost complete. Yet, she knew it would still be a week or two before it was ready for submission, more if she took the time to drive back to Virginia. Another reason her departure was beginning to seem untimely.

She moved from her bed and walked to her desk. A pile of unopened mail beckoned her. She sorted through it, separating the bills from other correspondence. One envelope caught her eye sporting a return address for The Texas Fly Fishing Tournament. She slipped her fingernail beneath the edge of the envelope and removed the contents. In addition to a letter acknowledging receipt of her entry fee, it held her tournament badge with her entry number prominently displayed in the center of the white rectangle. She closed her eyes, and Gus's face flashed into her mind. He was a man of few words and kept his feelings close to his chest. But she knew that her plans to leave before the tournament crushed him. He'd said very little to her since that day that she announced her departure.

Ali lay the badge on her desk and left the room. A heaviness in her heart followed her as she descended the stairs and went out onto the patio where Kate and Grace were rocking in a cushioned wicker rocker, a gift from Gus to Kate on Mother's Day. The significance visited Ali like a bucket of cold water.

"Here comes Gus and Joe," Kate announced, without looking up the Arroyo.

"You're something, Kate." Ali strained her ears. "I can't even hear a boat, much less see one."

"They're at the mouth. Be here in twenty minutes."

✳ ✳ ✳

True to Kate's prediction, Gus and Joe pulled up to the dock, laughing like a couple of young boys. Both had cigars dangling from their mouths. Ali sauntered to the dock to greet them, enjoying the scene before her. Joe's silver hair was slicked back, and he sported a bright yellow bandana around his neck. An air of relaxed camaraderie surrounded the men.

"Catch anything?" Ali asked.

Joe beamed at Ali. "I caught supper for our fine hosts." He jumped up on the dock, carrying with him a stringer of trout. "We're going out tonight."

"So I've been told." She smiled. Dinner with Joe was always the highlight of her week, a tradition that they kept for as long as she'd been at the magazine. "I've missed our dinners."

"I, as well, my dear." He flopped the fish on the cleaning table and began sharpening a fillet knife.

Gus joined them. "He's quite a fisherman. Spotted those two tailing trout moments after I told him what to look for." He slapped Joe on the back. "Never seen anything like it from a tourist before." Gus grabbed the hose and began washing off the boat.

"Where are you taking me?" Ali stood next to Joe, watching him deftly fillet the trout.

"Gus suggested a place called Pirates."

Ali nodded. "Fine choice."

"Stuffed flounder is the special." He glanced at Ali. "Perhaps we'll go dancing afterward."

She chuckled. "I haven't seen you like this in years."

"I haven't felt like this in years," Joe grinned.

Kate wandered down to the dock carrying Grace. Gus stood next to Kate. "Pirates is a good choice, don't you think?" He winked.

Kate smiled. "Perfect."

✳ ✳ ✳

Joe sauntered into the kitchen, wearing his white linen shorts, beige sandals, and a brown and beige tropical print shirt. His glasses were perched on his head. He set a bottle of wine on the counter and leaned over the cast iron skillet where a fillet was simmering in a lemon-thyme, white wine sauce. "Smells delicious."

"You'll have better," Kate chuckled.

"You underestimate your talents, Kate." Joe glanced at his watch. "Think he'll be there?"

"Skipper will see to it."

Kate stirred a helping of sour cream into the pot of boiled potatoes. "Gonna pour me a drink? Doc says red wine is good for my heart."

"Certainly." Joe uncorked the bottle as Kate whipped the potatoes with an electric mixer, preventing any conversation. When Kate finished, Joe lifted his glass. "To honorable endeavors." Kate clinked her glass against his.

"And what endeavors might those be?" Ali stood between the dining room and living room, with Grace on one hip and her hand on the other.

"Making sure you have a relaxing night on the town." Joe flashed a look at Kate before strolling across the room with a glass of wine for Ali. "All new mothers deserve a break now and again."

Ali raised the glass to her lips, eyeing him suspiciously. "Right." She returned to the living room and placed Grace in her bouncy chair. "Kate, I just fed Grace, so she should be fine for three or four hours." Ali walked back to the kitchen and opened the refrigerator. "Maybe some warm apple if she gets fussy."

"I can handle it." Kate regarded Ali. "I told you you've lost all that baby fat." She pointed to the dress. "Fits just like it did a year or so ago."

Ali's jaw dropped, remembering the night in Mexico with Jack. She glanced down at the gold tank dress, which hung loosely from her shoulders. On her feet were the same celadon sandals, and her multicolored pashmina waited in the hallway with her purse. Only her hair was different. Tonight, she wore it back, with short wisps framing her neck and face. Gold hoops dangled from her ears.

Sorry for her choice of words, Kate hurriedly excused them, "Now go on and enjoy yourselves." She shooed Ali and Joe from the kitchen.

"Yes, ma'am." Joe touched Ali's elbow as they left the room.

✳ ✳ ✳

As they drove along the farm-to-market road, passing expanses of South Texas pristine landscape with mesquite, ebony, *huisache,* and cactus, Ali savored the salty, pungent aromas wafting in through the windows. It was comforting, more so than crocus blooms in the spring or her grandmother's purple iris on Memorial Day.

"How are you doing?" She eyed Joe suspiciously.

"Just fine." His gaze was far off into the expansive horizon.

"Bleu says you've been out of the office a lot."

"Had some personal business that required my attention." He cleared his throat and then stared straight ahead.

"Still ready to retire?" Ali chanced another glance at him.

He shrugged.

"So, you may not need me right away?" Her heart thumped in her chest wildly, waiting for the answer, a little surprised that she dared to ask.

"We have options." He flicked on the radio. "Enough chatter. Let's enjoy this beautiful evening." He pointed across the bay to the west. "I've never seen a more beautiful sunset."

Waves of lavender and peach washed across the evening sky. Silently, she concurred. They traveled the remaining miles, saying little. Occasionally, Ali pointed out landmarks and explained how she included them in her book. Joe kept his comments brief.

Slowing as they entered Port Isabel, Joe turned off the radio and looked about. "Reminds me a little of Virginia Beach in the good old days, before too many tourists descended upon us and created a need for high-rise hotels."

"They're on the Island." Ali pointed across the bay. "Pirates is up here on the left, before the causeway."

✳ ✳ ✳

Jack parked his truck and scrambled out, glancing at his watch as he made his way toward the restaurant. He opened the heavy wooden door and stepped inside, taking a moment to survey the room. Skipper waved to him from the far corner where members of the club were gathered around a large round table.

"Have a seat." Skipper pushed back a chair next to his.

"Thanks." Jack sat in the chair and exchanged nods with a few of the other men at the table.

"I was worried you might not show." Skipper sipped his beer and then peered at Jack.

"I fell asleep."

"You need to go to bed earlier."

"I've been writing every night," Jack explained, a bit cautiously.

"About me, I hope." Skipper chuckled.

"Of course," Jack snidely remarked, before diverting his attention to the waitress. After placing his order for a beer, he let his gaze wander around the room. He stopped at the entrance, where a tall silver-haired man captured his attention, causing him to do a double-take. He tried to recollect where he'd seen the man before. Skipper noticed Jack's interest and lured him into a conversation, not wanting him to see Ali too soon into the evening. Joe needed time to set the stage.

Walking through the restaurant, Joe commanded the path well out of the gaze of Jack, acting a bit like a star-struck tourist as he bantered with Ali about the memorabilia hanging on the walls. Stepping out on the deck, he inhaled deeply. "Now that's fresh air." He grinned.

Ali smiled and shook her head. "You'll never lose that little boy exuberance."

"And why should I?" He held Ali's chair and then took his own across from her. The light evening breeze danced around them as they settled onto the deck. The lights on the causeway were beginning to glow, as were the ones from the hotels and beach homes on the Island.

"You have landed in a wonderful spot." Joe sighed, all the lines from his face eased.

Ali nodded. "I certainly have."

"Why do you want to return so soon?"

The waitress arrived with a bottle of wine and two glasses, giving Ali time to formulate her answer.

Ali took a sip and then set the glass back on the table. She folded her hands in front of her. "I guess I don't want to get so rooted here that it would hurt to leave."

"Something tells me you already are."

"You may be right." Her voice trailed off as she glanced out at the bay.

"So why leave?" He leaned forward and held her hand.

"There are no magazines nor publishing houses." She sounded exasperated. "How am I going to make a living?"

Joe pondered her question. "Let me think about that."

"For how long?"

"Until I come up with an answer."

She shook her head. "I hate limbo."

"That's your biggest problem." He reached into his rear pants pocket for the white envelope he'd hidden from Ali's view. "You're a control freak if you don't mind me saying so. You need to learn to go with the flow." He chuckled.

"That's one trait I've never seen in you."

"Ah, but it could have spared me and those I've loved many heartaches." Holding the envelope in his hand, he continued. "Fortunately, God has awakened me, and luckily I've heeded his call." He lay the envelope on the table. "I've been given a second chance."

Ali looked puzzled. She glanced from Joe's face to the envelope. "Are you going to let me in on your little secret?"

"You're not the only one who's witnessed a miracle of late." He pensively looked into his glass of wine. "My death sentence has been repealed, at least for a time."

Ali's jaw dropped. "What are you talking about?"

"Leukemia."

"Why didn't you tell me?" Ali's voice cracked with fear.

"I didn't tell anyone," Joe spoke softly. "Only my dear doctor and I knew."

Ali nodded. "We all suspected something. You took a lot of time from the office." She reached over and touched his hand. "I dismissed it as business."

"As well you should have." He smiled. "You had far more important things to concern yourself with than me."

"That's not true." She shook her head. "Before Kate and Gus came along, you were the only family I had."

"And now your family has grown." He picked up the envelope. "You have many more to consider now than me." He sighed. "I am sorry I coerced you into this agreement." He tapped the envelope against his fingers. "It was my attempt to control not only my life but yours. My apologies." He held the envelope over the candle and set it aflame.

"What are you doing?" Ali said, wide-eyed and with her mouth open.

"Releasing you from this selfish covenant." He grinned widely. "I'm not ready to retire, and you're not ready to return to Virginia." He tossed the blazing paper over the railing. He raised his glass and proclaimed a toast. "To new vistas and blessed adventures."

❊ ❊ ❊

Skipper had been keeping an eye on Joe, waiting for the cue. "Somebody just set something afire out there on that deck." He pointed as the flaming paper descended over the railing.

Jack followed the fiery trail and then retraced his visual steps until they rested on the gentleman with the silver hair. He allowed his gaze to slowly scan the table, coming to rest on the man's companion. His mouth fell open, much like Ali's had just moments before.

"You look like you've seen a ghost," Skipper prodded.

"I may have." Jack's voice was barely audible.

Skipper smiled. "Looks pretty lively to me. Darn lively."

Ali propped her elbows on the table and leaned close to Joe. Jack felt a surge of jealousy rip through his stomach. "It's her."

"That's what I thought." Skipper took a sip of his beer. "Sat there at that same table with Ali last August."

Jack glared at him. "What did you say?"

"I had dinner with her, right there at that table." Skipper picked up a piece of cheese from the hor d'oeuvres plate being passed around. "She interviewed me for the magazine article."

"Oh." Jack turned his attention back to the deck, letting his eyes follow the contours of Ali's cheeks before coming to rest on the corner of her lips. His loins ached as he remembered kissing them.

"You ought to go over and say 'hi' to her," Skipper nudged.

"She looks occupied," Jack responded, with a tinge of jealousy in his voice.

"No harm in reacquainting yourselves," Skipper taunted.

"Her companion might not think so." Jack hung his head. "Kate said she wasn't here."

"You believe that old witch?" Skipper chuckled.

"She wouldn't have said it if Ali hadn't made it clear that she didn't want to see me."

"That might not be the case. You know how conniving Kate can be."

Jack pondered Skipper's remark as he watched Ali's every move. She smiled and then laughed, pausing for a moment to wipe her eye. It caused him to imagine all sorts of things.

"Gus says she's becoming quite a fisherwoman."

Jack studied Skipper's face. "Did you know she was here?"

"Saw her a time or two." Skipper picked up his burger and took a big bite.

"Why didn't you say anything?" Jack glared at Skipper.

"Didn't know you were interested," Skipper paused. "Until now, that is."

Jack felt like fleeing and crawling into his cave again, to hide from the world and those in it, as he had for the past few years. The feeling was quickly replaced by a heaviness that kept him seated in his chair.

"Rumor has it she and Gus are fishing the tournament," Skipper added.

"Thanks for the warning. I'll bow out now."

"You can't do that. We got a wager."

Jack sipped his beer, keeping his eyes firmly fixed on Ali.

"What would it hurt to say 'hello' to her?" Skipper chuckled at Jack's lack of response. "Don't tell me I'm going to have to start calling you Captain Wuss."

After finishing the meal, Ali wrapped her pashmina around her shoulders. "I'll be right back." She brushed her hand across Joe's shoulder as she walked by, maneuvering between the two rows of tables on the deck. She opened the glass door and entered the main section of the restaurant. She walked intently across the room, averting her gaze from other diners. Her conversation with Joe and his surprising pyretic act left her feeling vulnerable. She pondered the vision of the flaming contract floating down into the bay as she ascended the two steps to the entryway before turning into the ladies' room.

It took her only a moment of being alone to realize she felt relieved. She now had options. She nodded to her reflection before reapplying her plum-colored lipstick. Squaring her shoulders, she stashed the tube back into her purse and whirled around. Two steps out of the door, she came face-to-face with Jack Cooper. Her eyes widened at the sight of him.

"Ali, I saw you from across the room." He stuck his hands in the pocket of his shorts, looking sheepish.

"I'm here with a friend." She glanced toward the table, where she and Joe were sitting, hoping the diversion would calm her wildly beating heart.

He nodded. "I noticed."

Her mind whirled. She had imagined meeting him for the first time over and over. But it wasn't anything like this. In her reveries, she was never caught unaware.

"I heard you might be in town."

Ali eyed him suspiciously. "There didn't seem to be any need to make that fact known." The tone in her voice was sharp.

"I deserve that," Jack said apologetically.

Pausing, she allowed herself to peer into his eyes. Her resolve to maintain her distance began crumbling.

"I'm sorry." He touched her arm, sending a jolt of energy straight to her heart.

She clenched her jaw to keep the tears at bay. The room seemed to fade around them. Her heart beat rapidly, as his words echoed through her mind.

"There you are, my dear," Joe appeared at her side and smiled gallantly at Jack. "A friend?"

Startled, Ali jumped, much like a lover caught in a clandestine meeting. After regaining her composure, she said, "Joe Driscoll, I'd like you to meet Captain Jack Cooper."

Joe extended his hand. "Captain Cooper, so nice to meet you in person. I feel like I've come to know much about you from reading in Ali's article."

Jack shook the man's hand, regarding him with disdain.

Joe turned his attention to Ali. "We must be going." He nodded to Jack. " Again, it was a pleasure to meet you."

Ali averted her gaze from Jack as Joe escorted her from the building, with his hand gently touching her back. The whole scene seemed surreal, as if she were watching a movie, instead of acting in her own life.

# Chapter Twenty-One

Jack drove slowly through the village. There was no need to be concerned with the speed limit. He had no desire to go fast. For the first time in ages, he dreaded going home to an empty house. Tonight, he knew it would feel emptier. In the past few weeks, the prospect of reuniting with Ali gave him hope. He'd written her letters that had yet to be sent. He called her office—and left voice mails, only to erase them when given the chance. The right words just didn't seem to come together, but he thought that they would. He thought he had time. Tonight, that dream seemed dashed. The image of Joe Driscoll's hand on her back smacked him like a 2 x 4.

His cell phone rang, ending the painful vision. As he fumbled for it on the seat next to him, he ran a red light. Glancing at the caller ID, he failed to see the flashing lights in his rearview mirror.

"Hey, Skipper."

"You al right?" The tone in his voice sounded unusually concerned.

A siren sounded, and Jack glanced up in the mirror.

"Going downhill fast. I'll call you later." He pulled to the side of the road.

"What's the matter?"

"I think I just ran a stoplight."

"You have all the luck."

"Don't I though." Jack signed off and rolled down his window, awaiting the next assault.

\* \* \*

Ali said not one word on the way back to Kate's. Joe allowed her the space for her thoughts. He had his own. He saw the look in Jack Cooper's eyes. He knew it well. He'd been the other man many times over. More than he cared to admit. The images of his more youthful days played one by one in his mind. He loved all of the women, but he was never able to commit to just one. He could have chosen differently. The woman sitting next to him would have made a great partner. He'd considered the possibility. But she was too available, too perfect for him. He would have destroyed the love that they did share. His choices had brought him to this place. They had left him a lonely man—successful, powerful, but still lonely.

He chanced a look at Ali. Over the piano music playing on the stereo, he heard her sniffle. He hated to see her in pain, always had. But if all went well, perhaps it would be short-lived. Tonight, he played his role to the hilt, but not for his own reward. He knew a man like Jack Cooper needed to be shaken into action. His photos depicted a man who had been lulled into complacency by life's challenges. Joe saw it in his eyes. He'd visited that psychic space in his own life on occasion. Reviewing the scene at the restaurant once again, there seemed to be something different in Jack Cooper's eyes this evening, for which he was grateful. Ali deserved to have a strong man in her life.

\* \* \*

Once home, Joe and Ali stepped quietly into the entryway. She turned and gave him a peck on the cheek. "Thank you for a lovely evening."

Joe held her hand. "The pleasure was all mine, my dear." He gave her a hug. "Sleep well."

Ali tiptoed into her room and looked into the crib at her sleeping daughter. She resisted the urge to touch her cheek for fear of waking her. She needed some time alone. Draping her dress onto the chair, she took her pajamas off the back of her door. After changing, she lay on her bed, staring at the ceiling; the events of the evening playing over in her mind, again and again. Joe burning the contract was the first startling act, seconded only by the chance of meeting with Jack.

She reached for the rosary on her nightstand. She'd taken to praying with it. The Holy Mother had of late been her only comfort, as was the Laguna Madre—the Mother Lagoon. She closed her eyes and touched the first rose-shaped gold bead. She'd bought the rosary in Mexico several weeks before when she and Kate went shopping for more dinnerware. It hadn't been her intention, but the gold and crystal beads beckoned her as she passed the jewelry counter.

As her reverie continued, her mind instantly shot back to the day on the bay with Jack, when the feeling first awakened in her that the Laguna Madre was more than a body of water. She was an entity in and of herself—and a powerful one. She seemed to have some teaching to bestow upon Ali. She'd been resisting it for some time. But that Divine Feminine essence had been working on her. It's what drew her back here in the first place. And it's what cracked her shell on the day she witnessed the murder of the tern.

Tears ran down Ali's cheeks. She didn't know much about surrender. That meant losing control. But she knew she had no strength to hold on any longer. She felt exposed to forces far greater than she had known existed, and the intensity was frightening. The words of the Hail Mary formed on her lips. "Holy Mary, Mother of God, pray for us sinners, now and at the hour of our death. Amen." After a pause, she added, "Show me how to surrender with your kindness and love."

Burying her face in her hands so as not to wake Grace, years of regret and sadness crashed down around Ali. She was so determined to be strong, so unlike her mother, who fell prey to a man not worthy of her love and who in the end was the cause of her demise. And in some ways, Ali's too. Trust came hard. Most of all, trusting herself and her wisdom was the toughest of all to accept. She feared being like her mother, and that fear attracted the men and the circumstances that derailed Ali time and time again, despite her warrior-like stance move on after being so greatly disappointed in her relationships. *It's time to learn a different way.*

This was the hour of her death, the death of the woman she had become or thought she should be. As the grief poured from her heart, her sobs shook her violently, wrenching her stomach until it ached. After a time, she became silent and slipped between the covers. With her eyes closed, she lie there, feeling nothing but a pleasant numbness, a void she had never in her life been aware could exist. And beneath, there was peace. The feeling diminished as she became aware of a palpable presence in the room. She opened her eyes, and the room was aglow, as was every cell of her being. And for the first time in her life, she felt supreme comfort as if she were snuggled in the embrace of a mother's arms, arms that would always be there for her.

As Ali surrendered to sleep, she had a knowing, more than a thought, more than intuition. It was as if it came directly from the Divine. Leaving the Laguna Madre, fleeing with her daughter, back to her life in Virginia, back to the safety of what was known, would be wrong. She knew she had to stay, at least for a bit longer, until the teaching of the Mother Lagoon had been conveyed upon her. To dismiss its importance would breach a covenant far more meaningful than her promise to Joe to return to Virginia. He'd seen that, for which she was grateful. She owed it to Grace to remain. More so, she owed it to herself.

* * *

Gus and Kate walked back and forth from the kitchen to the dining table, clearing the remains of their breakfast. They were lost in their own thoughts, both fearing that Ali's departure was imminent, but hoping otherwise. Neither had seen either Joe or Ali upon their return from dinner. And neither had they heard from Skipper.

Kate stood before the sink, washing and rinsing the dishes methodically. Occasionally, she paused to stare out the window overlooking the Arroyo.

"Got a read on it?" Gus ventured to ask.

"Something big happened last night." She turned, wiping her hands on her apron. "Not sure which way it went though," She reached for another stack of dishes. "You heading to the marina?"

He nodded. "Have to wait until the afternoon. Skipper's most likely out on the bay."

"Dang it, Gus." Kate's face was flushed. "Call him on the cell phone."

"I hate calling people when they're working."

"This is important."

"Patience, Kate." He picked up a dishtowel and began drying. "Let's see what Joe says. He should be up soon."

"They got in awful late." Kate sighed. "I thought I heard Ali crying."

"Grace will get her up soon."

Kate agreed. "Yes, but if she's in a mood, Ali will just stay up there until she's ready to come down."

"Maybe we can lure her down. You can feign like you're sick or something."

"Gus Lammons, I am not going to do that." She shook her head and put the last of the plates in the stack. "Leave them. Let's go on the porch and have more coffee."

Once settled onto the wicker chairs, Kate touched her rosary, moving her lips to the prayers she knew so well. Gus stared at the water, before the sitting became too much. He jumped from his chair abruptly, startling Kate from her meditation.

"Where are you going?"

"To the boat, to my gardens." His hand shook as he picked his ball cap up from the table and placed it on his head. "I just can't stand sitting around here anymore." He returned his attention to the water. "You know what I wish? I wish she would just leave. Today. If that's what she really wants. Why prolong the agony, especially for you or me." He turned and pounded his fist on the table. "If you ask me, Kate, she's nothing but a spoiled child, and I'm tired of coddling her. I wish she'd never have come here in the first place."

Ali froze in the living room, with Grace perched on her hip. Gus's words pierced her heart. She closed her eyes and allowed them to touch her deeply. When she opened her eyes, she witnessed Gus wiping a tear from his eye. Kate offered no defense. Ali knew one couldn't be made.

She walked forward and opened the door. Gus and Kate stared, mouths agape, as she stood in the doorway. Gus blushed. "I'm sorry, Ali."

Holding up her hand, she said, "No need. You spoke the truth." She stepped forward and sat next to Kate, allowing Grace to play with a spoon left on the table. As the child banged the table, Gus joined the ladies, clasping his hands as they rested on the mosaic surface. "I deserve everything you said, and I deserve your anger." She looked into Gus's eyes. "I'm the one who is sorry."

"It's just that we love you, Ali—and little Grace, and it's going to hurt like heck when you leave. For both of us," Gus offered.

"I've decided to stay." She averted her attention to Grace, smoothing the child's light brown hair down on the back of her head. "If you'll have me."

"For how long?" Kate asked cautiously.

Ali shook her head. "I haven't a clue." She sighed. "I haven't seen the rest of the script. But I do know that this is the chance for me to learn how to receive love and not worry it's going to be taken away or that I don't deserve it." She choked back her tears. "There's something I need to share with you."

She paused, momentarily to survey Gus and then Kate. She kissed the top of Grace's head as if to summon courage. "I grew up without my mother and my father. He died in prison where he was serving a life sentence for murdering my mother."

Kate gasped. Gus shook his head silently.

"I was a little older than Grace when I crawled through the blood seeping from the back of my mother's head. There were suitcases by the door. My grandparents were heading over to pick us up and save us from my father's torture. He'd beaten my mother repeatedly. Somehow I had been spared."

Tears were now steaming down Ali's face, and she paused to look out over the Arroyo. Joe stood in the doorway, witness to the testimony.

"Through the years, while my grandparents loved me, I didn't know how to receive their love. I was angry—at my mother, my father, and God. I survived all these years by building a cage around myself, and only a few were allowed inside. Most of the time, I chose badly when it came to men, and that drove me to hide behind my work. It was easier."

She took a deep breath and gazed at Kate and then Gus. "I think it's time I learned how to let people love me so I can really show this little girl what it's like to be loved."

"A wise choice," Kate smiled and touched Ali's hand. *"Mi casa, su casa*, my dear."

"Hallelujah," Gus slapped his knee. "I knew there was a God." He glanced at Kate, Grace, and then Ali. "I'm sorry you've had to go through such terrible things in your life. But I promise you, Ali, You and Grace are always welcome here—in our houses and in our hearts."

Ali felt years of tension melt away, as her vulnerability took center stage, perhaps for the first time in her life.

Joe stepped out onto the porch. "Seems I'm missing out on a meaningful conversation."

Ali looked up at him. "You'll have to return to Virginia alone, my friend." She winked. "I've got a tournament to fish."

Gus squeezed Kate's arm tightly. "Our girls are staying!"

Kate beamed. "I heard Gus. I was sitting right here." She rose from her chair. Silently, the words "Thank you" crossed her lips as she looked at Joe. She cleared her throat. "I say it's time I fix another breakfast."

# Chapter Twenty-Two

**D**awn was an hour away when Ali made the trek from the porch to the boat. A single light illuminated the dock, shrouding the skiff in a mystical glow. Gus was aboard, stowing food in the ice chest, and checking the lights. He looked up as Ali stepped onto the dock. "You all set?"

She handed him her rod and gear bag. For an instant, she flashed back to the first time she did the same with Jack. It was a cause to pause and feel his presence once again. This time she didn't run from it. Without him, she would not have Grace. She took a deep breath as she looked up at the sky, a lone bright star twinkled above her. "As I'm ever going to be."

"Well, let's get going then." Ali unhooked the rope and took her place next to Gus, allowing him to take the helm. She needed the time to be quiet, to finish her prayers, and align herself with the force of the Mother Lagoon. Her success depended on it.

The motor started, sending a reverberating "putt, putt, putt" through the early morning silence. The night herons in the neighbor's tree squawked their displeasure as Gus eased the boat off the ramp. Once clear of the dock, he punched the throttle. "Trout Bar, here we come. Yeehaw."

For a moment, she wondered how her fate ever brought her to deep South Texas and into the lives of Gus Lammons, Kate McGregor, and the man who made one of her most cherished dreams come true. She never saw it coming. And she wasn't sure she'd believe it if a psychic had laid the vision before her. It seemed all too bizarre and so far from the life she was used to leading.

She sipped her tea, pulling the collar of her jacket around her neck to protect it from the salty air rushing at them as they boated along the Arroyo. Gus, too, was quiet, seemingly lost in his own thoughts. He never was much for idle chit chat, for which Ali was grateful this morning. An uneasiness was working on her. If she was at the helm, she might just turn back for the dock. Slowly, the feeling subsided as Gus maneuvered the boat into the mouth of the Arroyo and veered north. The same path she and Jack had taken on her first day on the Mother Lagoon.

Her time in South Texas was about to come full circle, and Ali had no clue what the fates held in store for the next phase of her life. Her stomach tightened, warning her that it most likely depended upon this tournament and how she responded to the tests that Mother Lagoon set forth for her. She held that thought in mind as Gus pulled the boat off the channel, and she prepared to embrace her first challenge of the day.

Shrouded in darkness, Ali slipped from the boat and entered the water, feeling the chill of the water seep through her pants. A faint glow illuminated Green Island, where the morning songs of gulls, egrets, and terns echoed across the flats.

"Ten minutes to starting time," Gus called from the boat. "Remember, stand still. Let Grandmother Trout get used to your presence. Do that yoga stuff or whatever you do."

Smiling at Gus's comment, she nodded, knowing he most likely couldn't see her response. She did as she was told. Closing her eyes, she said a prayer asking for protection from the stingrays, and for her child and Kate back at the lodge, and for Gus. Her throat tightened, realizing how blessed she really was. She belonged here. She now knew that. She sighed and an intense weight lifted from her shoulders. She returned her attention to the fishing and aligned herself with her intended quarry for the day. "Mr. Redfish, be with me," she whispered. "Mr. Flounder, grace me with your presence." She took a deep breath. "And Grandmother Trout, bring to me your highest teaching, as only you can."

While she hated taking any life, she knew that God had put these creatures on the planet to provide not only physical sustenance but spiritual teachings as well. Over the course of interacting with these inhabitants of the Mother Lagoon, she understood that any fish that took her fly that day had made a sacred contract to offer themselves to her. And not only for her. All of the fish from the tournament were to be served at a dinner for the area homeless. Then, as she relaxed, her vision sharpened in the growing light, and her hearing became acutely sensitive to the distinct sounds of trout smacking the water as they fed.

"It's time," Gus announced. "Go gettum, girl."

Minutes passed as Ali slowly waded away from the tip of the spoil island, carefully eyeing the surface of the water for the telltale black triangle. She watched as schools of mullet streamed off the channel. *Go toward the channel marker.* Heeding the voice, she angled to the left, blind casting as she continued her wade. She felt the tug on her line, and she strip-set the hook, but the tension immediately eased. "Oooh."

"What happened?" Gus stood on the bow of the boat.

"Missed one."

"Keep at it. It's still early." He wrung his hands. "Call her in."

*Grandmother Trout, be with me.* A surge of energy moved through her. Once again, her awareness heightened, shutting out everything but the inhabitants of the water around her. She only vaguely noticed the cries of the gulls, making their way inland. The din of far-off boats reminded her that she was not alone on the water or in this contest. But they were a mere ripple on her consciousness as she remained calmly focused.

Out of the corner of her eye, something caught her attention. She turned her head slowly, scanning the water as she swept her gaze in the direction of the movement. There, the black tail of a trout came fully out of the water. *Here I am.* Ali whirled around, careful not to make a noise. She made one false cast and let her black topwater fly sail through the air. It landed inches from the trout's head. Time stood still. A trance overcame Ali as the trout's head came out of the water and nabbed the fly. Her heart raced, keeping time with the trout's flight toward the channel.

"What is it?" Gus yelled.

"It's the Grandmother." Ali reeled the excess line onto her spool. "Keep her tight."

Ali knew that if she lost the tension, the trout would slip from the hook. The trout ceased her run, and Ali took the opportunity to reel her in, facing resistance she had never experienced on the end of her line before. Her rod bent dramatically. Her mind whirled with the possibilities. She knew the area well and wasn't aware of any structure that could snag her line.

"She won't budge, Gus." Ali stepped forward, moving any slack in her line to the reel.

"She's buried herself in the grass." Gus paced the edge of the boat. "Keep on her." He took his cap off and swept his hand over his head.

A boat zoomed by on the channel, sending a high wake toward Ali. Waves lapped to the top of her thighs, making her lose her footing. She stumbled backward. "Shit."

"Daggum it." Gus shook his fist at the boaters. "Your mama didn't teach you any manners. Slow down!"

The trout darted toward Ali. She watched as the bow in her rod lessened. She frantically reeled to keep the line tight.

"You're not going to do this to me." She said aloud, as she took several steps backward, praying that no stingrays were in her mud trail.

She held her rod high, as the trout banged into her legs. She thrust her hand onto the back of the trout's head. Struggling to tuck the rod under her arm, Ali's heart raced.

"You okay?" Gus was floating the boat toward her, steering it with the pole.

Ali said a silent prayer of thanks, as she raised her up to show Gus while he eased the boat to a halt. "What do you think?"

He whistled. "Five pounds." He dug into the console. "Let's weigh her." He reached down and clipped the end of the BogaGrip to the trout's mouth and then handed the scale to Ali. "Looks like five and a half to me."

"Is that good?"

"I'd say she's a keeper." They had agreed before leaving that trout five pounds and over would be kept. The rest would be released, even if she returned to the dock empty-handed.

Ali handed the trout to Gus, watching as he placed the fish reverently into the ice chest. He removed his hat, holding it over his heart, and closed his eyes. She scooted onto the deck of the boat. "Thanks, Gus."

He turned to her, with tears glistening in his eye. "No, thank you, Ali." He took a handkerchief from his pocket and blew his nose. "Enough of this. Time to go after your redfish."

The day passed, and Ali achieved greater success than she had dreamed possible. By the time they eased into the dock, she had a redfish that weighed over six pounds and a three-pound flounder, in addition to the trout. Kate paced the edge of the seawall, with Grace in her stroller, as the boat came to a halt and Gus killed the engine.

"How'd you do?" Kate inquired, a look of concern etched into her brow.

Gus beamed. "Over thirteen pounds out on the water." He glanced at his watch. "No time to dally. We need to get to the weigh-in before these fish dry up and lose a couple of pounds."

Grace began crying at the sight of her mama. Ali reached into the stroller and picked up her daughter. "Do I have a couple of minutes to feed her?" She strode up the hill toward the house. "My breasts are so full."

"Ten minutes." Gus hauled the ice chest from the boat. "I'll meet you in the truck. Gotta put fresh ice on these fish."

Ali took a seat on the wicker chair and unbuttoned her wet fishing shirt. "Sorry, sweetie. Mama's kind of dirty and smelly right now."

"Didn't you pump?" Kate asked, surprised.

Ali shook her head. "There wasn't any time."

"That's what I call tending to the task at hand." She patted Ali's shoulder as she moved to the door. "I'll get you something to drink and a snack."

✳ ✳ ✳

Forty minutes later, Gus pulled into the marina parking lot in Port Isabel. "You two go on ahead. I'll bring the baby along." Kate shooed them onward. "Good luck. We'll be rooting for you."

Opening the tailgate of the truck bed, Gus took one side of the ice chest and Ali the other. As they walked along, she reached into her pocket and pulled out her Tournament ID. She waved it at the checkpoint as she joined the line of anglers waiting to be weighed in. She nervously scanned the crowd. "Think he'll be here?" She peered at Gus, her eyes concealed by her sunglasses, and her face shielded by her teal trucker cap.

"Most likely." Gus scanned the dozens of faces, some reddened by the wind and the sun, all looking weary from the day on the water. "I'll take a swing about. Looks like Skipper's coming in." He pointed to the seawall, as the blue skiff came to rest. Ali's heart raced, knowing that Jack might not be far behind. She honestly didn't know what she'd say to him if he approached her again.

She moved along in the line and came to the measuring table. She opened the ice chest and lovingly placed each fish on the surface. "Twenty-seven and three-quarter inches." The man behind the counter yelled out as he measured the redfish. The trout came next. "Twenty-five inches." The flounder followed. "Nineteen inches."

The t-shirted man, sporting the tournament logo, said, "Nice going. Best I've seen yet."

Ali's heart skipped a beat.

"Let's see how much they weigh." He handed the fish to the next person in line, and the weights were called out in succession.

"I want you on my boat next time." Skipper's voice startled Ali, and she whirled around. He extended his hand. "Congratulations. I didn't come up close to that." He gestured toward the seawall. "Let's see how Jack has done."

Ali watched as Jack hoisted his ice chest to land. Gus came along and placed Ali's fish in the ice chest. "Better move out of this line, so the other folks can weigh in." Stepping aside, Ali rested her eyes upon Jack.

"Buy you a beer?" Skipper asked.

She shook her head. "No, thanks. Better be going. " She reached down and picked up her end of the ice chest. "Let's go, Gus."

He glanced at Skipper and shrugged. Looking over his shoulder, Gus caught Jack's eye and tipped his hat briefly.

Ali kept her eyes averted, knowing that Jack was watching her every move. She could feel him, his gaze sinking beneath her skin, sending a jolt of energy through her much like Grandmother Trout had that very morning. It was unsettling, and she did her best to push him from her mind.

Kate met up with them by the bleachers. Grace was in her stroller, with a bright pink balloon tied to the seat. "How about getting some supper here? They've got hot dogs and pizza."

"I want to go home." Ali quipped. The steely resistance so familiar to her was forming its fortress around her heart.

Kate touched Ali's forearm. "He knows you're here. He's looking right at you."

"Great. Think it will take him long to question whose baby this is?"

"He's got a right to know."

"I'm not ready." She set the ice chest down and hung her head, one hand placed on her hip. "I've got to concentrate on this tournament."

Kate's straw hat shielded her face from the afternoon sun. "Maybe this tournament is about more than catching fish."

Ali's hand dropped to her side. She sighed. Her resistance melted. "I can't go up to him in this crowd."

Kate glanced at Grace, and then at Gus, and then at Jack. She held his gaze for a moment and nodded her head. "Fair enough."

✳ ✳ ✳

Jack inched along in the line, scooting the ice chest with his foot. He occasionally glanced over his shoulder, hoping he'd see Ali coming toward him. Yet, he knew it was a wish that might never come true.

"Looking for someone?" Skipper appeared at his side and handed him a beer. "She turned me down."

"What?" Jack looked puzzled.

"I offered to buy her a beer, and she turned me down." Skipper clutched his heart. "Not sure if I can stand this rejection much more."

Jack rolled his eyes. "What did she weigh-in?"

"Thirteen, two, and three-quarters." He glanced at Jack's ice chest. "How much you got?"

"Maybe twelve."

Skipper chuckled. "Should be an interesting day, *mañana.*"

# Chapter Twenty-Three

A loud clap of thunder shook the house, startling Ali out of a deep sleep. Grace, too, was awakened and began to cry. Ali reached for the light, only to find that the electricity had gone off. As she picked the baby up from the crib, a bright flash of light illuminated the room, followed immediately by another thunderous clap.

"You okay?" Kate peeked her head around the door.

"Just a little startled."

"Not a good sign for the day."

"What time is it?" Ali sunk back onto the bed, holding Grace close to her breast.

"Around four."

Ali groaned. Every bone and muscle in her body ached.

"You won't be going any place right quick." Kate sat in the rocker chair next to the crib. "Forecast calls for showers all day." Another crack echoed through the room. "Not sure they predicted this, though."

"Ali? Kate?" Gus's voice floated into the room.

"Up here."

A flash of lightning lit up Gus's face as he entered the room.

"What do you think, Gus?" Ali didn't like the pit in her stomach.

He paused, and Ali could see him take a deep breath. He held his hat in his hands, slipping the brim back and forth between his fingers. "I say we wait until dawn before we decide. Better get ready, though."

"I'll finish feeding Grace and be down." She looked at her daughter's face, pondering the day ahead. She furrowed her brow, unable to contain her worry about leaving her daughter.

"I'll get breakfast ready." Kate rose from the chair, pausing to regard Ali and Grace. "I wouldn't let you go out if I thought anything bad would come of it."

"I know, Kate." A weak smile crossed Ali's lips. "I'm just feeling something, and I can't put words to it. It feels big."

She wished for Joe's presence and reassuring words. Yet, his absence seemed to be the vote of confidence she needed. She was on her own. He essentially had kicked her out of the nest, trusting that she had made the right decision. Bleu, too, had urged her to make a choice for herself. Not as a way to ward off the past, but as a way to embrace a new future. Now she had to trust herself and her decisions, particularly this morning—on whether to fish or stay onshore. *This is about more than the fishing.*

The lights flickered on and off a couple of times before staying on.

"Say a few prayers while you're sitting there. It'll make you feel better." Kate reassured as she left the room.

Twenty minutes later, dressed in her tan pants and a bright blue fishing shirt, Ali sauntered downstairs, with her arms full of Grace and her fishing tote and hat. She reached the archway between the living room and dining room and placed Grace in her swing. The bright-eyed little girl happily sucked her fist and occasionally giggled as she propelled herself into the air by kicking her feet against the floor. Ali continued into the kitchen, plopping her gear bag on the dining table as she passed by. She stopped at the coffee pot and poured the dark, steaming liquid into a large mug.

"No tea?" Kate looked up from flipping an omelette.

"I need a jumpstart this morning." She groaned. "I don't think I've ever been so tired."

"Just a few more hours and this will be behind you." Kate slipped the omelet onto two dishes. "You might just out fish these South Texas rednecks. Show them a thing or two." Kate grinned as she placed two pieces of toast next to each slice of omelette. "I can see it now, not only a lady but a Yankee lady at that."

"I must admit I like the sound of that," Ali chuckled.

"Time to eat up then." Kate shooed her toward the table.

Gus burst through the back door. "Boat's all ready." He hung his raincoat on the doorknob. "Now all we have to do is wait for a little cooperation from Mother Nature."

Ali took a bite of her egg, as Gus settled into his chair, and poured a couple dashes of hot sauce on his eggs.

"What's the plan?" Ali sipped her coffee while waiting for his reply.

"I ain't got one."

Ali's eyes widened. "Great."

"Just gonna have to go with the flow today." Gus piled the egg on his toast and took a bite. "But that's all we ever do. Ain't really nothing different, except today we have a little rain put in the mix." He wiped his lips with a blue cloth napkin, and then glanced first at Kate and then Ali. "Storms all around us. Might not let up according to the weather bureau." He took a swig of coffee and then looked pointedly at Ali. "We don't have to do this." His eyes held a look of concern.

Ali ran her hand through her hair and stared off into space. She closed her eyes and rubbed her temple, her lips moving in silent prayer. A mantle of comfort wrapped around her, followed by a surge of energy up the back of her neck and around to the crown of her head. She opened her eyes, gazing first at Grace, then Kate, stopping with Gus. "We'll do it." She stood up and took her plate to the kitchen. "I'll be ready in ten minutes."

"Last one to the boat is a rotten egg," Gus quipped, before taking another swig of his coffee.

✳ ✳ ✳

Ali stood at the helm of the boat, steering the skiff northward at the mouth of the Arroyo. Their plan was to fish the edge of the west side of the channel for half an hour and then cross over into Peyton's Bay, counting on tailing reds.

Surveying the Trout Bar, she noted three boats had already staked their claim, as Gus predicted. There was no way to squeeze into a spot without causing an outcry from the anglers. Traveling several hundred yards up the channel, they passed Woody's Hole. A lone skiff was staked in the center of the lagoon, preventing passage into the south end of Peyton's.

"Look's like Jack got out early." Gus pointed to the boat.

Her heart skipped a beat as she spotted a lone fisher casting elegantly in the morning light. They continued onward for another mile and pulled off to the left side of the channel. Game fish was crashing bait along the edge, sending small minnows scurrying along the surface of the water. "Good sign," Gus said as he hoisted the anchor from beneath the deck.

Ali snapped on her stripping basket and her fanny pack. Taking her rod from the rod holder anchored behind the seat, she rechecked her knots and her tippet. All was in place. In the distance, a rumble of thunder echoed across the morning sky.

"I'll keep an eye on the storms. You fish."

She saluted him. "Aye, aye, captain."

"Another day like yesterday, and you'll have it in the bag."

She glanced at the sky. "It's not like yesterday," she said, as she slipped into the water. The morning air was thick with humidity, so much so that she left her light fleece hoodie on board.

Wading carefully to the edge of the channel, she proceeded to blind cast to the right and to the left, relying on her backcast to help her cover more water. She pulled in several trout, between the sixteen to twenty-inch range, letting each go free. As promised, she'd keep nothing smaller than the trout she caught the day before.

The sky grew dim as she reached the channel. She glanced toward the north and to the east. A storm was brewing, and it appeared to be wrapping around them to the south as well. She shot a look at Gus. He studied the sky, sharing her concern. "Fish," he called out. "We got a little time."

Ali cast over the edge of the channel and retrieved the fly without so much as a hit. She stripped it back in and checked the fly, making sure it wasn't wrapped around the tippet. She sent the white and black topwater sailing through the air and stripped the line back. A loud bolt of lightning in the distance sent a shiver through her bones. An instant later, she had a strike on her fly. Instinctively, she set the hook, and the chase was on. The fish turned and headed for deeper water. Another crack of thunder followed, and it began sprinkling.

Gus pulled the stake and began drifting toward her. The extra fly rods in the holder were humming from the static electricity in the air. "Bring her in fast."

Ali applied pressure to the fish, reeling whenever she sensed the fish eased off on any attempt to escape. Her heart raced as another clap of thunder rumbled through the morning air. The sky grew darker with each passing moment.

"Better bring her in or break her off," Gus called out.

Ali took a reading of the situation, tuning first into her body for a hint of intuition and then looking at the sky. Taking a deep breath, she whispered to the fish. "Come on, Grandmother. Teach me what I came to learn." She knew instantly she would not break off intentionally. She steadily applied pressure and walked toward the fish, reeling with each step. A bright flash lit up the sky. The fish was within reach. Gus closed in with the boat. "Now, Ali." The rods were humming loudly, and the hair on the back of his neck stood on end.

The boat was within two feet of her when Ali landed the fish. She raised it out of the water, handing it to Gus. He clipped the tippet and threw the trout into the ice chest. Ali hoisted herself onto the deck as a bolt of lightning streaked across the sky, followed within seconds by a clap of thunder.

"Damn that was close," Gus said as he started the motor, and Ali placed her rod in the holder. "We better take refuge at Smitty's place." He pointed to a white shack a hundred yards south of them on the other side of the channel. He maneuvered the boat across the choppy waters, with white caps spraying them as they made their way across the deeper water. Ali slipped on her turquoise rain jacket and then carefully inched toward the front of the boat, holding first to the console, then to the ice chest in front of it. Beneath the casting platform on the bow of the boat, lay their tie rope. She needed to have it in her hands as they approached the shack. Taking a deep breath, she lunged toward the platform, keeping it sharply in focus. A wave lobbed the boat, sending her sprawling to the deck and landing hard on her right elbow. She groaned as she grabbed the platform with her left hand and pulled herself to her knees.

"You okay?" Gus yelled over the din of the motor and the crashing waves.

"Yes," she shouted, hoping that the blow to her elbow wouldn't affect her casting for the rest of the day. She eased onto the platform, with the rope poised in her hand. Gus directed the boat to the backside of the shack. Ali slipped the noose of the rope around a piling and then hopped onto the walkway. Standing beneath the overhang, she glanced around at her surroundings. The doors and windows were boarded and padlocked. Peregrine castings were scattered under various perching spots on the eaves, and the edges of the walkway were covered in gull and pelican droppings. The aroma was far from appealing.

"We better hunker down in that corner." Gus pulled on his rain gear. "This might not be much fun."

"That's comforting." Ali sunk down into the corner, pulling her legs close to her chest. She wrapped her hands around her knees and began to pray. The light show continued, and the sky turned an eerie green, a sure sign of tornado activity.

"I don't like the looks of that." He handed Ali her cell phone. "Call Kate. See if we can make a run for it."

Ali dialed the number. Three rings chimed before Kate answered.

"Are you okay?" Kate sounded worried.

"A bit held up, I'd say." Ali offered. "What's it like there?"

"Terrible. Hasn't let up a bit since you left."

"Shit."

Gus raised a brow.

"We're surrounded," Ali said, with a catch in her voice.

"Tell her to call us if it lets up," Gus said.

"I heard." Kate replied.

"Take care of my baby, Kate."

"Ali, you listen to me. You're going to be all right. Just keep your wits about you."

A crash of thunder echoed in their corner. "Jesus."

"It might be nice to elicit his help," Kate quipped. "His mother as well."

An involuntary smile formed on Ali's lips. "We'll call you later." Ali stuffed the phone into her pocket and retrieved her rosary.

✳ ✳ ✳

Three miles south, a water spout was ripping through the flats and heading in a northwesterly direction. Jack had been warned. Skipper had seen it forming. As Jack waded toward the boat, he watched the monstrous formation heading his way. It was near the channel, and given its speed, Jack knew he'd never make it to his boat in time. Sizing up the situation, he made a dash for the spoil island. There was a small bluff to the west side, and he decided that terrain was the best cover.

The whirling sound of a freight train drew nearer, and the thunder and light ning continued with a vengeance. He dashed to the ground, tossing his rod far from him. The redfish and trout on his stringer struggled, as they lay beached alongside him. He clasped his hands behind his head and pressed his forehead against the cool sand. Rain pelted his back, stinging like buckshot through his rain gear.

Visions of being stoned flittered through his mind. But it wasn't his safety that most concerned him. Ali figured most in his thoughts. He had seen her and Gus traveling north. He hoped they had taken shelter, but he also knew that a shack was no match for this water spout.

The fifty-foot spinning cloud bounced along the channel and veered sharply to the left. It headed straight toward Jack's boat. It bounced twice on the white surface, snapping the pole that had held the boat firmly in place. The skiff spun around and was set free to find its own course up the channel. It altered the path of the water spout as well, sending it across the channel and in a more northerly direction.

Jack raised his head and watched as it hugged the edge of the east side of the channel, bouncing off several of the fishing shacks like a spinning top, and sending shards of wood and glass into the air. A streak of fear coursed through his body as the rain continued its assault. He watched the spout head toward where Gus and Ali were probably seeking shelter. There was nothing Jack could do but wait. He closed his eyes and placed his head against the cold wet sand, praying harder than he ever had in his life.

As sheets of rain pelted the flats of the Lower Laguna Madre, and dark clouds hung low in the sky, the hair on the back of Ali's neck stood on end. She had never remembered being more frightened in all her life. She knew that this adventure was far from over. In the distance, she noticed a strange sound approaching. It was like nothing she'd ever heard. "What's that noise?"

"Most likely a water spout." Gus struggled to his feet.

"What is a water spout?" Ali joined him, and together they walked around to the front of the shack and peered down the channel.

"A tornado on water."

Her knees buckled as she watched the twisting, dark funnel cloud roaring toward them. "How do we get out of this?"

"Pray." He jumped onto the boat and opened the door to the storage compartment beneath the deck. He pulled out a blue tarp and tossed it up to Ali. He, too, had a feeling about the day and, as a last-minute precaution, had stowed the tarp beneath the deck. "Get under this and hurry." He took one last glance toward the channel. "Holy Mary Mother of God. Be with us," he muttered as he scrambled to join Ali beneath the only protection they had from the monstrous formation heading their way.

"This will at least protect us a little from flying debris," he offered. "As long as we don't take a direct hit, we should be okay."

Ali clutched her rosary in both hands as her body shook with fear. "I won't leave my daughter."

Gus put his arms around her and held her close. "Just hold on tight."

The thunderous noise descended upon them, and the wind whipped the unsecured ends of the tarp. Sheets of rain bounced off their protective covering. Ali and Gus fell silent. Then suddenly, a whirling gust of wind whipped the tarp off of their heads. "Oh, God," she cried out. The rain pelted her face as she fought to regain her hold on the only thing protecting them from the elements. Gus struggled to do the same.

"It'll pass soon." Gus offered as he caught hold of his edge of the tarp. "Just hang on. Kate will be doing her magic for us."

"I hope so." Ali croaked, as she tucked the tarp beneath her. Her emotions twisted and turned inside of her at a dizzying pace. Silently she prayed, *I'll do anything you want. Just let me see my daughter again. Please.*

The deafening roar faded. Gus peeked his head out from beneath the covering. The sky was growing lighter, and the rain had lightened to a soft, steady shower. "I think we're out of the woods."

Shaking from fear, Ali got to her feet, stashing the tarp in the corner of the building. She followed Gus to the channel side of the shack, and they looked northward. The funnel cloud had jumped the channel and was heading northwest, with the town of Port Mansfield firmly in its sights. "Doesn't look too kindly for those folks," Gus said, and he turned around to survey the expansive horizon, now showing signs of blue sky between the light grey clouds. "I think we're out of the woods now."

Behind them, to the southeast, rays of sunshine were pouring through the dissipating clouds. "Let's venture to Woody's see if we can catch you a flounder." Gus made his way toward the boat. "Then we'll head to the sand, get you a redfish, maybe two."

Ali let his words settle into her consciousness. Part of her wanted to run home and hide for the rest of the day. But as she looked around at the blue sky spreading over the flats, she knew there was no reason to retreat. She took the helm of the boat and gently steered it back to the channel. Gus sat next to her, and they headed southward toward a spot Gus knew should produce a fine flounder. Soon, the aftermath of the storm would be nothing but a memory, and the redfish and even the trout would return to the open waters of the Lower Laguna, grubbing for worms and crabs as they cruised along a stretch of white sand along Padre Island.

As they approached Woody's Hole, a lone angler stood along the channel. Ordinarily, this would pose as no unusual sight, except he was missing his mode of transportation.

"Looks like Jack lost his boat." Gus pointed to the east side of the channel where a boat floated aimlessly. The winds had subsided, so there was no chance that it would reenter the channel and return to its master.

Ali's heart raced frantically as they approached. She came within fifty yards of him and could see Jack looking in their direction, but she hadn't yet slowed her pace.

"You gonna stop?" Gus questioned.

"I don't know." She was closing in on Jack quickly. As she struggled to make her decision, the gentle reminder that she'd promised to do anything to see her daughter again popped into her mind. Then, without warning, she pulled back on the throttle and steered toward him.

Jack reached out and grabbed hold of the bow, slowing the boat to a halt.

"Lose something, captain?" Gus hollered.

Jack shook his head. "A hell of a storm." He looked at Ali. "I'm glad to see you two weathered it nicely. I was worried."

"Aw, piece a cake," Gus said. "Right, Ali?"

Ali remained quiet, allowing the men to carry the conversation. Jack handed his stringer of fish to Gus. "Nice bunch of fish here." Gus opened the ice chest and lay the fish on top of Ali's trout.

Ali glanced first at the fish, then at Gus. Jack's trout was larger than hers by an inch.

Jack hoisted himself on board. He walked toward the helm of the boat. "Thanks for stopping."

"You better sit down so I can take you to your boat." She motioned to the ice chest, where Gus had already taken a seat. As she turned the steering wheel, the tips of her fingers brushed his shoulders. Struggling to remain centered amidst a whirlwind of emotions, she putted the boat across the channel. When near his craft, she killed the motor and allowed the skiff to gently float toward his.

With the agility of an antelope, he hopped over to his boat, his long legs easily making the leap. Gus sat on the bow and prevented the two from banging together. Jack started the motor and nodded his head. "That's a blessing."

Ali reached into the ice chest and pulled out his stringer of fish. She stood at the edge of her boat and extended her arm. Jack did likewise, bringing them once again face to face. "Appreciate the rescue," he said with a tender smile.

"See you at the weigh-in." She mirrored his smile.

He nodded. "Good luck."

"Thanks, you too." She returned to the helm, noticing that inwardly she was experiencing another tornado.

Gus pushed the boats apart, and Ali headed to the west side of the channel. She knew without turning that Jack's eyes were upon her. She could feel them burning through her flesh and once again, into her soul.

# Chapter Twenty-Four

Ali and Gus paraded past the growing crowd of spectators with her day's catch in hand. The smell of popcorn, pizza, and hot dogs filled the air. Lively pop music played over loudspeakers, intermittently interrupted by the announcement of a phenomenal catch. Kate walked along side of them, in her customary wide-brimmed straw hat, and a blue flowered cotton sundress, straying from her daily attire of cotton shirts and shorts. Grace was dressed in a matching sundress and sucked on her fist as they moved along. Occasionally, she pointed to a dog and voiced her comments in baby babble.

"You ladies sure look beautiful today," Ali offered.

"You look mighty pretty, Kate," Gus concurred.

"Cause for celebration, I'd say." Kate grinned. "Surviving a storm, Ali completing her first tournament. Who knows what else? Magic is in the air." She stopped at the foot of the bleachers. "You two hurry along. We'll be in the stands."

As she held her place in line, Ali inched her ice chest along with her foot. She was much calmer than the day before and most certainly a lot more at peace than she was earlier in the day. A shower and fresh change of clothes contributed to her ease, but she knew there was more. She glanced around the crowd, this time not fearing the sight of Jack Cooper, but hoping he'd be near. She didn't know how the change in her heart had taken place. It just had, and she was grateful.

She spotted Skipper at the front of the weigh-in line and waved. Gus stood near him, and the two were exchanging words. Ali turned to look at Kate and Grace in the stands. Her eyes falling upon her daughter. It did indeed seem like this tournament was about more than catching fish.

The length and weight of her fish were called out, and she signed her weigh-in card. She'd come up a few ounces short of 13 pounds. She strolled toward Gus and Skipper, leaning against the railing by the sea wall. "Take that beer?"

Ali smiled. "I'd love to."

"I'll fetch us one. Kate might want to join us." Gus chimed in and headed toward the concession stand.

"Heard you had a time of it today."

Ali nodded. "So did Jack."

"Heard that, too." Skipper paused and sized her up for a moment, chewing on his toothpick. "He was worried about you."

Ali acknowledged the information and then glanced around the crowd. The weigh-in line grew shorter.

"He's on his way." Skipper pulled his toothpick from his mouth. "Had to talk him into coming."

"Why?" She couldn't hide her concern.

"He saw that his trout was bigger than yours." Skipper studied her. "He's coming to claim his prize."

The words hung in the air as Gus and Kate approached. Grace cried out for her mother, and Ali reached down to pick her up out of the stroller. Grace voiced her pleasure by blowing bubbles around her fist.

"Looks a lot like her mama." Skipper touched the baby's cheek. "And a little like her daddy."

Ali glanced at Kate, who shrugged and then took a sip of her beer.

"Speakin' of the devil." Skipper looked in the direction of the bleachers. Jack was carrying the ice chest through the crowd. "I'd better give him a hand." He tipped his hat. "If you'd excuse me."

"Thanks for the beer," Ali said.

"Thank Gus. He paid for it."

"I'll take it out of your hide." Gus waved a crooked finger at Skipper. "Don't you worry."

\* \* \*

"Folks, Folks!" The announcer's voice boomed over the loudspeaker. "We're just about finished tallying the results of the 56th Annual Texas Fly Fishing Tournament. We've had some great fishing today, despite a few harrowing moments with a water spout that almost took out a handful of our anglers. Thankfully, no injuries were reported. A couple of boats went missing, but all made it back to port safe and sound." The applause sent the gulls flying off until it subsided. "Just a reminder. All of the fish are going to the charity fish fry. Volunteers are needed for tomorrow's event. The sign-up sheet is under the blue pavilion."

With Grace perched on her hips, Ali paced along the seawall, pointing to pelicans and seagulls, hoping to divert her own attention more than Grace's. Her stomach churned, making it impossible to finish her beer. She struggled to keep from finding Jack and introducing him to his daughter, which she knew was imminent.

"Now for the moment we've been waiting for." The man's voice lulled the crowd into a low murmur. "The results."

Ali returned to the stands, and as she approached, she noticed that Gus and Kate were holding hands. She raised an eyebrow and smiled at Kate as she took a seat next to her.

"They'll announce the junior divisions first."

Kate glanced at her. "You al right?"

"No," Ali said, with a shaking voice. "My stomach is in more knots now than it was during the storm."

Kate patted her hand. "It'll all work out just fine."

Grace became fussy, squirming in her mother's lap. "Got a bottle for her?" Gus asked.

"Some juice." Kate reached into the diaper bag and handed Gus the bottle.

"Give her to Grandpa Gus." He reached out and took the baby. "Your mama's got to claim her prize."

"Do you think I won?" Ali asked, with doubt.

"More than you realize," Kate said, as she handed Gus the bottle.

"And now for our final results. Third place with 25.7 pounds, Captain Skipper Jones." The crowd roared.

Still dressed in his salmon fishing shirt and dark green shorts, Skipper strode to the podium and accepted his plaque with a hearty handshake. He raised it over his head, sending the crowd into another frenzy. "Thanks, folks." He grinned his toothy smile.

"And now in second place. This was a tough call, folks, a real close one."

Butterflies took up residence in Ali's stomach.

"Ms. Ali Stephenson, with 26.3 pounds, and all three species on both days. And the first woman to ever place in our contest."

In a daze, Ali maneuvered through the applauding crowd, aware of heads turning as she passed. She shook the announcer's hand and accepted the second-place plaque, a one foot long wooden carved redfish. After murmuring her thanks, she took her place next to Skipper.

"Good work, kid." Skipper poked her with his elbow.

She smiled. "Thanks. Coming from you, that means a lot."

"And finally, in first place. Drum roll, please."

The crowd booed.

"Jeez, what's a little more suspense today." The announcer adjusted the cap on his head, obviously buying more time. "Captain Jack Cooper, with 26.5 pounds."

Ali took a deep breath, stunned by the outcome of the day's events. When entering the contest, she had no idea that she would even come close to placing, let alone beating one of the best anglers on the bay and coming close to out angling another.

Jack accepted his plaque and took the microphone.

"Thank you. I have to admit, though, that I owe this prize to something other than my angling expertise." He glanced at Ali. "In today's storm, my skiff pulled loose and wound up on the opposite side of the channel. Ali Stephenson came along and rescued me, despite seeing that the trout in my possession was larger than her own." He looked directly at her. "Thank you."

The crowd whistled and shouted their support as Jack joined his fellow anglers on the podium.

"Come on, Gus." Kate nudged him. "We gotta get a picture."

Gus followed along, carrying Grace in his arms as Kate pushed the stroller.

The trio held their prizes high as camera's flashed from all directions. "Reminds me a little of this morning's storm," Skipper quipped.

"Smile, Ali." Kate weaseled her way to the front of the crowd, holding her smartphone close to the prize winners.

"Take one for me, Mama Kate." Skipper held his trophy up next to his face, his Cheshire grin sweeping across his face.

"Grace, there's your mama." Gus held the baby up so she could see her mother.

Ali felt Jack's gaze fall upon her.

"She's beautiful.'"

"Thank you," Ali said, swallowing hard to choke back her emotions.

"You and Joe must be very happy."

Ali chuckled, as she stepped off the podium and walked toward Gus. "I'll trade you." She handed him the trophy and took Grace in her arms. Taking a deep breath, she looked into Kate's eyes. "Wish me luck," she whispered.

Walking back toward the podium, she approached Jack. Their eyes locked on one another as she took each step slowly, deliberately until she stood before him.

"Jack, I'd like you to meet my little miracle." Grace looked up into his eyes and cooed. Then she looked at her mother and then back at Jack before she went off into a babble. Ali used the exchange to calm herself before continuing the introduction. Jack took his gaze off of the child and searched Ali's face. A tear was slipping from the corner of her eye. "Her name is Grace Azalea Stephenson. She's your daughter, too."

Jack took a deep breath. He glanced first at the little girl and then at Ali. Then stunned, he began walking away, taking a step off the podium, passing Kate and Gus, who stood by witnessing the event.

Ali's heart sunk as she watched him recede into the crowd. Skipper came alongside of her. "Give him a minute."

"Really?" Ali asked, feeling like once again she had fallen into her fantasies. Anger boiled in her belly. Glancing at Kate and Gus, she shook her head. "I'm so done with this," feeling her knees buckling beneath her.

Kissing Grace's head, she said, "Let's go, baby. We can do this on our own."

*Go back.* Jenna's voice stopped Jack in his tracks. Tears welled in his eyes. "Really, Jenna? How can anyone ever replace you or our memories?" *They won't. I will always be with you—all of you.*

Taking a deep breath, Jack lifted his gaze toward the sky, now blue as a robin's egg. Slowly, he turned toward the podium. Ali and Grace were gone. Scanning the crowd, he saw Ali carrying Grace, walking alongside Gus and Kate, with Skipper following behind.

"I was right all along, Kate," Ali said. "I should have just accepted my gift and moved on. I am such a fool."

Gus chimed in. "It might be too much for him to take in right now. Give him time to think about everything."

"Gus may be right, Ali," Skipper added. "Guys don't take too well to surprises. We like to think we have everything under control."

Ali shook her head, unable to accept the encouragement from Gus and Skipper.

Suddenly, Kate stopped and put her hand on Ali's arm. Turning, she motioned her head. Jack was dashing between the people milling about, drinking beer, and talking about the tournament.

"Ali, wait." Jack stood before her, glancing at Kate, Gus, and Skipper, who remained close to Ali and the baby, sending a message of support for her. "I'm sorry. I panicked. I didn't know what to think." He glanced at Grace. "I still don't."

Ali nodded. "Fair." Her voice was cold. "I had months to get used to the idea of being a mother." The iciness in her voice began melting. "I can see why you would be shocked."

"I know, and I'm sorry." He looked at Skipper for encouragement.

"Sounds like you two have some talking to do," Skipper said.

Jack nodded. "This has been quite a day." Then he returned his attention to Grace and then looked deeply into Ali's eyes.

"Do you think it might be possible..." Jack paused. "Would you have dinner with me tonight?" He glanced at the child in her arms. "You and Grace." He stroked Grace's cheek.

Ali smiled, her heart thumping wildly in her chest. "Dinner would be lovely."

Kate looked at Jack. "There's hope for you after all."

"You're too quick to give up on me, Kate," he grinned.

She winked and then turned to Ali. "There's some extra clothes for Grace in her bag. We won't wait up."

"Thanks." She leaned over and gave Kate a hug. "You are the best."

"No, you are," Kate glanced at Jack before turning her attention back to Ali. "Now go on."

✳ ✳ ✳

Gus put his arm around Kate's shoulders as Jack and Ali watched them work their way through the crowd.

"Can I interest you two in dinner?" Skipper spoke softly as he stepped up behind them.

Gus piped up. "No, thanks. You'd only stiff me for the bill again." He grinned and glanced at Kate. "Besides, Kate and I have some of our own catchin' up to do, now that we got the kids settled in."

"We sure do." She kissed Gus on the cheek. "We make quite a team."

Gus blushed. "I've been trying to tell you that for years."

"I can be a bit stubborn at times." She took his hand and began leading him through the crowd. "But when I catch on, watch out."

"Hee doggy." Gus tipped his hat as they walked away.

"Hey, what about me?" Skipper yelled after them. "I had a part in this conspiracy."

Kate turned to look at Skipper, with a gentle smile on her lips. "We'll invite you to the wedding."

# Acknowledgements

Writing may be a solitary experience, but the production of a book is far from a solo-adventure. There were many people who assisted me in bringing this book into its current form.

Scott Sparrow, without your presence in my life, I would never have learned to fly fish and would never have set eyes on the Lower Laguna Madre. Even though our paths have taken different directions, you continue to be a great supporter, particularly in providing me photos for the creation and marketing of this book—and being a trusted sounding board for many of my powerful sojourns into the world of dreams.

Merril Boruchin-Spielman, you play multiple roles in my life—friend, assistant, and sometimes "mom." Your love and support of not only this project, but all of my work has helped me over the hurdles I've encountered in my "writable life."

Wanda Hair Taylor, the South's First Lady of Fly Fishing, you are an inspiration to me in many ways—both on the water and off.

Alex Ramirez, I hear your voice whenever I'm in the surf, chasing whatever fish may be present. I am so grateful for the many conversations where we explored the concept that fly fishing is about a lot more than catching fish. It's so much deeper.

Jeffrey Pill, you were one of the first readers of this story. Your encouragement to create a stronger, more courageous protagonist inspired me to grow as well.

Skipper Ray, you taught me how to be in the presence of Grandmother Trout.

And for all my readers who provided me with feedback for improvements on various drafts of this book, I thank you. You have each contributed to this story through your insights. Amanda Johnson, Mara Karpel, Molly Lord, Mike McCleish, Bill Hornbostel, Becky Weiss, Kevin Greisiger, Vanessa Springett, and Kathi Burns.

To my editors Bronson Herr and Alyssa Coehlo. Even though I've been writing professionally for over thirty years, your professional eyes have ensured that this book is the best we could make it.

Karen Floyd, you captured the essence of this story beautifully with the cover design.

And to my friends and family, who saw in me, what took me so long to see in myself, thank you.

# About the Author

An award-winning author, leadership and empowerment expert, and university professor, Kathy Sparrow is the CEO and Founder of A Writable Life™ Publishing. She has been mentoring aspiring writers of non-fiction, fiction, and poetry, for over two decades, many of whom have penned best-selling books and whose works have been included in anthologies.

Kathy was the co-founder and manager of Kingfisher Inn, a dedicated-only fly fishing lodge located in Arroyo City, Texas, just a short boat ride from the Mother Lagoon, the Lower Laguna Madre. She was also one of the first female saltwater guides in the nation.

Her memoir, *On the Mother Lagoon: Fly Fishing and the Spiritual Journey* (to be re-released in the Spring of 2022.), chronicles her experiences as she learned to fly fish and discovered more about herself and the importance of connecting to nature. She is the co-author and project lead of *Ignite Your Leadership: Proven Tools for Leaders to Energize Teams, Fuel Momentum, and Accelerate Results.* She also is the co-author of the children's book, *Stanky & Cece: Break the Rules.*

Kathy has studied transformational methodologies with Jack Canfield, Dr. Deb Sandella of The RIM® Institute, Laurie Seymour of The Baca Institute, and Renee Moorefield of Wisdom Works. She is a Certified Canfield Trainer in *The Success Principles* and Canfield Methodologies, Certified Be Well Lead Well Pulse® Guide, and Master RIM® facilitator.

When she's not working with her clients or penning her own blogs and books, Kathy enjoys yoga, hiking, fly fishing, and adventures with her family. Her basecamp is in San Diego, but you can also find her in Colorado—or wherever her travels take her.

For more information about Kathy Sparrow, visit
*www.kathysparrow.com*

# Kathy's Commitment to Tithing a Percentage of Sales

I have a deep appreciation for the work of **Project Healing Waters Fly Fishing** and the organization's commitment to the healing of disabled veterans through the world of fly fishing. There were times when in my role as Media Lead for the Colorado Springs Chapter, I received more than I gave. I made good friends and experienced the beauty of Colorado waters. Most importantly, I witnessed the incredible transformation of men and women through fly fishing. Because of this, I will be donating 5% of the net sales, split between the national headquarters and the Colorado Springs Chapter.

Being on the water, learning to fly fish, and eventually becoming a guide, taught me a lot about myself. I became more confident both on the water and off. I also deepened my connection to myself and my inner wisdom. I believe all women would discover much about themselves and grow into who they really are meant to be through this sport.

**FFI Women Connect** is dedicated to creating a community of women fly fishers where sharing inspiration is offered in a fun, non-intimidating environment as women develop and improve fly fishing & tying skills.

Learning to fly fish was one of the most empowering activities that I ever experienced. Fly fishing allows me to "meet" myself and stretches me beyond my comfort zone every time I step into the water. I want to support other women in this transformational adventure, and

FFI Women Connect will also receive 5% of the net sales of this book.

# Fly Fishing Transformational Adventures

When Kathy Sparrow first embarked upon the sport of fly fishing, she thought she was learning a new sport to catch fish. However, she soon learned that there was another plan in store for her as the Lower Laguna Madre. The Mother Lagoon and the sport of fly fishing brought her face-to-face with her fears, self-imposed limitations and challenged her to grow beyond who she thought she was. Ultimately, she discovered that the changes she made on the water influenced all aspects of her life on land.

And so, Kathy would like to offer that opportunity to you.

You'll begin with the Be Well Lead Well Pulse® assessment, which measures our ability to thrive even when facing life's most difficult challenges. "The theories of adult development shaping Be Well Lead Well Pulse® emphasize psychological wellbeing as an innate resource that people can actively nurture as the basis of human potential, adaptability and growth, fulfillment, and sustainable performance"

Thriving—not just surviving—personally and professionally is vital for us to positively impact everyone around us–our families, our organizations, and our community.

Your fly-fishing destination is chosen based on your skills and budget. Your days with Kathy will revolve around fly fishing and intentional conversations. You'll also have time to reflect upon the lessons and discoveries made throughout your day. Many of your discussions with Kathy will be based on the Be Well Lead Well Pulse® assessment outcome, the challenges you're facing in your life, and your goals.

Kathy will walk alongside you, witnessing how you show up for the opportunity that nature offers. She'll guide you in recognizing limiting beliefs and patterns that prevent you from living *your* life to your highest potential as they are revealed to you on the water. Together, you'll create a plan to strategically make the necessary changes in your life to create the results you desire—and to positively impact and influence your world and those around you.

Whether you're a solopreneur, small business owner, or leader in a large organization, we give those around us permission to be who they are and to rise above their challenges by first doing our own work. This is especially more meaningful and impactful when you're away from the distractions of your daily life, immersed in nature, and having fun!

Fly Fishing Transformational Adventures are suitable for individuals, small groups, or teams—with or without fly fishing experience. For more information, contact Kathy at kathy@kathysparrow.com or visit www.kathysparrow.com/flyfishingadventures

Made in United States
Orlando, FL
04 May 2022

17510823R00135